THE
BILLIONAIRE'S
PET

The Winters Saga
Book Three

IVY LAYNE

GINGER QUILL PRESS, LLC

Contents

ALSO BY IVY LAYNE

Don't Miss Out on New Releases, Exclusive Giveaways, and More!!

Join Ivy's Readers Group @ ivylayne.com/readers

THE HEARTS OF SAWYERS BEND

Stolen Heart

Sweet Heart

Scheming Heart

Rebel Heart

Wicked Heart

THE UNTANGLED SERIES

Unraveled

Undone

Uncovered

THE WINTERS SAGA

The Billionaire's Secret Heart (Novella)

The Billionaire's Secret Love (Novella)

The Billionaire's Pet

The Billionaire's Promise

The Rebel Billionaire

The Billionaire's Secret Kiss (Novella)

The Billionaire's Angel

Engaging the Billionaire

Compromising the Billionaire

The Counterfeit Billionaire

THE BILLIONAIRE CLUB

The Wedding Rescue

The Courtship Maneuver

The Temptation Trap

CHAPTER ONE
ABIGAIL

I sat on the plush leather sofa and stared at the thick wool carpet, trying not to count the scuffs on my shoes. John would have been so disappointed. The soft leather of my beige sling-backs was marked from walking through the wet grass before sunrise.

Small flecks of grass stuck to the soles. John loved for me to look nice. He always bragged that he had the prettiest wife in town. But John was gone, and I was doing the best I could. Lately, my best had not included polishing my shoes.

This morning, my best had included a pre-dawn trek through the field behind the house I'd shared with John, a half-mile hike through the woods separating the house from my cousin-in-law's small cabin, then a clandestine ride to the bus station two towns east.

I hoped no one found out that Tina helped me get to Atlanta. If I'd known any other way, I'd never have put her at risk. But I'd had to get to Jacob Winters.

He was the only one who could help me. I'd called his office from the bus station, arguing and pleading with the receptionist, then his assistant, to tell him I was on the line.

After ten humiliating minutes, Jacob had clicked on, verified I was me, and told me he could fit me in at eleven for fifteen minutes. I'd spent the time in between lurking in a bookstore, knowing that would be the last place the people looking for me would think to search.

Jacob's office wasn't what I expected. I don't know where I got the image in my head, but I'd pictured it as slick and modern, filled with sleek black leather and chrome, his assistant as a svelte blonde Valkyrie.

The couch was leather. I'd gotten that part right. But instead of cold black, it was a deep espresso, punctuated with dull brass tacks. The rug was a Persian design, the furniture not sharp and shiny, but antique, polished wood.

And the woman at the desk, guarding the door to his office with disapproving eyes, was older than my mother, with a neat, chin-length bob of grey hair that was heartbreakingly familiar.

An ugly irony that his assistant reminded me of my mother. My mother was the reason I was here. The reason I'd made almost every one of the disastrous mistakes I'd made in the last five years.

If Anne Louise Wainright had any idea I was sitting in Jacob Winters's office, prepared to make him an offer I hoped he wouldn't refuse, she'd have passed out from the shock. Ladies did not consort with men who were not their husband.

I'd been raised to be a lady, first, last, and always. It was why John had married me. But my mother no longer recognized me and my husband was dead. I'd made more than my share of bad decisions since my father had died and my mother had fallen ill.

This would likely be one more. I was prepared to live

with that. If Jacob could give me what I needed, I could find a way to live with anything.

A tone sounded at the assistant's desk. She pressed a button, then murmured something I couldn't hear. My stomach clenched. I still had time to change my mind.

I could stand up, make some flimsy excuse, and be out on the city streets in no more than a few minutes. But what then? I couldn't go home.

When Big John discovered me gone this morning, he would have been furious. I didn't want to imagine what he would do to me if I came crawling back.

His first proposal had been so appalling, my imagination recoiled from trying to picture what my father-in-law would consider an appropriate punishment for my defiance. If Jacob turned me away, I would lose everything. Not just my home and my mother, but my life as well.

"Mrs. Jordan?" The assistant stood in front of me, waiting with expressionless patience. The tension in my stomach congealed into a frozen ball of fear. I stood, wobbling only a little on my narrow heels.

They were the sexiest pair I owned, a gift from John in the early days of our marriage. They pinched my toes and were the worst shoes to wear when I'd spent a good part of my morning walking, but paired with my cream linen shift, they made my legs look a mile long. I needed every advantage I could get.

I tugged at the hem of my dress, smoothing the fabric as I followed the assistant to Jacob's door. I caught a whiff of her hairspray tangled with a perfume that smelled of roses and baby powder. She seemed too normal to be working for a man as magnetic as Jacob.

The assistant turned the brass handle, and the door

swung open on silent hinges. With a gesture, she indicated I should enter, then closed the door behind me.

The click of the handle sent my heart thudding. No turning back now. All I could do was hope Jacob didn't throw me out when he heard what I had to say.

He walked toward me, his hand extended, a distant, vaguely curious expression in his arresting silver eyes. Not a good sign.

The way he looked at me was most of the reason I was here. That and the fact that he was the only man I could think of with the power to untangle my troubles.

The power was the *how*, but the way he'd looked at me was the *why*. Or I'd hoped it would be. I hadn't met Jacob many times in the five years I'd been married to John. Only a handful of encounters, but each time, I'd come away shaken.

He was always controlled, gracious, and reserved . . . except when I caught him watching me on the sly. Then, his cool silver eyes had burned with desire and intention.

Jacob Winters wanted me. Not enough to risk his business with my in-laws, or maybe he'd known I'd never have cheated on John.

Our marriage was so far from perfect. It had devolved into a nightmare, but I still owed John too much to think about cheating. He hadn't deserved that kind of betrayal.

Steeling myself, I raised my hand to take Jacob's. His fingers were firm around mine, sending a shiver down my spine. I did my best to pretend confidence as I smiled up at him.

He smiled back, his eyes warming a shade. A lock of thick, dark hair fell over his forehead, softening his sculpted face.

Jacob Winters had the kind of looks that stopped a

room. I'd seen it happen at a cocktail party when John and I had been early and Jacob had been uncharacteristically late.

He'd walked in and conversation had literally stopped, all eyes on Jacob handing off his coat as he brushed raindrops from his dark hair.

He was taller than most men, at least a few inches over six feet. Broad shoulders, narrow torso, muscled but lean, and every woman who caught sight of him knew that without his trademark grey suits, he'd look even better.

Smug gossip from the women who'd been there affirmed that as hot as he was when dressed, a naked Jacob Winters would ruin you for all other men.

Hard to tell how much of that was bragging from women who wanted everyone to know they'd captured his elusive attention, even if it was only for a short time.

I'd always thought they were understating his appeal. I never would have cheated on my husband, but if Jacob had asked, I would have been painfully tempted.

"Thank you for seeing me," I said, following Jacob deeper into his office. The space was divided into two sections, including a sitting area with a couch, love seat and coffee table in the same style as the front room.

Further into the long room was a huge desk of warm, caramel toned wood. A dark leather desk chair sat on the far side, two smaller leather armchairs opposite.

To my surprise, Jacob led me to the desk. I'd thought that with my being the widow of a former business associate, he'd treat this more like a social visit.

Wrong.

There was no bullshitting Jacob that this was a social call. He'd sent flowers when John died. The niceties had been covered. The last-minute call this morning and my insistence that I had to see him today told him this was business.

So, the desk.

I took a seat in one of the armchairs, crossed my legs, and pasted a polite smile on my face. The training of my marriage. Don't show anything but what they want to see.

Hide the panic. Hide the desperation. Slow, even breaths. Hands lightly clasped in my lap. I was the picture of calm elegance. Always.

"What's wrong?" Jacob asked, his sharp eyes pulling apart my facade.

The instinctive protest that nothing was wrong jumped to my lips. I beat it back. Ridiculous to say nothing was wrong when everything was wrong.

"I'm in some trouble." I sat up straighter, tugging on the hem of my dress. It was just a hair shorter than it should be, making it an alluring combination of classy and sexy.

I'd worn it hoping it would sway Jacob in my favor. Now that I was sitting here in front of him, the amount of leg the cream linen exposed made me feel more vulnerable than confident.

"Do you know why I married John?" I asked, deciding to get straight to the point. It was a long story, and he'd only given me fifteen minutes. Jacob sat back in his chair and shook his head.

"I'd always wondered. You never seemed like a good fit to me."

It was funny that Jacob would say that. Everyone else seemed to think we were the perfect fit. Me, the sweet, spoiled banker's daughter and John, the son of one of our small town's most powerful men.

His family hadn't exactly been above-board, but John was supposed to change all that.

Marriage to me had cemented the image that his family was moving in more legitimate directions. Shortly after our wedding, he'd been invited to join the country club. In the beginning, I'd taken over for my mother as a lady who lunched.

No one had seen beneath the surface because we hadn't let them.

"No," I said. "We really weren't."

Taking a breath, I prepared for the confession I had to make. Five years later, and I was still ashamed of what I'd done.

"When I was sixteen, my mother began to develop early onset Alzheimer's. By the time I graduated high school, she needed round-the-clock care. The summer after my sophomore year in college, my father had a fatal heart attack."

"I'm sorry." Jacob leaned forward, compassion warming his demeanor. "That must have been very difficult for you at such a young age."

I let out a bitter laugh, the harsh, short sound completely unlike the careful image I'd cultivated over the past few years.

"It would have been easier if I hadn't discovered that my father had lost everything. The only miracle was that he'd kept things at the bank clean. I don't know what I would have done if I'd had to pay them restitution."

"So you had nothing?"

"Nothing. The house, cars, artwork, my mother's jewelry and my grandmother's engagement rings they were all sold. If it had just been me, I could have handled it."

"Your mother," he said. "I take it there wasn't any insurance to cover her care?"

"No. My father had her in an excellent facility by that

time, but it was too expensive for me to handle on my own. And I wasn't qualified for the kind of job that could cover the bills and pay my rent. If I'd brought her home with me, I couldn't have gone out to work. I was trapped. And terrified."

"Let me guess. John walked in with the solution?"

I should have known Jacob would grasp the situation with a minimum of explanation. He might have lived and worked in the city an hour from our small country town, but he made it his business to know everything about the people who might impact his interests.

He knew all he needed to know about the Jordan family — far more than I had when I'd married John.

I'd grown up the sheltered, indulged daughter of our town's two leading citizens. I wasn't one of those privileged little snots who looked down on the rest of the world for not having the newest cars and clothes.

My mother had, along with lunching at the country club, spent much of her time volunteering in our community. She'd taken me with her to food drives and literacy clinics, always wanting to make sure I understood how fortunate I was, and in my good fortune, to remember to take care of those with less.

While she'd managed to instill a sense of humility in me, my upbringing had not prepared me for the various ways life could turn ugly.

I'd known about John's family. His father, Big John, was spoken of with respect and awe. Not the same kind of respect people had used when they'd spoken of my father. This was tinged with fear and a vague threat.

I was never quite clear on what Big John did, or didn't do, to earn this type of regard. As far as I knew, he owned a plumbing supply company on the edge of town.

When I asked, my father had told me to stay away from the Jordans. By the time I was in high school, I had the idea that some of Big John's enterprises weren't quite legal, but I hadn't understood what that meant.

Not really. Not until it was too late.

"Yes." I straightened in the chair, as if correcting my posture could pull the shreds of my dignity together.

"He offered to marry me. He was just back from college, ready to settle down, and he said he'd always had his eye on me. He said that if we got married, he'd take over my mother's care. I didn't know what else to do."

"Like a lamb among the wolves," Jacob commented, a wry smile on his face. "You had no idea what you were marrying into, did you?"

"None." I looked away from those knowing silver eyes, afraid I'd see pity. "It was the wrong thing to do. I know that. I told him I didn't love him. And I did my best to be a good wife."

"You played the role he married you to play. Even when you knew what he was."

"Yes." I nodded. I'd married a man for his money. A man I liked, but would never love. The more I grew to know him, the less I even liked him.

But I did my best to be what he wanted, always aware that he held my mother's life in his hands. She was far too fragile to leave The Shaded Glenn, and only John's continued goodwill kept her safe and cared for.

"So why are you here?" Jacob leaned back in his chair, hands folded, resting on his chest. His eyes flicked to the clock on the wall. Time was ticking away, and I wasn't doing a very good job of getting to the point.

"Big John moved into the house a few days ago. He said that with John gone, my debt was transferred to him. And if I wanted to see my mother taken care of, I'd do as he said."

"And what, exactly, did he say he wanted you to do? Sleep with him?" One dark, elegant eyebrow raised as if to ask if that was all it took to scare me off.

"Sleeping with him and keeping his house were just the beginning," I said.

"He and John fought a lot at the end. One of the things they were fighting about was me. Big John felt that I was too big a drain on their resources. That I needed to earn my keep. He wanted to trade me out to some of their associates. John refused."

"You're kidding." Jacob's face darkened, his eyes shading from silver to a dark, forbidding gray.

"I wish I were."

"What did he say when you told him you wouldn't do it?"

"He said he had ways to keep me in line. I acted like I'd go along and said I knew I owed him, but I had my period. Then I snuck out in the middle of the night."

I fell silent, waiting. Jacob watched me, not speaking, for several endless minutes. Every muscle in my body was tight, tense to the point of pain.

Jacob was my only chance. I had no money and no friends I'd risk to Big John's fury. Nowhere to go. Finally, he spoke.

"What do you expect me to do?"

This was the sticking point. The truth was, I didn't know. I wasn't asking for a job. After four years of marriage to John, I still had no marketable skills. All I had was my willingness to do anything to protect my mother.

"I can't take my mother out of the facility she's in. I can't afford to pay the fees. And I'm not sure, even if I turned my back on my mother, that I can stay clear of Big John. I need help with all of it."

Jacob remained silent, studying me. I swallowed. It was against my temperament to push, but I didn't have a choice.

"I know it's too much to ask. But I'll do anything." I stared him in the eye, daring him to doubt my commitment.

"*Anything* is a dangerous promise." Jacob tilted his head to the side.

It should have been endearing. Instead, it made him look like a predator studying his prey. Me. I swallowed before I spoke, my throat thick with nerves.

"Before I left, Big John said he was going to shoot me up with heroin and chain me to a bed while a gang of bikers rapes me. I'll do anything that stops short of drugs and rape."

More silence. Then Jacob picked up the phone on his desk.

"Rachel, reschedule my 11:15." He hung up the phone and studied me another long minute before he spoke. "I want you. I wanted you the first minute I saw you. You know that. It's why you came to me."

"I—" I stopped speaking. Without knowing where he was going, I didn't want to dig myself a hole. I fell silent, waiting to hear what he would say.

"I have a circumstance I find difficult to handle, Abigail," he went on. "Over the years, I've tried various methods of dealing with it, and none have met with success. I've been thinking it's time to try something new. And you're going to be my something new."

My mind raced.

Jacob's lips had curved into a smile at the word 'new'. His top lip was severe, the bottom lushly full. Together, they drew the eye. Especially in a half-smile with a hint of mischief.

His words, the smile, all sounded like he was going to help me. Now I just had to see what being his 'something new' would entail. Unable to force my mouth to move, I lifted my chin, inviting him to continue.

"I like sex," he said. "I like a lot of sex. I like variety. Kink. You've probably never heard of half of the things I've thought about doing to you. What I don't like is inconvenience."

Jacob leaned forward, his eyes locked to mine, elbows resting on the polished wood of his desk.

"Relationships are inconvenient. They involve compromise, accommodation, and time. I don't have the patience for the first two or enough of the last. I don't want to get to know a woman. I'm not interested in intimacy outside of sex. What I want is to fuck when I want to fuck. And I want to fuck a woman I'm attracted to who will let me do anything I want to her."

"Will you hurt me?"

My voice was high and tight. I don't know what I was expecting, but this matter-of-fact, efficient speech wasn't it. It was, however, far less scary than Big John's proposal.

"Yes," he answered. My stomach pitched. "But I won't damage you. And the kind of hurt I'm talking about? You'll like it."

"So how does it work?"

"You move in with me. You don't leave the house. Ever. You do nothing without my permission. I'm not looking for a woman. I'm looking for a pet. An obedient, available pet. Can you do that?"

I stared, not sure I could answer. I'd walked in prepared to trade my body for my mother's safety. It wasn't honorable, but it was the only thing of value I had to offer.

But this, his dehumanizing description of what he

wanted from me, had shocked the speech from my brain. Lips and tongue frozen, I forced myself to nod.

I couldn't afford for Jacob to think twice. No matter how terrifying this sounded, I couldn't run away. He stood, pushed back his chair, and rounded his wide desk. Standing in front of me, he rested his hands on his hips and said,

"I think, before we go any further, I need a sample."

I stared up at him in dumb confusion. If my brain had been working, I'd have known exactly what he meant. Since I was slow, he clarified.

"Suck my cock."

CHAPTER TWO

ABIGAIL

S *uck my cock.*

I felt my eyes flare wide. I must have looked like a virginal child in my creamy white dress, staring at the bulge behind his well-cut suit pants, my hands trembling.

"Abigail," he said, voice even and treading the edge of impatience, "I dislike asking twice for something I want."

A gracious warning, but I knew it for what it was. This was my one chance. If I blew it, or didn't blow it, he'd continue looking for his 'something new' and I would be walking down the street, praying for a miracle that wasn't going to come.

Lifting my unsteady hands, I reached for his black leather belt.

Once I started moving, Jacob was silent, apparently prepared to let me work through my nerves as long as I wasn't balking at his order. Sliding to the edge of the armchair, I unfastened his belt and lowered the zipper of his pants.

Beneath the gray flannel wool, he wore fine cotton

boxers in a dark blue. Involuntarily, I smiled. I don't know what I'd been expecting. Maybe commando? His dick to pop out and slap me in the face? Instead, he was clothed like any other man. Easing his boxers down, it hit me.

This was Jacob Winters.

I was about to suck Jacob Winters's cock.

Take it in my mouth. Lick it. Stroke and cup his balls. If I did a good job, he'd have his hands all over me. Fuck me, and more. He'd said he'd do things to me that I'd never even heard of.

I'd seen him across more than one crowded, stifling charity event and dazed out imagining all the things I'd love to do to his beautiful body, knowing I'd never get the chance because I was married to John.

And now I wasn't married. I had Jacob's cock in my hand, swelling and lengthening to a full, steely erection.

Holy Christ, there was no way that was going to fit in my mouth. At the sight of him, my pussy flooded with wet heat. Apparently, my body was on board with Jacob's proposition, even if my brain hadn't quite caught up.

Leaning in, I drew in a breath. His scent flooded my brain—so male, the scent of heat and sex and lust.

Unable to help myself, I rubbed my cheek along the side of his fully erect cock before licking the swollen head. His size was intimidating. When I'd peeled down his boxers, he'd been half-hard and already bigger than any cock I'd ever seen, not that I'd seen that many.

None that looked like Jacob. I wrapped my fingers around his girth and stroked, realizing that my fingers didn't come close to meeting.

This arrangement wasn't about my pleasure, but I couldn't deny that part of me was melting at the idea of having this cock fucking me on a regular basis.

Aware that the clock was still ticking, I devoted myself to the task at hand.

There was no way I could take Jacob's cock all the way. Not without a lot of practice. But there were other things I could do. Slowly, savoring the masculine flavor of him, I licked every inch of his cock until he was wet enough for my hand to move easily.

Sliding my lips down as far as I could, I sucked hard, giving his length a stroke in rhythm with my mouth. And again.

My brain clicked off as I got into the groove, allowing my saliva to escape the tight ring of my lips, keeping the movement of my hand tight and slick. He was literally mouthwatering. I'd never liked going down on John. But now, with Jacob?

Maybe it was the illicit nature of what I was doing, bartering myself for his protection.

Or maybe it was just that this was Jacob, the man I'd been secretly lusting after since I'd first met him four years ago.

I didn't care. The rest of the world dropped away, narrowed down to his cock in my mouth and my hand sliding over his hard flesh.

I drew back, stroking again, sliding my tongue over the head of his cock, tasting the first drops of pre-cum. Above me, Jacob was silent, his hands still on his hips.

His cock didn't lie. He loved my mouth on him. I ran my tongue against his salty skin on the upstroke, eager to coax out more of his come.

I had a feeling that Jacob was about control in the bedroom. I might not have many chances like this, to have him at my mercy. I wanted to give him everything I had while I could.

Leaning forward in the armchair was getting awkward. Pulling back, I released him for only a second before dropping to my knees in front of him. Tugging down his pants and boxers, I dove back in, but not before I caught the look in Jacob's flashing silver eyes.

He might have been silent, but his eyes were molten, burning with lust. At his look, my nipples tightened into hard, needy beads.

I wouldn't lie to myself. I wanted this. Wanted to be his. His pet. I wanted his cock in my mouth. Wanted it in me everywhere I could get it. Greedy to touch all of him, I slipped my free hand between his legs and cupped his tight sack, squeezing it with a gentle touch.

Above me, I heard a moan. The low, hungry sound drove my arousal higher. Heat pulsed between my legs. I sucked harder, stroking my tongue up the underside of his cock over and over as my hand slid around the length that didn't fit in my mouth, twisting and sliding, close to frenzied.

I needed too much. Needed him to come for me, to make him feel the same rush of pleasure and heat that I felt having him in my mouth.

With a moan of my own, I reached behind him, sinking my fingers into the warm skin covering his perfect, tight ass, dragging him closer, driving his cock deeper into my mouth. He hit the back of my throat before I was ready and, for a second, I choked.

Jacob tried to pull back, but I wouldn't let him. I held him as deep as I could bear, my throat convulsing on the head of his weeping cock, wishing it was my empty pussy.

Jacob gave up trying to pull back and gripped my head, holding me still as he stiffened in orgasm, spilling his come down my throat. I drank it, eager for the taste. I didn't know what had come over me—why I'd needed him so much when I'd never wanted a cock in my mouth before.

I wasn't going to wonder about it. I was just going to be happy I'd loved every second of it.

It was a revelation. Epiphany by blow-job.

I wasn't going to worry for a while. Wasn't going to be afraid. I was going to enjoy everything I could and get through what I didn't like. Good to know blow-jobs weren't going to be a hardship.

Jacob released his hold on my head, easing back until his cock popped from my lips, leaving a trace of his come on my cheek.

With the same faint, mischievous smile I'd seen earlier, he wiped it off with one long finger, offering it to me. I opened my mouth and sucked it in, licking the few drops of come off his salty, sweet skin. Another thing I'd never been into before. But I liked the taste of Jacob's come.

Lucky for me, given how this was going. He watched me sucking his finger, the banked heat in his eyes sending another pulse of desire between my legs. I already knew better than to ask if he was going to take care of me. That was the question of a lover. I was to be a pet. I didn't get to ask questions like that.

He withdrew his finger and gave me a pointed look, then flicked his eyes to his boxers and suit pants, slouched around his knees.

I got the message and carefully slid his underwear, then his pants, back into place. He took over, tucking in his shirt and fastening his belt. Reaching out a hand, he helped me to my feet, then gestured for me to take a seat back in the armchair.

I did as he ordered, crossing my legs, conscious that my panties were soaked. Thankfully, the linen shift was lined, or I'd probably leak through my dress and leave a wet spot on the leather.

My body felt like a foreign thing, disconnected from my uncertain emotions. Fear and hope were a roller coaster in my brain, but my body was on a different track. At the idea of touching Jacob, fucking Jacob, my body was all in.

"So." Jacob leaned back in his chair, watching me with eyes almost as cool as they'd been when I'd entered his office a short time before.

"Terms. For every month you stay with me, I pay for your mother's care. If you stay more than a year, we'll discuss a more permanent arrangement for her. You will remain inside my home at all times, at least in the beginning. Among other things, I want to assure myself that you'll be safe. Big John won't want to let you go."

He stopped, seeming to want some kind of response from me. My head was spinning, the taste of his come on my tongue a heady distraction as he talked about terms as if we were going over a contract. Which I guess we were.

I nodded, not sure I could trust myself to say anything intelligent.

"I'll arrange for you to have a laptop and a credit card. You can buy what you like, within reason."

"What's within reason?" I asked, before my brain could tell me to shut up. Definitely couldn't trust myself to say something intelligent. He raised one dark eyebrow at me.

"No diamonds or cars. Clothes, make-up, books . . . whatever you need to be comfortable is fine."

More than fair. Considering the cost of my mother's care, it was beyond generous. I nodded again. At that, he stood. I copied him, not sure what was going to happen next.

Was he taking me home? Would he bend me over the

desk and fuck me? The very un-demure, unladylike part of me, the part that would have appalled my very proper mother, was hoping it was the latter.

Sadly, he turned toward his office door, and with his hand on my back, propelled me into the reception area. With a nod for his assistant as we passed, he pressed the button for the elevator. Over his shoulder, he said,

"I'll be back shortly, Rachel."

"Yes, sir."

I'd barely noticed the elevator on the way up, too nervous to pay attention to detail. Like Jacob's office, it had an old-world elegance, all polished wood and thick carpeting with what I was sure was an original oil painting hung on the back wall.

The elevator rose in a smooth surge, surprising me. I'd assumed he was bringing me to his home. Did he live upstairs?

Taking a closer look at the panel beside the door, I saw that the button labeled with a 'P' was lit. Jacob lived in the penthouse. He probably owned the whole building. As the elevator glided to a stop, a dizzying sense of vertigo hit me.

Of course he owned the building. He owned a good portion of the city. Including me.

The doors slid open to reveal the gleaming hardwood floor of a foyer, surrounded by smooth, creamy walls, the heavy, complicated moldings at the ceiling a soft white. More oil paintings like the one in the elevator.

A narrow table sat against one wall with a stack of mail on top, a half-open gym bag slouching beneath. The human touch in all this elegant beauty reminded me where we were. Jacob's home. And now mine, for however long this lasted.

A long hall, lined with white wainscoting, led to the rest

of the penthouse. I followed Jacob, intensely curious about the space this man would call his home.

For someone who was so contained, who preferred a pet to a girlfriend, I'd expected cold and austere. Instead, his home was as warm and elegant as his office.

The long hall opened into a wide space with a kitchen and breakfast area on one side and a huge sitting room complete with couches, an armchair and an oversized television on the other. Filled with more polished antiques, except for the television, the space managed to be both impressive and welcoming.

Without a glance at me, Jacob continued through the great room and turned down another hallway. I spotted what looked like a dining room on one side, then an office behind glass French doors on the other.

Another turn, and Jacob stopped to open a door. He entered the room and held the door open for me to follow.

Inside, I saw an enormous black canopy bed covered with a snow white, fluffy duvet, the dark headboard partially blocked with matching white pillows. I got the vague impression of bedside tables in the same deep black, and an armchair in the corner, but the bed had most of my attention.

It was both the most inviting thing I'd seen in ages and somewhat intimidating. Not unlike Jacob himself. It didn't take much imagination to picture some of the things Jacob could do to me in that bed.

I shifted, rubbing my thighs together, suddenly aware of how aroused I'd been only a few minutes before, kneeling in front of Jacob after sucking his cock.

His taste lingered on my tongue. I wasn't sure if I was hoping he'd brought me here to fuck me, or afraid he had.

My head spinning with nerves, relief, arousal and heavy

exhaustion, I looked at Jacob, waiting for him to say something. That half-smile was back, giving me the uncomfortable sense that he was reading my mind.

"This will be your room for the duration of your stay. I need to get back to work, but I'll be back after six tonight."

"Would you like me to make dinner?" I asked, sounding far more wifely than I'd intended.

"I forgot," he said, a gleam of new interest in his eyes. "John used to brag about your cooking."

"I took classes," I said, feeling stupid. I was a college drop-out, but I'd been to every cooking class in a hundred-mile radius.

John hadn't wanted a wife with a degree in education. He'd wanted one who could hold dinner parties with intricately folded napkins and complicated gourmet food.

"Not tonight," Jacob said. "I'll have something sent in. We'll talk about what you can cook over dinner tonight. I wouldn't mind coming home to a hot meal once in a while."

I nodded, not sure what else to do. Normally, I was fabulous with small talk. Large groups or one-on-one, I was one of those people who always knew what to say.

Even with Jacob, when we'd met during my marriage, I was never at a loss for words. But back then, I'd been the wife of a colleague. Now I was his pet. An indentured sexual servant.

On top of all the other shocks I'd experienced since John's death, this one seemed to have frozen my social skills. I felt as though I'd used every ounce of intelligence and resolve to get away from Big John.

Once Jacob had agreed to my plan, I'd hit empty, run down like a wind-up toy at the end of its cycle. I glanced at the huge, fluffy bed again. It looked like heaven. Following my gaze, Jacob said,

"Why don't you relax? Take a nap. There's food in the fridge if you're hungry." He started for the door to the bedroom, not waiting for me to respond. Before he disappeared into the hall, he turned back, pinning me with those brilliant silver eyes.

"I'm glad you came to me, Abigail. I think we'll solve each other's problems nicely. Now get some rest."

"Is that an order?" I asked, the question somehow sounding both flirtatious and uncertain.

"Yes," he answered, his gaze serious. "Everything that you are is mine now. And I take care of what belongs to me."

At that scary pronouncement, he vanished, leaving me alone. I stood in the center of my new bedroom, undecided. I wasn't hungry. I knew I should be. I hadn't been eating much lately.

Too much coffee early in the day, on top of the fear twisting my stomach since the moment I'd slipped from my bed before dawn, left me disinterested in food. But a shower —that was a different story.

I felt like I'd been wearing these clothes for weeks. And if the bedroom was this nice, what did the bathroom look like?

I didn't wait to find out. Crossing the room, I pushed open the door to find it was about the size of the master bath in the home I'd shared with John. We'd had a very nice house, a semi-custom two-story with a basement on a few acres on the edge of the Jordans' land.

Spacious and new, it was nicer than most, though not as nice as the home I'd grown up in. Jacob's place left both my former homes in the dust.

The guest bath was all white marble, with a huge shower, garden tub, and a long marble counter highlighting the wide, deep custom, glass sink in a delicate sky blue. The towels, neatly hung beside the shower, were the same blue, as was the frame around the mirror over the counter.

It was lovely and feminine, without being so girly a male guest would feel out of place. I loved it. The tub beckoned, but I had a feeling if I got in, I'd be in danger of passing out. The longer I stood there, the more I knew exactly what I wanted. A long, hot shower and a nap.

Poking around, I discovered a thick robe hanging on the back of the bathroom door. The linen closet held more towels, a hair dryer and a basket of unopened toiletries.

Grabbing what I needed, I headed for the shower, shedding clothes as I went. Bliss. Enveloped by hot steam, I tilted my head back into the spray, letting the water wash it all away.

For the first time since I'd heard John and his father arguing about my 'obligations' to the family, I felt safe.

It was stupid. I knew Jacob little better than I'd known John before we married, and look how that had turned out. I'd thought I was marrying a nice guy who was getting ready to go into business with his father.

I'd actually married the only legitimate member of the biggest criminal family in central Georgia. Jacob had done business with them. Why was I so sure he was any better?

I didn't have an answer. As I washed my hair and shaved my legs, I pushed the thoughts from my mind. I'd had two goals—to secure my mother's care and get away from Big John.

Jacob had taken care of both. I wasn't going to question it. For now, I was going to stick with my post blow-job epiphany.

Enjoy what I could, and get through the rest.

And stop being afraid.

CHAPTER THREE

JACOB

I walked back into the reception area of my office, triumph swelling in my chest. In a million years, I'd never imagined I'd get my hands on Abigail Jordan.

And now she was mine. Completely mine.

Stopping at Rachel's desk, I waited a moment for her to finish her call. She met my eyes with the cool, bland expression I loved. I was sure she was curious, but Rachel was the consummate professional.

She might be dying to know who Abigail was, but she'd never ask. Perfect, especially considering what I was about to tell her to do.

"Almost lunch time?" I asked, knowing she went to lunch at noon every day like clockwork.

"Yes, sir. Would you like me to pick up something for you?"

"No, I'll order in. But I'd like you to leave a little early and pick up a few things for my guest."

Always prepared, Rachel picked up a pen and pulled a notepad in front of her, ready for my list.

"A laptop. Enough clothes for a few days. Casual, but not boring. You can guess her size?"

"Yes. And I can find a few things that will work even if I'm off. What about shoes?"

"She won't need shoes." I waited, sure I'd catch a hint of prurient interest in Rachel's expression, but her eyes remained alert yet impenetrable.

She was good. I grinned at her, too pleased with the world just then to get annoyed that I couldn't ruffle Rachel's composure. I was used to it, and she knew me too well to let me put her off her game.

"Is that it?" she asked, her pen still poised above the paper.

"Anything else you think she might want until she has time to get online and order a few things for herself. Don't worry about hurrying back. You have a light afternoon."

Despite my offer to take her time, I knew Rachel would be back at her desk not long after one o'clock. Most assistants would take advantage, lingering over lunch and stretching out the shopping list to eat up the afternoon.

Not Rachel. Her honesty and reliability were just two of the reasons she'd worked for me for over a decade.

Closing my office door behind me, I scanned the papers on my desk. Earlier that morning, the real estate deal I'd been putting together had captured every ounce of my attention. Now I couldn't summon my former enthusiasm.

Abigail Jordan was in my penthouse. More than that, she was mine. Mine. I'd told her she would be my pet, and she hadn't even flinched.

I could hardly believe I'd dared to make the proposal. There wasn't much I wouldn't dare, but making a pet of Abigail Jordan? The possibility had never crossed my mind.

The fantasy, absolutely.

But the reality? Not once.

If I hadn't seen the faint tremble in her hands, I never would have imagined she'd agree. For a woman as composed as Abigail, that tremble had said it all. That and the scuffs on her shoes.

The idea of her running from her home in the dark of night sent a rush of anger coursing through me. I wasn't offering her a return to the life she deserved, but at least I could keep her safe. I had no doubt she'd been telling the truth about Big John's plans for her.

Her husband had been a decent enough guy for a man raised in a den of snakes. I knew John had been proud of Abigail even if he hadn't loved her.

Big John was another story.

While John had been the public face of the family, educated and somewhat refined, Big John was their leader. His interests were far more dangerous than his son's. He'd want Abigail back. I wondered if Big John would guess where she was.

My decree that Abigail stay in the penthouse had been mostly for her safety, though I wouldn't deny that a dark part of me loved the idea of Abigail as my prisoner, tucked away in my home, her entire existence focused on me.

My needs. My pleasure. Everything that was her, living just for me. A seductive image, even though it was an illusion.

Abigail's entire existence was focused on her mother. She'd sacrificed herself for her mother when she'd married John, and now she was doing it again. Only this time, she'd lost the dignity of marriage.

She'd enslaved herself for a woman who, to be entirely honest, probably didn't even recognize her anymore. She'd fucked up her life, no question, but at least her motivation was noble.

I liked Abigail even more for her reasons, even though I knew I should feel pity, not admiration. It didn't matter. I'd always been a bastard. What kind of man would blackmail a woman like Abigail into servitude?

Not a good one.

I had more than enough money to help her out of her problem without feeling a pinch. And while Big John could cause some difficulty, I had the power to handle him. But this would be so much more fun.

If Abigail had balked at the blow-job, I might have written her a check and sent her on her way. I had no interest in coercing reluctant women. I liked control, but only when the woman wanted it as much as I did.

But Abigail hadn't balked. She'd hesitated for a second, then handled my cock like she'd been dreaming of sucking me off for the past four years. About as long as I'd been dreaming of feeling her mouth on me.

I'd never forgotten my first glimpse of Abigail Jordan. I'd been at a gallery showing, bored to tears, dragged there by one of my failed attempts at dating. The woman with me had been intelligent, gorgeous, and dull as hell.

She'd even managed to be boring in bed. I couldn't remember her name, but she'd lasted long enough to drag me to the opening of an unknown post-modern sculptor.

Not my style.

I'd been sipping awful wine and scanning the room when the door had swung open, letting in a swirl of frosty winter air, a goddess at its center, sparkling with the snowflakes that had just begun to fall.

She'd worn a navy dress, long sleeved with a simple

wide neckline that bared a hint of creamy shoulder, exposing no cleavage and very little leg.

Diamonds had flashed at her ears, around her neck, and on the ring finger of her left hand. I still remembered the shock of disappointment that hit me when I spotted her ring.

I'd barely noticed John on her arm, but that was John. The affable good old boy, handsome enough, smart enough, but never more than that. Beside his wife, John had disappeared.

It hadn't taken me long to realize that was the point. I'd often wondered just how much of her situation Abigail understood.

John had wanted a wife to lend him legitimacy. She gave him an excuse to mingle with the people he'd need to bribe, or forcefully convince, as part of doing business. And with Abigail around, no one paid attention to John.

It wasn't that she was loud or bold. Every time I'd seen her, even that morning when she was wound tight with nerves, Abigail had been calm. Serene. A perfect lady.

She could hold an intelligent conversation on economics or world events and had a knack for making those around her comfortable. I'd seen her introduce people in just the right combination to spark a party into something memorable, then step back to let them run the show.

More than once, she'd sought out a newcomer to their circles and drawn him or her out, making sure they found their place.

In truth, she really wasn't my type. Too cool and refined. The things I liked from a woman were too dark, too demanding, for someone like Abigail. But still, she'd drawn me.

The few times we'd spoken at length, her dry sense of

humor had startled a laugh out of me when I'd least expected it. And she had a look in her eye when she smiled that suggested she might be more than she seemed.

Her body didn't hurt either. Abigail dressed with elegant restraint, sexy but never obvious. Again, not my type. But a body like hers couldn't hide under sedate linen and appropriate hem lengths.

She had long legs, round tits, a firm ass, and thick, silky, dark hair I'd always wanted to pull down from the complicated twists she favored for formal events. She wasn't skinny, like so many of the women in our social set. From what I'd seen, she enjoyed eating, and it showed in her figure.

I'd seen other women sneer at her curves, but more often, I'd spotted the admiring glances of men as they lingered on her ass or her discreet cleavage. I'd caught Abigail looking at me more than once, a heated longing in her warm brown eyes.

She'd always looked away, her cheeks flushed, careful not to get near me for the rest of the night. She'd wanted me, but she hadn't been the type to cheat. If she had been, she wouldn't have been Abigail.

I didn't fuck married women as a rule. If a man wanted simplicity in his lovers, he didn't get in the middle of a marriage. That was the definition of messy.

I'd put her out of my mind and relegated Abigail Jordan to an occasional fantasy, a source of entertainment during otherwise boring social events. I couldn't get my brain around the idea that she was a few floors above me, waiting for me to come home.

Ready and willing to do anything I wanted. Remembering the heat of her eager, sucking mouth on my cock, I gave into temptation and opened my laptop.

Flipping through the open windows, I pulled up the security controls for my penthouse. I should probably feel guilty for not telling her that every inch of the place was under surveillance. Then again, it wasn't her business if it was.

I wouldn't do anything with the recordings that would embarrass her. No one else would see them. The cameras had been installed for security after a break-in. So far, I hadn't used them for anything other than their intended purpose. But I had to see.

What was she doing? Exploring the penthouse? Rifling through my underwear drawer? Trying to crack my safe so she could take off with a wad of cash without having to work for it?

The last wasn't her style, but desperation drove people to do things they'd never consider otherwise.

Like enslaving themselves to virtual strangers. All the same, I doubted she was packing a pillowcase with my mother's silver.

Shifting from one camera to the next, I was surprised to find her tying the belt to a white robe, exiting her en-suite bathroom.

A minute or two earlier, and I'd have seen her naked, wet from the shower, her body slowly emerging from the steam. I groaned at the mental image, my cock swelling at the thought of a naked, slippery Abigail.

She'd sucked my cock, but I hadn't touched more than her face. With that robe tied tight, it looked like I wouldn't get to see more until later.

I ignored the pulse of my erection as I watched Abigail walk to the bedroom door and turn off the light. After a second, the camera switched to night vision. Though the picture was a little grainy and shaded with gray, it was surprisingly clear.

I should have turned the cameras off and gone back to work. There was a deal to put together for my meeting tomorrow, and Abigail was just going to take the nap I'd suggested. Only my pet for an hour, and already, she was following orders.

The sense of satisfaction was absurd, but very real. Forcing myself to focus on my papers, I left open the camera focused on her bed, just to remind myself that she was real.

It wasn't until I went to pull up a spreadsheet on my laptop that I realized she wasn't asleep. The last time I'd checked the monitor, just before I'd gone back to work, I'd seen her tuck herself beneath the white duvet and had assumed she'd be out cold in no time.

She'd done a good job with her makeup, but she hadn't been able to hide the signs of her exhaustion. I wouldn't have been sleeping either if I'd been a woman alone with Big John.

Setting my papers aside, forgetting the spreadsheet, I watched Abigail twist and turn under the heavy duvet.

I almost expected it when she tossed the cover off, kicking it to the end of the bed. She rolled over, tucking her head into her pillow as she stretched, then relaxed.

The robe fell open over her hip, giving me a tantalizing view of long, pale legs and the beginning of the curve of her ass. For a minute, she didn't move, and I thought she'd finally fallen asleep.

She shifted again, her jerky movements betraying her frustration. Her chest heaved in a sigh before she raised one hand and rested it on her chest. She bit her lower lip once, her open eyes flashing like a cat's in the night vision of the camera.

Before I registered what she was thinking, her other hand dropped to the tie on her robe. Finally, I understood.

Abigail was too aroused to sleep. She'd gotten off on sucking me. If she'd dared to touch herself, I was sure she would have come along with me. But she hadn't had the nerve, and her hands had been too busy with my cock.

Selfish bastard that I was, I hadn't taken care of her before I'd left her alone. Her first day as my pet, and she was about to break the rules, big time. Not her fault when I hadn't explained what it meant to be mine. That wouldn't save her from her punishment.

My own hands drifting down to free my hard cock, I watched, my breath held, as she untied the robe. If I'd been there, I would have spread it wide.

Abigail only opened the thick terry cloth enough to cover her breast with her hand. Her other hand slid between her legs.

Wiggling a little, she spread her legs further, giving the camera, and me, a direct view of her pussy, glistening with moisture in the dim light.

CHAPTER FOUR

ABIGAIL

I couldn't remember the last time I'd made myself come. Married to John, sex was never about me. He'd tried, in the beginning. I don't know if he was inexperienced or he just didn't get it, but he never managed to make it good for me.

Fortunately, I knew how to take care of myself. But the last few months, since John had died, I hadn't exactly been feeling sexy. Now, lying in this bed, in Jacob's guest room, my own hands on my body felt foreign. Exciting.

I knew, instinctively, that Jacob would not approve. But I was tired and restless and very, very aroused.

Who knew when he'd be home? And even when he got back, what was to say he'd take care of me?

This arrangement wasn't about my needs. It might have reminded me of my marriage to John, if Jacob hadn't been a completely different man.

Based on my reaction to sucking his cock, I already knew I'd find more pleasure in this arrangement with Jacob than I ever had with John. That was great, but right now, I needed to come.

Cupping one breast with my right hand, I let my left slide down my torso and drop between my legs.

I was wet.

I couldn't believe how wet I was, even after taking a shower. Letting my mind drift, I wondered what Jacob would do with me when he got home.

Would he want me to suck him again? Or would he realize the fantasies I've had for years and fuck me until I couldn't walk?

I dipped one finger deeper between my legs, spreading the slick moisture up to my clit. Just a quick one. Jacob would never have to know.

Pressing and sliding my fingers over my slippery clit, I squeezed my breast, pinching my nipple hard, the way I imagined Jacob would do it.

The need inside me grew, my arousal a demand I had to answer. Giving in completely, I closed my eyes and imagined exactly what I wanted Jacob to do to me.

He would come home from work tired and distracted to find me lying here, naked in his bed. In my mind, this might be the guest room, but it was still his bed.

Everything in this penthouse belonged to Jacob, myself included.

He would see me here, my body exposed, my eyes hot and my pussy wet. He would come to the edge of the bed and begin stripping off his clothes.

First, his dark suit jacket, then his silk tie and his crisp white shirt. He'd undo the shirt buttons and shrug it off, baring his torso to my greedy gaze.

And finally, his hands would go to his belt. A flick of the leather. A button. A zipper.

The shove of two hands on fabric, and he would be naked.

I had to imagine his naked body, but I knew his cock already. It would be thick and hard, reaching for me.

My pussy clenched at the thought of Jacob's cock forcing its way into me.

He would grab me by my ankles and drag me to the edge of the bed, spreading my legs wide. It might've been a fantasy, but I could feel the demand as his eyes raked my body.

One second more, and he would drop to his knees at the end of the bed, fitting his cock to my pussy. He'd have to work to get inside me.

It'd been months since I'd had sex, and then only with John, who was nowhere near Jacob's size. My fingers squeezed my nipple and my clit at the same time, sending a jolt of white-hot pleasure arcing through my body.

I'd never much been into virgin and conqueror fantasies, but in my imagination, fucking Jacob would be like getting fucked for the first time.

There would be that painful stretch as he made room for himself inside my body. I knew it would hurt, and I didn't care. I wanted it. Wanted him. Wanted him to fill me up and fuck me until I lost myself in it.

At the thought of his strong body moving over me, his cock thrusting hard, the need in my body tightened. It wasn't enough.

I didn't want my hands. I wanted Jacob.

For now, this would have to do. Driving two fingers into my pussy, I ground my palm down against my clit, pressing in tight circles that pulled my rising pleasure and need into a tension that had to shatter before it cracked me in half.

I pulled my knees up around his phantom body and the imitation of sex, the familiar touch of my hand between my legs as the thought of Jacob set off my brewing orgasm.

Pleasure flowed through my body, erasing the stress of the day, the fear, the uncertainty, and the sheer exhaustion of worry.

The physical release of the fantasy combined with the reality of being in Jacob's home washed me clean. I dried my wet fingers on the robe, suddenly too tired to even think about getting up.

Pulling the thick duvet over me, I rolled over and let sleep take me under.

Chapter Five
Abigail

I woke from a dreamless sleep to an itchy tickle between my shoulder blades. Sprawled on my stomach, the robe twisted out of place, I was acutely aware that I was not alone in the dark room.

I had no idea what time it was, but I felt like I'd been asleep for hours. The blinds in the guest room were closed, the heavy drapes still drawn as I'd left them before my nap.

Weak, gray light leaked in around the edges, suggesting it was either early evening, or I'd slept straight through until morning. I didn't feel rested enough to have slept all night, so it must have been option number one.

If I rolled over, I knew I would see him. Jacob. Watching me sleep. My stomach turned with anticipation and dread.

This was the beginning.

The interview in his office, and the blow job, had been nothing more than an appetizer. Now it was real. I was in his home, and he was waiting for me to wake up and begin serving him.

With a deep breath for courage, I rolled over, searching for his tall form in the dark room.

He stood at the end of the bed facing me, his hands tucked into his pockets. I didn't need to see his face clearly to feel the weight of his silver gaze. Tension strung tight in the room.

Whatever was going to happen next, it was safe to say Jacob was not as relaxed as his stance implied. Ignoring the flutters in my stomach, I pushed free of the duvet and sat up, reaching for the light on the nightstand.

"Leave it off," he said. "Come with me."

I rolled out of the bed and followed him through the dark room, tightening the belt on my robe as I walked, aware it was a futile gesture since he was probably about to order me to strip naked.

Jacob led me down the long hall, back into the main living space of the penthouse. When we reached the comfortable sitting area in front of his flat screen TV, he gestured at the couch for me to sit down.

I followed his direction, not sure exactly what he wanted and not ready to piss him off. Jacob took a seat in a leather armchair facing the couch. He leaned back, crossing his arms over his chest, and studied me, a faint smirk on his face.

"Sleep well?" he asked.

"Yes," I said, uncertain what he wanted.

"Good." Jacob nodded, the smirk blooming into a full smile. "Did I remember to tell you that there are cameras in every room of the penthouse?"

I felt the blood drain from my face. Cameras? In every room? The only reason he would bother to mention them now was if he'd been watching me.

And if he'd been watching me, he'd seen what I'd done. Seen me touching myself. Watched me make myself come.

As fast as my face had paled, I flushed a deep, hot red. I wasn't a child. I'd made myself come before, but never for an audience. Especially not one I didn't know was there.

"No, you didn't tell me."

Despite my raging embarrassment, I did what I always did when I was confused. I straightened my spine, cleared all expression from my face, and gave Jacob a cool smile.

"I'll keep it in mind for the future."

"Did I also forget to tell you that you belong to me?"

"No, I understood that," I said.

"Then I must have neglected to inform you that I don't just own your body. I own everything about you. Including your pleasure. So when you made yourself come without my permission, you stole from me."

"Jacob," I began.

"Quiet." He sat forward in the chair, bracing his elbows on his knees, eyes intent on my face. "Stand up. Take off the robe."

It didn't occur to me to disobey. His voice had a physical presence, heavy and solid, demanding complete obedience.

You would think, after the life I'd lived with the Jordan family, I would balk at being told what to do. Oddly, coming from Jacob, the orders were a relief.

After so much confusion and fear, there was something freeing about knowing exactly what I should do.

Wobbling just a little, I came to my feet, my hands working the knot of the belt. I'd tied it tight as I'd walked down the hall, and it took me a minute to loosen the fabric.

As soon as I had it free, I shrugged the thick terrycloth robe off my shoulders, leaving me naked to Jacob's hot gaze.

Even as my cheeks flamed, my nipples hardened into two tight points.

I was wet. Again.

Or still.

It was hard to tell, but standing in front of Jacob bare ass naked was definitely a turn-on. The grin melted from his face, leaving only a serious, set expression.

"Another thing I may not have explained adequately," he said. "Is that when you disobey me, you will be punished."

My throat suddenly bone dry, I had no idea what to say to that. I couldn't say 'no'. Besides, my body was thinking something more like 'yes, please'.

"Come here."

I crossed the room to Jacob slowly, not sure if I hung back out of apprehension or to build my growing sense of anticipation. From the way he was sitting, knees together on the edge of the chair, I had the feeling I was about to get an old-fashioned spanking.

I didn't have the time to wonder how I felt about that. Seconds after his command, I stood before him.

When he took my hand and pulled me down, draping me over his knees, I gave him no resistance. His legs were hard muscle under my stomach, my breasts pressed to the side of his thigh.

His hand on my back made me jump, and I heard a chuckle from above me. Long fingers smoothed over my spine, spreading tingles of heat. Without warning, he dipped two fingers between my legs, going straight for my wet pussy.

"Fuck, you're soaked. Is this from before or now?"

"Both," I said.

Jacob drove his fingers deep inside, twisting them,

stretching me. I'd been right. If his fingers were almost too much to take, his cock really was going to feel like getting fucked for the first time.

Just as I was getting used to his fingers inside me, he slid them out, raised his hand, and smacked his palm against my ass.

I squealed. The sound was high-pitched and embarrassing, but I couldn't have stopped it.

The first smack was followed by a second, and a third in rapid succession. His skin against mine stung, then burned, my tender flesh unused to such abuse.

He didn't count, didn't ask me to keep count. He just smacked my ass over and over, moving his hand from one side to the other, first low, then high, so that he always had a fresh target.

My emotions tangled in my chest as I tried to process what was happening. This was supposed to be a punishment.

In a way, it was.

God knew, it hurt like hell.

But I'd felt pain before, and this was no regular pain. This pain was alive. Strongest in the reddened skin of my ass, it spread through my body, somehow both sensitizing and numbing all my nerves.

After the first few shocking spanks, my brain relaxed.

Every strike hurt, but once I got used to it, with each touch of his palm to my skin, I felt a surge of desire between my legs.

I squirmed against him, not sure if I wanted to get closer or get away from his relentless punishment. One of my nipples scraped the upholstery of the chair, sending a desperate flare of pleasure through my body.

A tiny, panicked voice in the back of my brain was

begging, 'please, stop', 'please, let me go', but I kept my mouth shut.

Partly because this was the deal that I'd made. Jacob owned me. If he wanted to spank me for masturbating, that was his right. I'd given it to him willingly, and it was a far better deal than what I would have gotten from my father-in-law.

But the real reason I didn't ask him to stop? It was because every time he smacked me, it made me want him more.

The pain tangled with need, tangled with pictures in my head of Jacob pushing me to the floor, coming down on top of me, and fucking my brains out.

After an undetermined amount of time, he stopped. One arm lay tight across my back, pinning me in place. With his other hand, the hand he'd used to spank me, he rubbed light, soothing circles across the sore skin of my ass.

I froze, waiting. Was he done? Was that it? The punishment had short-circuited something in my brain. That tiny part of me that hadn't liked it was relieved. But the rest of me was mystified at how I'd given myself over to him.

If I'd been wet before, now I was dripping. Every time my thighs rubbed together, I felt trails of moisture running down toward my knees. It was insane. I'd never, ever in my life been this wet. Been this desperate.

In a way, it wasn't that hard to understand. I'd always had a crush on Jacob, had fantasies about him for years, and I'd spent those years in a loveless and somewhat scary marriage.

I wasn't confused about being attracted to Jacob. There'd been a time or two, at a boring party after too much champagne, when just watching Jacob got me a little wet. But the spanking part—I didn't know what to make of that.

I'd only been struck a handful of times in my life, those few by my father-in-law, and I had not enjoyed it. I understood that getting hit by Big John was not the same thing as a naked spanking from Jacob.

Still, Jacob had draped me over his knees, stark naked, and he'd smacked my ass until it burned with pain. So why had I liked it so much? And there was no question that I had liked it.

Even if I tried to pretend I hadn't, my pussy gave me away.

As if he read my mind, Jacob stopped his soothing strokes and moved his hand between my legs. It was embarrassing that he didn't even need to get close to my pussy to feel my need for him.

He traced his fingertips up and down my inner thighs, running them through the slick moisture. I trembled, my lips falling open, ready to beg.

Forget that I had come only hours before. It was like that release had never happened.

As he touched me, skating his fingertips around but never actually on my pussy, I became aware of the hard bar of his cock pressing into my stomach. It was a relief and a promise.

He had to fuck me soon, didn't he? I knew better than to think I could take care of this myself. Unless I wanted another punishment, which I was pretty sure I did, just not right now.

I fought my own body, desperate not to squirm against him. It was silly to try to hang on to dignity in the aftermath of the spanking that had ignited a desperate need to fuck.

I already felt so vulnerable, my brain still spinning, my body glowing with pain and need and an odd, floating peace, that I just didn't want him to know exactly how badly I wanted him.

I lost the fight.

Without my permission, my hips pressed back into his fingers, searching for contact. I knew it wouldn't take much to push me over the edge. I was right there already.

A finger, a little pressure on my clit. Just one more touch.

"Time to get up," he said.

His hand left my thighs, and he reached to take my elbows, lifting me carefully to a standing position. I wobbled a little and couldn't help leaning into him.

The thump of his heart echoed against my cheek through the cool, fine cotton of his shirt. A comfort next to the exquisite pleasure of my nipples sliding against the same fabric.

His arms came around me, holding me for the briefest moment before stepping back. He turned away and headed for the kitchen, saying over his shoulder,

"Time to eat. Leave the robe."

CHAPTER SIX

ABIGAIL

When I walked into the kitchen, Jacob was leaning into the oven, looking at two tinfoil pans. He must've brought home takeout.

The faint smell of garlic, tomatoes, and spices drifted into the room, and I realized I was starving. I hadn't eaten much that morning. I'd been so overwhelmed and relieved, by the time Jacob brought me to his penthouse, that all I'd wanted to do was take a shower and go to sleep.

Now I wasn't sure what I wanted more, that food or the orgasm Jacob had denied me. He closed the oven and turned to the counter, picking up a small black box sitting beside his keys.

"Come here, Abigail," he said.

I crossed to him, not bothering to conceal my curiosity as I stared at the black box. He opened it to reveal a length of shining silver chain with sparkling pale blue gemstones at either end.

As he lifted it, I realized that it was not a necklace, as I'd thought, but something else. The blue stones set off two silver clamps shaped like long Vs with tiny metal teeth at the end.

A delicate circle of silver wrapped the V of the clamp, and as he lifted it and slid the circle up, I saw that it would control how tightly those teeth would grip.

I'd seen pictures of nipple clamps before, but I'd never seen any in person. Definitely none this beautiful. Jacob didn't have to prepare my nipples for the clamps. They were already two tight beads, ready for whatever he wanted to do with them.

"Have you worn clamps before?" he asked as he placed the first silver clamp against my left nipple. I shook my head.

"No," I whispered.

"Given how you responded to the spanking, I think you'll like these."

I nodded my head, unable to speak. The bite of those tiny silver teeth into my hard nipple sent shockwaves through my hyper-aroused body.

He fastened the second clamp, and I swayed on my feet. I hadn't imagined it was possible to feel this much sexual need at one time. Then it occurred to me.

He was going to make me eat dinner like this. Naked. My nipples clamped, my pussy soaked. I was swamped by confusion.

What kind of game was this? I understood the punishment, but I'd felt him. He was rock hard and ready to go. Why didn't he just take me? I belonged to him, after all.

"Why?" I whispered. Jacob ran his finger down my nose and smiled. I'd always loved his smile, even now when he was being a bastard.

"Why did I spank you? Why did I clamp you?"

"No. Why aren't you . . . Why don't you want to—"

"Why didn't I fuck you?" he asked, his smile growing even wider.

I nodded in response, not sure I trusted myself to speak. Jacob tilted his head to the side and studied me standing before him, fighting not to squirm.

"Did you think the spanking was the punishment?"

At that, he turned around, took the foil pans out of the oven, and began to plate our dinner. I stood there dumbfounded, marveling at the depth of his evil.

The chain on the clamps swayed, tugging on my nipples, sending jolts of pain and pleasure from my breasts straight to my pussy. For the first time, I felt like a pet.

Clearly, he enjoyed this—having power over me, playing with me. Making up arbitrary rules about my body and then punishing me for my transgressions.

I wished I could say I wasn't enjoying it too, but that would be a lie. This was too new, and all I had to offer, aside from my intense arousal, was confusion. And obedience.

Fine. I could obey. I had a lot riding on keeping Jacob happy. But that didn't mean I wouldn't be myself at the same time.

Trying to ignore the clamoring demands of my body, I checked the kitchen drawers and found silverware and napkins. While Jacob dealt with the food, I set the table.

The dining room was tucked beside the entry hall, separated from the rest of the penthouse by glass French doors, currently propped open.

The long and rectangular formal dining table, polished to a fierce shine, was surrounded by upholstered chairs that looked comfortable. The type of chairs that invited long, intimate meals.

I swallowed. I didn't want a long, intimate meal. I wanted to eat fast and then get fucked. By Jacob.

My own mind felt foreign, as unlike me as my nudity and the glittering jewelry pinching my nipples. I didn't usually think about sex. I never called it 'fucking', even in my own head.

Jacob had done this to me.

He made me so hot, so needy that I was devolving into a creature of sheer carnality after less than a day. I was going to set the table, but my head wasn't thinking of domestic skills.

My head was thinking, *eat, then get to come. Please, please, let me come.* Or, preferably, come first, then eat. But that wasn't going to happen. With a small sigh, I focused on the task ahead.

Half of the long table was covered with shopping bags. I took that to mean that Jacob didn't want us to eat opposite one another, the whole of the table between us. That worked for me.

I'd always hated when two people sat that way, raising their voices to be heard just for the sake of formality. My parents had done it every evening, sticking me in the middle, translating from one end to the other.

Setting the napkins and silverware at our places, I turned to get drinks and almost crashed into Jacob. Suddenly, I was acutely aware that I was naked in his dining room and acting like his hostess.

He didn't seem the least bit surprised, handing me the warm plates, piled high with what looked like lasagna, before he headed back to the kitchen, asking over his shoulder,

"Wine or beer? Or a cocktail?"

"Wine, please." I arranged our plates, folding the napkins in precise triangles. Silly when we were about to use them, but setting an attractive table was one of the frivolous, wifely things John had expected that I'd enjoyed. Fussy, but it could be fun.

I waited for Jacob to return before I sat, not sure what he expected of me. He walked back into the room carrying two glasses, a plate of garlic bread, and a wine bottle clamped under his arm.

"Sit," he said.

I did as ordered, watching him open the wine with easy competence. A deep, rich red, the scent of the wine drifted across the table, teasing my nose.

I had a feeling Jacob had good taste in wine. Taking a small sip from the glass he handed me, I confirmed my suspicion.

"Good?" he asked, nodding at the wineglass in my hand.

"Very."

I put the wine down and picked up my fork and knife. My mother always told me, 'A lady is never the first to eat', but I was starving and I didn't think Jacob would mind. I could be about to earn another spanking.

I was willing to take the risk for a bite of that cheesy, meaty lasagna. My guess was safe. Jacob smiled at me and picked up his own silverware.

For the next ten minutes, we barely spoke. I did my best not to shovel food in my mouth. It was hard. The lasagna was perfect, with just the right amount of garlic and extra Parmesan, the sauce almost, but not quite, spicy. Forget about the garlic bread.

Light, crispy, buttery—I could have eaten the whole plate on my own. The food was so good that I forgot I was sitting at the table naked, despite the abrasion of the chair on my tender ass.

Reality didn't trickle back in until my stomach was mostly full and a glop of sauce fell off my fork to land on my bare thigh. I looked down in surprise, still chewing, to see the warm, red sauce sliding across my skin.

The sight was so incongruous in the formal dining room that I immediately began to feel uncomfortable. I put down my fork and swallowed, the food sticking in my throat.

"Am I eating dinner naked, with clamps on my nipples?" I asked, watching Jacob for his response. I earned another one of those grins.

"You are. Do you mind? Because I'm enjoying the view."

He took another bite of lasagna. His eyes followed my blush, raking me from my hairline to the tips of my clamped breasts, all the way to the napkin barely covering my legs, now stained with sauce.

"I don't know that I mind," I said. "But I do feel like I left home this morning and stepped into the twilight zone."

"You may feel that way for a while," he said. "If you decide you want to stay."

I raised my eyebrows, deciding the only way to deal with this was to brazen it out. I had the feeling that a few weeks with Jacob, and I would not be blushing quite so much.

Lifting my wine glass, I took a sip, finally able to appreciate how good the wine was now that my stomach wasn't grinding in starvation.

"If I decide I want to stay?" I asked. "I thought I'd already decided."

"That was this afternoon. You might've changed your mind."

"I haven't changed my mind," I said. I thought about adding something like *maybe I will if you don't let me come*, but that felt like it would be breaking the rules.

I wasn't willing to subvert my entire personality in the

service of Jacob, but I had to remember what this was. I wasn't his girlfriend. I wasn't his lover. I was his pet.

"Good. When you're done, please clear the table and bring back the white box in the refrigerator with one fork."

I was finished eating, and the thought of what might happen next drowned what was left of my appetite. I did as he asked, carrying both our plates into the pristine kitchen, taking a minute to rinse and load them into the dishwasher.

I wasn't sure if Jacob had a housekeeper, but he didn't seem like a man who did his own dishes. If I was going to end up doing them, I did not want to be stuck scraping off dried tomato sauce.

The refrigerator held a white bakery box, not large enough for an entire cake or pie but too big to hold just one slice. I took a clean fork from the drawer and brought it and the box back to the dining room.

Placing the box and the fork in front of Jacob, I returned to my seat. Jacob didn't open the box or touch the fork. Instead, he lifted his glass of wine and took another sip. I did the same, noticing that he'd refilled our glasses while I'd been gone.

"So you're staying," he said.

"Yes, I'm staying." Despite my embarrassment, my uncertainty, and the outright confusion at how I was going to handle all of this, I did not want to leave.

I wasn't entirely sure if that was my pussy talking, still hanging on in the hopes of an eventual orgasm, or my long-standing fascination with Jacob.

Probably both. And let's not forget that his power and money were the only things standing between my mother and a life on the street. Then there was Big John . . . I had a lot of reasons to stay.

"Do you have any questions?" Jacob slid his seat back

from the table, crossing one ankle over his knee in a comfortable half-slouched position.

I'd been right again. The plushy upholstered chairs really did invite lounging at the table. If I hadn't been naked, I might have been tempted to imitate his position. Instead, I sat up straight, knees together, acutely aware of my upthrust breasts and the chain dangling between them. Did I have questions? More than a few.

"Are you . . . is this . . . are you into bondage?"

My inexperience was showing. I knew what I wanted to ask, but I didn't have the right language to ask it.

"Are you asking if I like to tie women up for sex, or if I practice BDSM?"

"Both, I guess. I'm not sure I understand the difference," I said.

"Then I'll explain. BDSM refers to a lifestyle, at least the way I think you're asking. And the answer to that is no. I'm not a trained master, and I don't generally engage in dominant/submissive relationships with women. I'm neither a sadist nor a masochist. However, I do enjoy a variety of activities, sexually, including bondage. And in most things, but absolutely when it comes to sex, I like to be in charge."

"So this is the first time you've had something like this?"

I gestured between us, not comfortable using the word 'pet' to refer to myself out loud.

"It is," he said. "As I said earlier, I'm trying something new."

"Because you don't want a relationship," I said.

"Exactly."

"But—"

"Abigail," he said. "Don't overanalyze it. I'm going to be sexist for a minute, so bear with me. Women tend to think everyone wants a relationship. That everyone needs to partner up. I'm not interested. I have work. I have friends. I have time for very few outside interests. Relationships are demanding. Frankly, I've never been involved with a woman who was worth the trouble. At least, not outside of bed."

"Don't you get lonely?"

"Were you lonely with John?" he asked.

That was a direct hit. He was right. I had been lonely with John, desperately lonely.

"Okay, but what happens if while we're doing this," I gestured between us again. "You meet someone and—"

"Not going to happen. What we're doing right here? This is stacking up to be my ideal situation. As long as you're good with it, you don't have to worry about any other women."

"All right," I said.

Maybe it was sexist. *Did* all women think everyone had to pair up? I didn't know. The assumption that people were meant to couple had always felt like a given part of life.

And here was Jacob saying that, now that he had me, he had everything. Some part of me, the part that was still innocent, that still hoped, felt like he was giving up. As if, even with all he had, he was settling for a barren existence by denying a need for love.

Who was I to tell Jacob Winters how to live? I'd made a mess of my own life. And I certainly hadn't had any luck finding love for myself. Maybe this was the best I could do as well.

"Any other questions?" he asked.

"Yes. When can I visit my mother?" I asked.

"Not yet. As soon as I think it's safe, I'll arrange for you to visit her. How often do you normally go to see her?"

"At least three times a week," I said. "I'll need to call and let them know I won't be in for a while."

"I'd rather you didn't," Jacob said. "You're more secure if you have zero contact with the outside world. I already called them today and had your mother's account transferred to my name."

"They let you do that?"

"It turns out that Big John hasn't been overly prompt in paying her bills. They were more than happy, with a little extra incentive, to move her account to a more reliable source of income."

"He wasn't paying for her care?"

After all that he'd put me through, the idea that big John wasn't even covering her bills enraged me. Our position had been more precarious than I'd known, a thought that would have terrified me if Jacob hadn't already come to our rescue.

"He was paying," Jacob said. "Just not on time every month. He was delinquent often enough that they felt secure, legally, in terminating his access to her account. You remain the primary contact person. Don't worry."

"And you really think it's that dangerous for me to leave the penthouse?" I asked.

"For now, I do." Jacob paused, taking a sip of his wine, thinking. "How much do you know about what the Jordans are into?"

"Not a lot," I said, embarrassed that I was so ignorant of my in-laws' activities.

In a wry, self-deprecating tone, I said, "Based on the people I've seen coming through the house and the business, I figured out that they don't run a plumbing supply company."

To my surprise, a laugh burst from Jacob's mouth, showing a line of straight white teeth. The sound was lighthearted, amused, and it made him look years younger. I couldn't help but smile back.

"Have you been inside the business?" he asked.

"Just the front offices. And only a few times. A long time ago, when we were first married, I wandered into the warehouse by mistake. John was furious, and I never went near it again."

"What did you see?"

"Nothing that looked like plumbing supplies," I answered. "Not that I know a lot about what plumbing supplies would look like, but I'm pretty sure they don't come in soft, plastic-wrapped bales."

"No," Jacob said, shaking his head. "They don't."

"I was very young when we got married. I didn't realize what I was seeing. Not until more recently."

"And how much of my business do you think intersects with Big John's?"

A disorienting rush of horror sent my stomach plunging to my toes. Icy fear washed my skin.

I'd assumed, since I'd known Jacob through John and not his father, that Jacob's business interests were entirely legitimate.

Thinking of his office, this penthouse, and the power I knew he held in the city, that assumption suddenly seemed very, very foolish.

"Relax," Jacob said. "I'm not the next in line to serve you up to a gang of bikers. I'm not a criminal. I don't do business with criminals. John was trying to take the Jordans legitimate. His efforts were failing when he died, but our work together was in commercial real estate, not running drugs or guns or any of the rest of the shit your father-in-law's got going on."

"Okay." I could barely get my breath.

"I only asked because I wanted a clearer idea of who you thought you were getting into bed with. But the look on your face tells me everything I need to know."

"If you're not involved with that side of their business, how do you know so much?" I dared to ask.

"Information is essential, Abigail. I make a point of knowing everything there is to know about the players in my city. Especially if I'm working with them. The money John invested with my projects was technically clean, but I had to make sure I understood where it originally came from. I know more about what Big John has going right now than he'd like. And I've heard rumors that he has a tasty new treat to offer his partners as an incentive."

"You mean he's been telling people . . .?" My stomach turned.

"That's what I heard," Jacob said. "There's interest in John's widow, and he's going to be very unhappy when he can't find you. I don't know how hard or long he's going to look for you. He might be willing to cut his losses, or his ego might make this difficult. Some of it depends on what promises he's made involving you, and to whom he's made those promises. I don't want to keep you from your mother. I think I understand how important she is to you. But I won't risk your safety."

"How long do you think I'll have to wait?"

"I don't know. As soon as I think it's safe, I'll arrange for you to resume your regular visits."

I couldn't argue with that. As much as I wanted to see my mother, whether she knew I was there or not, it would be a disaster in every way possible if I fell into Big John's hands.

I was just going to have to be patient.

"Now," Jacob said. "Let's have dessert."

Chapter Seven

Abigail

J acob's words sent hungry shivers through my body. For once, I wasn't interested in dessert. Not if, by dessert, he meant food.

Something in the tone of his voice, predatory and intense, suggested he wasn't talking about whatever was in the white box.

"Come here." Jacob held out his hand for me. I stood, as if in a daze, and rounded the corner of the dining room table, my hand reaching for his.

When he had me in his grip, he arranged me in front of him, my sore ass pressing to the edge of the table, my body bracketed between his knees.

Giving my hip a light slap, he said,

"Up."

Without thinking, I hopped up onto the table. Either I was getting used to being naked, or I just didn't care anymore. My inhibitions were distracted by the hard bar of Jacob's cock tenting his suit pants.

Naked was good.

Naked meant that as soon as he got those pants off, I

would be that much closer to having that cock inside me. He pulled his chair closer to the table, using his elbows to spread my knees.

My center of gravity shifted, and I fell back, propping myself up on my palms. Maybe I was dessert. I felt like it - as if I were serving myself up to him, my breasts swelling, nipples hard and so red, and my pussy still wet, soaked, and very needy.

After a long moment staring at me displayed before him, Jacob turned and opened the white bakery box. Inside, I saw a small cake only large enough for two, maybe three, servings.

I couldn't see the inside, but the frosting was a deep chocolate decorated with tufts of whipped cream. My mouth watered.

I was a sucker for chocolate. Jacob picked up the fork and scooped the bite of cake right off the side, not bothering to slice it.

Lifting the fork, he brought it to the edge of my lip and scraped the tines against my skin as if requesting entry. I opened. The chocolate and sweet cream hit my tongue in an explosion of decadent flavor.

Before I got used to it, the fork was gone. Jacob went back and dug out another bite, this time all frosting, no cake. Pressing my thighs further open, he swiped the loaded fork down the center of my pussy and dove in for his dessert.

At the first flick of his tongue, I almost choked on the cake still melting in my mouth. Nothing we had done today was normal for me.

But this . . . this was one of those things I'd read about but never experienced.

It was heaven.

Not that I would know, but I didn't think Jacob was

using any special technique. At least, to start, he was just licking off the frosting. That was enough.

His tongue had barely touched me before I was back on the edge of orgasm, teetering, dying to crash down on the other side, to drown in the pleasure that had been tormenting my body since I first dropped to my knees in his office.

He knew. So far, he seemed to know exactly what my body wanted. Lifting his head, he said,

"Don't come."

"What?" The word was a scream, desperate and offended.

"Not until I tell you that you can."

He had barely enough time to smile, that mischievous glint in his eye, before he went back to work. How was I supposed to wait? What was he even talking about, *don't come?*

Was he insane? And when had I gone from a woman who'd only ever come on her own to one who couldn't imagine holding back another second?

How was I supposed to hold back? Didn't guys think about baseball? I didn't know anything about baseball.

And while I sensed he wanted me to let the pleasure build without spilling over, I had no idea how to find that kind of discipline.

He laughed at me, holding back my pubic hair with one hand to bare the glistening lips of my pussy and my hard red clit. I couldn't keep up.

He alternated between soft, slow licks, teasing my eager flesh, before focusing his attention on my clit and sucking hard. The first time he did that, I almost lost the battle.

I twisted under him, every movement sending the chain between my nipples shifting to one side or the other, pulling on the clamps, the painful, tugging pressure driving jolts of pleasure straight from my breasts to the spot between my legs, where Jacob had focused all of his attention.

In the distance, I heard a voice, thin, high, pleading.

"Please. Please. Please. Jacob, please."

Finally, he stopped, pushing back just enough to stand. I heard the rustle of fabric, the crinkle of foil. Then he was right there, between my legs, his hands reaching for my sore ass.

I was so aroused, so needy, that I didn't even flinch when his fingers closed over my red skin. He yanked me closer, and the press of his cock to my weeping pussy was the answer to every prayer running through my fevered brain.

"Yes. Please. Yes."

When he pressed into me, the stretching pain only pushed me higher. Like the nipple clamps and the spanking, it brought an edge I'd never known I wanted.

My head dropped back, eyes staring blindly at the ceiling. It took more than one thrust to fill me completely. I was too tight, and he was too thick. I could tell, despite his own tension, that he was trying to hold back.

I wiggled closer, trying to take as much of him as I could get. Finally, he was seated to the hilt.

When he pulled back and thrust in the first time, I thought I was going to explode. There was no way I could stop myself from coming.

I knew I had to, knew it was important to him, but my entire body had been on the edge for too long, and every stroke of his thick cock pushed me that much further.

"Jacob. Jacob, I can't. Jacob, please," I babbled, logic and sense long gone.

I teetered, feeling the orgasm cresting everywhere. My

pussy, my breasts, and on the skin of my stomach, where the chain slid back and forth, teasing my sensitized flesh.

His eyes burned into me, and I knew he felt it too. I heard myself begging, words of entreaty spilling through my lips as I writhed beneath him. He gripped my hips, pinning me to the table, holding me perfectly still.

I was a vessel, there only to receive his pounding cock, and it was the best thing I'd ever felt.

"Now. Come now," he said, his voice a rasp.

At his words, the pressure inside me detonated in a white-hot wave that swept me from my head to my toes. I heard myself screaming, felt my hands clawing at him as I arched and stiffened and twisted.

He fucked me through it, driving me higher, dragging it out until I thought I'd drown. I have no idea how long the orgasm lasted, but when I came back to myself, I knew two things.

One, I would be willing to do a lot of things for that kind of pleasure. And two, Jacob was still hard inside me.

What kind of discipline did it take for Jacob to have held off his orgasm through my own? I didn't know the answer, but the question itself was a little scary.

Opening my eyes, I met Jacob's. His silver gaze was hot, intent and pleased. A slow, dreamy smile spread across my face.

His hands slid off my hips and began to stroke my skin. Not with the intent to arouse—at least, he wasn't going for any of the obvious targets.

As his fingers trailed from my shoulders, down my arms, across my stomach, and up between my breasts, it felt less like he was trying to get me hot and more as if he were soothing me.

I stretched, arching my limbs into his touch. He stopped

fucking me, and instead remained completely still between my legs, filling me without moving. It didn't take long before the relaxing strokes of his fingers had me wanting more.

Just when I was beginning to wonder exactly what he was up to, Jacob's hands stopped between my breasts. He lifted the chain and tugged.

A bolt of sharp, pained pleasure shot straight between my legs. He tugged the chain again, and my head dropped back as my pussy clenched around his cock.

Another pull on the chain, and I thrust my hips at him, trying to take more when I was already full, restless and needy all over again.

Only a few hours as Jacob's pet, and I was getting quite an education. I'd never really understood the connection between pain and pleasure.

I always thought it was fiction, one of the many things you read about that isn't real. Now I knew, not only was it real, but I was one of those women for whom pain could be a turn-on.

Not with just anyone, but I trusted Jacob. I wasn't exactly sure why, but as much as there were things about him that scared me a little, I knew I was safe with him.

"Are you ready to come again?" Jacob asked, pulling on the chain with his right hand and then his left, sending flares of exquisite need through my body.

I couldn't answer with words. I was beyond language. The only thing I wanted as much as another orgasm was to feel Jacob let go.

I needed it. To feel him come inside my body, to know that I was giving him at least a fraction of the pleasure he was giving me.

My legs were still wrapped around him, though they'd fallen loose after I came. In answer to his question, I pinned him between my thighs and used all my strength to work my pussy back and forth on his cock.

Jacob growled.

Dropping the chains, he took a clamp in each hand, slid down the rings, and released my nipples. Agony swelled in my breasts as the blood rushed back into my tortured flesh.

As quickly as it hit, the pain faded to be replaced by a pleasure so sweet, it was almost an orgasm in itself.

I gasped a sob as Jacob slipped his hands beneath my knees and pulled my legs from around him. He leaned over me, pressing my knees back, opening me obscenely wide.

This morning, being this exposed to anyone would have shocked me unconscious. Not now. Now, all I knew was the need.

Jacob hammered into me, fucking me hard, harder than I'd ever been fucked before. At his groan of release, my own orgasm tore free, along with a keening cry.

He collapsed over me, his hard chest pressing my breasts flat, as my arms came tight around him. I held on, gasping and sobbing as my orgasm took me under, then slowly eased into a glow of sated pleasure.

We stayed like that, pressed together, collapsed on the table, until we'd both gotten our breath back.

Then, before I could think about what might be next, Jacob was moving, sliding out of my sore pussy and walking away with a firm, "Don't move," tossed over his shoulder.

Good. Because I wasn't sure I could move. At least, not yet. I drifted, eyes half-open, every muscle in my body relaxed. Not only had I never had sex like that before, but I'd never even imagined sex like that.

My every secret masturbatory fantasy seemed pale and dull beside what Jacob had just done to me. I wasn't doing this, being Jacob's pet, for the orgasms.

I knew our arrangement wasn't about me. The only way I would get to come like that was if it did something for Jacob. But as long as I got that every once in a while, I was going to be more than okay with the situation.

He was back before I'd really gotten my head in gear, carrying something in his hand. I tried to sit up, but he pushed me down with a firm hand, moving between my still-open legs. Warm, gentle heat on my tender parts.

He was cleaning me, sliding the washcloth up my inner thighs and along my pussy. In the back of my mind, I was embarrassed.

I'd gotten so wet, I'd leaked down my legs. I didn't even know my body could do that. I was naked, sprawled on his dining room table, and Jacob stood between my legs, fully dressed.

When he was done, he set the washcloth off to the side and carefully helped me off the table. I was unsteady on my feet, my head still stuck in the clouds. As soon as I had my balance, he stepped away.

Suddenly, the whole scene was surreal. I was stark naked, and he was fully clothed, his suit and tie straightened with precision.

Only minutes before, my uncertainty and embarrassment had been held at bay by need and pleasure and want. Now, it all came flooding back, and I stared at the carpet beneath my bare feet, unable to meet Jacob's eyes.

"I have work to do," he said. "You can take those things back to your room with you." He gestured at the bags on the other end of the table. "I won't see you in the morning. I leave early. I have meetings all day. Plan dinner for seven."

I nodded, not sure how to respond to his suddenly brisk and businesslike tone.

"Sleep well." And with that, he was gone. I stood where

I was, frozen, wishing desperately for clothes. Where had I left my robe?

The living room. In front of the TV. Where Jacob had spanked me. Somewhere down the hall, a door closed. Jacob was in his office. The coast was clear.

I scuttled to the living room, snatched up the white robe, and slipped it on, pulling the belt a fraction too tightly. It was a flimsy defense, but I felt immeasurably better, less vulnerable, than I had when I was naked.

Re-entering the dining room, I scanned the table. Our wine glasses sat, half-full, on either side of the box of cake. Remembering what Jacob had done with that cake sent a flush through my body.

Thoughts and emotions tumbled in my head. Smug satisfaction warred with shame and anxiety. Could I really do this? Reduce my entire life to being nothing more than a sexual pet?

I remembered my epiphany in Jacob's office. All I had was right now. And right now, I was safe, my mother was protected, and I'd just had the most intense, amazing sexual experience of my life.

I wasn't going to worry. I was going to live in the moment.

And in this moment, I had wine, decadent chocolate cake, and shopping bags to explore. So much better than the way I'd started my day, running through the predawn woods, cold and terrified.

I carried Jacob's wine glass and the cake into the kitchen. Cutting myself a generous slice of the cake, I returned the white box to the refrigerator and rinsed Jacob's wine glass.

Then, balancing my plate of cake and my wine glass in

one hand, I scooped up the handles of the shopping bags on the table and carried my booty to my new room.

I ate the cake and finished my wine while sorting through the selection of clothes that Jacob, or probably his assistant, had purchased for me.

The sizes were close enough, and everything was casual rather than tailored, so I could make them work, at least, for now. Casual they might have been, but they were also luxurious and expensive.

A luscious, slouchy cashmere cardigan in a soft violet with a matching camisole and stretchy lounging pants. Another matching camisole/pant set with a pullover hoodie in feather-light pink merino wool with a pocket in the front.

Cute, comfortable, and I knew, expensive. There were a few more outfits like that, two long silk nightgowns, one ivory and one black, along with some necessities.

Panties but no bras, basic toiletries, and a few essentials like eyeliner & mascara.

Thinking ahead, and aware I couldn't go back to Big John's, I'd chucked a few things into my purse when I fled my home that morning.

I'll admit to a certain degree of vanity when I say that my makeup bag was one of the things I'd taken with me.

I'd had no idea where I was going to end up, but wherever it was, I'd had no intention of looking washed out and tired when I got there.

Buzzing a little from the wine and exhausted from my dinner with Jacob, as well as all the sleepless nights in the past few months, I put my new clothes away in the walk-in closet, pulled on the ivory silk nightgown, and fell into bed without washing my face and brushing my teeth.

For the first time in what felt like an eternity, I drifted into a dreamless sleep feeling safe and protected.

Chapter Eight

Abigail

I slept late.

There was no clock on my bedside table, but I knew it when I woke up.

I had that sticky, sludgy feeling you get when you sleep too long after too much wine, worse because I hadn't brushed my teeth or washed my face before bed.

Sliding from beneath the heavy duvet, I stumbled into the bathroom and stepped into the shower. I didn't have to wash my hair again. Long and thick, it took forever to dry, so I didn't wash it every day, but the rest of me needed more than a quick rinse.

After a few minutes of standing beneath the spray of steaming hot water, I felt like a new woman.

Teeth brushed, light makeup, and my hair in a messy bun, I put on the camisole and stretchy pants that went with the violet cashmere cardigan and ventured out of my room.

The penthouse was silent. When I got to the kitchen, the clock over the stove told me that it was ten thirty-seven. I couldn't remember the last time I'd slept that late.

My first order of business? Finding coffee. Since I

couldn't leave the building, I hoped Jacob kept coffee in his kitchen.

The coffeemaker on the counter indicated he did, but it took me a few minutes of searching to find the filters and the canister of ground coffee in his well-hidden pantry.

With coffee brewing, I turned to study the items on the kitchen island—a note, an envelope, a brown box, and a small white shopping bag.

The note read:

Abigail,

You have a laptop and a phone. In the envelope is a credit card under my name. As discussed, use it to purchase anything you need, within reason.

DO NOT use either the laptop or the phone to contact anyone but me. Both have been equipped with monitoring software and will report unacceptable activity to both myself and my security team.

This is for your safety. Do not take it lightly.

Rachel will be by later today with a doctor. He will give you a brief exam and draw blood for some tests. Cooperate with him. I'll provide the results of my own tests.

You are free to use any room in the penthouse with the exception of my office. I have a service that comes to clean, so don't bother with that.

In the envelope, along with the card, is my account information for a grocery store that delivers.

Plan whatever menu you prefer to cook. Stock what you need and instruct them to deliver the groceries to my office. Rachel will bring them up to you. DO NOT open the door for anyone but me or Rachel.

Jacob

.   .   .

I WOULDN'T HAVE EXPECTED A LOVE NOTE, NOT FROM Jacob.

It sounded exactly like him—clear, to the point, and bossy. So he was going to spy on me? He said it was for my safety.

I guess I'd see if the spying would continue after the danger from Big John was gone. And the doctor? I didn't have to think too hard to figure that out.

I was on the pill, and John and I hadn't been using condoms. Before he died, sex had been infrequent, but it probably wasn't a secret that by that time, he'd been nailing half the women in town.

In John's world, fidelity was for wives. The husband's job was to screw anything that moved, as often as possible.

I doubted Jacob would want to use condoms with me, and he was smart to verify that I was clean. I'd had a checkup recently and had asked the doctor for the same tests that Jacob's doctor would likely run.

By some miracle of fate, if John had picked anything up, he hadn't passed it to me.

But telling Jacob that, admitting what my marriage really was, would be more humiliating than just letting his doctor do what he had to do.

It meant something that he wasn't going to make me ask for his own results.

But hey, I had a computer and a phone. And carte blanche at what was probably a pretty nice grocery store. On top of that, aside from the doctor's visit, I didn't have a single obligation all day except to plan dinner.

Fortunately for me, not only did I like to cook, but I kept all my favorite recipes in an online database I could access from anywhere.

At the time, I'd done it for convenience. Now, it was

comforting to know that I hadn't lost one of the few good parts of my marriage when I left home.

I poured myself a cup of coffee, added a little cream and sugar, and set off to explore Jacob's penthouse.

I'd already seen the kitchen, the living room with its comfortable couches and big TV, and of course, the dining room and my bedroom. But down the long hall where my room was located were a few doors I hadn't opened.

I walked through the living room first. Though I'd been in it the night before, I hadn't exactly been paying attention. His flat screen hung on the wall, framed like a painting over the gas fireplace.

On either side of the fireplace, he had built-in shelves with cabinets on the lower half. A quick look revealed stereo equipment, a DVD player and some other black boxes I couldn't identify.

A set of heavy double doors were set into the wall to the right of the fireplace. I was betting that was Jacob's office. It was tempting to peek, but I thought better of it, remembering the cameras.

I couldn't say that I hadn't enjoyed my punishment the night before, but I had a feeling that had been a gentle introduction. I wasn't ready to push the boundaries of what Jacob considered 'punishment'. Anyway, there was more penthouse to explore.

Down the hall that led to my bedroom, I found more closed doors. The first was a powder room, its custom porcelain sink set into a repurposed antique chest. Above it hung a gilt-framed mirror.

I've been in some nice bathrooms before, but not many that had chandeliers. This one was perfectly sized for the small room, but the glittering crystal reflecting the gilt of the mirror frame made me feel as if I were in an English manor house and not a penthouse apartment in the middle of the city.

The next door was my bedroom. Nothing new to see there. On the opposite side of the hallway, I discovered a game room, complete with a pool table, wet bar, poker table, and a screen that covered most of the far wall of the room, framed on either side by red velvet curtains.

In front of the screen, Jacob had a semicircle of movie theater seats in black leather that looked so soft and comfortable I thought you could sit there all day. This was a serious man cave.

Back in the corner beside the wet bar and behind the pool table, I spotted an old school pinball machine. I loved pinball.

I hadn't had my hands on one of these in years, but when I was younger, I used to sneak off to the town arcade with one of my cousins and waste quarter after quarter chasing the sounds and lights, trying to rack up as many points as I could.

I'd never been very good, but I didn't really care. To my delight, I quickly realized that Jacob had set the machine to work without quarters, and I killed a good half-hour losing myself in the game.

When I was done, I headed back to the kitchen to pour out my cold coffee and replace it with fresh. Then back to my search. The next door past the man cave turned out to be a workout room.

Jacob had said he never had enough time, so it made sense to have a gym at home. I was thrilled. I missed working out. I'd never been an athlete, but I'd always been fairly active.

In the last few years, John had stopped my going to the

gym in town, claiming he didn't like me out in public, sweating in tight clothes.

I used to do yoga at home, but as Big John and his business acquaintances started to drop by the house unexpectedly, I wasn't comfortable getting caught alone, in yoga pants, in the middle of downward-facing dog.

It looked like I could do almost anything here. Jacob had a treadmill, an elliptical, an impressive rack of free weights, and open space with a padded floor and yet another enormous, wall-mounted flat screen TV with a DVD player on top of the cabinet in the corner.

Now that I had a laptop and Jacob's credit card, I could order some yoga videos and some workout clothes. Putting aside the way I was earning my keep, I was starting to feel like I could get fragments of my old life back. Or at least fragments of the old me.

The last stop on my self-guided tour was the doorway at the far end of the hall. I opened it slowly, aware this could only be Jacob's bedroom.

He'd said I could explore any room except his office, so his bedroom was fair game. Still, sneaking in felt naughty.

I don't know exactly what I expected. I'd already learned that Jacob favored the old over the new, so I didn't think his bedroom would be filled with chrome and black leather.

Given his appetites, I guess I thought there'd be something to give him away. Chains attached to his bed? Handcuffs on the dresser? I didn't know.

The king-size, four-poster bed in warm, polished chestnut with matching dressers and armoire wasn't it.

Actually, his bedroom was similar to mine, except larger and with a little more furniture. On the far side of the room, most of the wall was taken up by windows and a panoramic view of the city.

In front of the window, he had two comfortable looking armchairs with an ottoman and a small table between them.

The dresser opposite the bed had the expected wall-mounted flat screen above it. For a guy with no time on his hands, Jacob had a lot of TVs.

I imagined him lying in bed after a long day of work, catching a few minutes of *SportsCenter* before passing out for the night.

Did he wear pajamas to bed?

No, definitely not. My imaginary Jacob was shirtless, and I realized I hadn't seen him fully naked yet.

I'd seen his cock. I was intimately acquainted with that part of his anatomy. But the night before, in the dining room, he hadn't gotten undressed. In fact, he'd barely pushed his pants down.

Maybe that should have made me feel degraded, with me naked and Jacob not bothering to remove his shirt. It didn't. Instead, it made me feel wanted, as if he'd needed me too badly to bother taking his clothes off first.

Shrugging off the thought—no sense in getting all worked up thinking about naked Jacob when I wouldn't see him for hours—I went back to the kitchen and brought my laptop, the envelope with Jacob's credit card, and my new phone to the kitchen table.

The phone was already charged and powered up. The only numbers in the phone were Jacob's—his office and his mobile.

Not a surprise.

The laptop was. It had been set up with most of the programs I usually used, as well as a new email address.

One I was sure someone on Jacob's security team was monitoring.

It was a little creepy that they were watching me, on the cameras as well as on my laptop and phone, but I'd gone to Jacob for protection, and if he thought this was necessary, I wasn't going to argue.

The truth was, Jacob knew my former father-in-law and his business associates far better than I did. It seemed sensible to trust his judgment, at least for now.

Just the thought of Big John's reaction to my escape sent a shiver of fear down my spine. I was more than willing to hide myself away until Jacob was sure that Big John had lost interest in me.

For the next few hours, I occupied myself browsing on the Internet. Jacob had said to cook him my favorites, so I pulled up my recipes for pot roast and lemon icebox pie.

Not gourmet, by any standards, but they were both delicious, and I loved them. If he didn't agree, I'd find out soon enough. Those would do for tomorrow, since they took a day of prep.

Tonight, we'd have salmon with a light Dijon sauce and fresh green beans, along with the leftover chocolate cake from the night before.

Once I had my shopping list and had placed my grocery order online, I picked up a few of my favorite yoga videos as well as some cute matching yoga outfits, a pair of sneakers, and some other clothes I thought I'd need.

I was leaving the best for last. Books. Reading was another thing that had been curtailed by my husband. He preferred that I read literary fiction, the kind of books you showed off on your coffee table and dropped in the conversation at cocktail parties.

I liked those books well enough, though they could be

depressing and a little boring. My favorite type of fiction was romance.

Needless to say, the husband who had married a 'perfect lady' did not approve of my reading books with half-naked men on the cover.

I was fairly sure Jacob wouldn't give a damn. In fact, I thought he'd be perfectly happy if I got myself an e-reader and filled it with books that would keep me thinking about sex.

I already knew he wouldn't be in favor of the 'happily ever after' part of romances, but I could compartmentalize.

I had almost soothed myself into thinking my new life was going to be almost normal when I heard a knock at the door.

Panic hit first, my heart thumping in my chest before I remembered we were in a secure building.

I sat frozen in my chair for a long moment before a second knock reminded me that I had a visitor. I rose and went to answer it, knowing it couldn't be Jacob and hoping it was all the same.

CHAPTER NINE
ABIGAIL

I wasn't supposed to open the door to anyone but Rachel or Jacob. I knew that. And I wasn't going to.

Fortunately, Jacob's door had a discreet peephole hidden behind a white metal disk that matched the paint on the door.

I rotated it out of the way, suddenly thinking of the action movies I'd seen where the bad guy shoots as soon as he sees someone put their eye to the peephole. Not going to happen, I told myself. Jacob said this building was secure.

I was a little nervous anyway when I looked, my shoulders tight with the anticipation of bad news.

It was with relief, and some disappointment, that I saw Rachel standing on the other side of the door, an unfamiliar older man beside her.

Aware that I had made them wait, I unlocked the door and swung it open, saying, "I'm sorry it took me so long."

"Don't worry about it, dear. This is Dr. Whitmore. He's going to give you a quick examination, and then we'll be out of your way."

I stepped back to let them enter, reassured by Rachel's

polite efficiency. I'd tried not to think about what this must look like to her—a strange woman showing up in her boss's office, moving in less than an hour later, and Jacob sending her shopping to buy me clothes.

It was all very sketchy. At first glance, I would have said Rachel wasn't the kind of woman to do sketchy, but now, she seemed unflappable.

If Jacob hadn't already told me I was the first woman he'd kept, I would have wondered if she did this every day.

Dr. Whitmore, on the other hand, seemed less comfortable with our circumstances. As I followed Rachel down the hall, I noticed that the older man couldn't seem to look at me.

He carried a black leather bag that looked like the stereotypical doctor's kit and walked beside Rachel, saying nothing, his posture stiff, his jaw clenched.

"Will the kitchen work, Dr. Whitmore?" Rachel asked.

"That's fine," he said. Turning to me, he said, "Mr. Winters requested some simple blood tests and a very basic exam. Do I have your consent?"

The doctor was still unable to meet my eyes. I opened my mouth to answer and found I couldn't get a word out. Instead, I nodded.

That wasn't good enough.

Narrowing his eyes, the doctor said, "I need your verbal consent, Miss."

Condescension dripped from his tone. Clearly, he thought I was beneath him and was annoyed with Jacob for asking him to get his hands dirty with a woman like me.

I'd had second thoughts about my deal with Jacob. I'd be even more of a fool than I already was if I hadn't questioned my decision to trade my body for Jacob's help.

I refused to be ashamed.

I was taking care of my mother and saving myself from a fate far worse than consensual sex with a smoking hot guy like Jacob. It wasn't for this doctor to judge me.

Still, I felt a little sick as he prompted, "Miss?"

Somehow, it was worse that he didn't seem to know my name. As always, when I was anxious, I defaulted to dignity, even in a situation completely devoid of that quality.

Raising my chin, I said, "Jordan. Abigail Jordan. I had my last physical seven months ago, and everything was normal. After my husband died four months ago, I had myself tested and had my annual exam with my OB/GYN. I was clean and everything was normal. I have no reason to think that my health has changed since then."

I met Dr. Whitmore's eyes and saw his disdain. I didn't need him to like me. At this point in my life, the only person who needed to like me was Jacob Winters.

"Fine, that's good," he said. Opening his doctor's bag, he removed an old-fashioned stethoscope and gestured for me to turn around.

He placed the stethoscope between my shoulder blades, over my cashmere cardigan, and ordered me to breathe deeply. Checkups never changed.

I remembered being a child, sitting on the tall examining table in my pediatrician's office, legs swinging while my mother waited patiently, breathing deeply for the doctor and dreaming of the lollipop to come when it was over.

I didn't think this disapproving man was going to give me a lollipop. Jacob was enough of a treat, and if he felt better because I'd had a few blood tests, that was understandable.

He'd promised to provide me with the results of his own tests. As invasive as it felt, he was only being sensible.

I tried to hang on to that thought as I removed my cardigan and held out my arm. Saying little, Dr. Whitmore prepared the needle and the collection vials. I looked at the ceiling as the needle pierced my skin.

I was fine with minor pain. Apparently, when it was connected to orgasms, I was fine with more than minor pain, and I didn't mind the sight of blood, but that didn't mean I wanted to watch.

The vials filled slowly, all three of us pretending that we were happy to be there together. Rachel was the only one whose act was believable.

She sat at the island tapping away on her smart phone, and I instinctively knew she wasn't playing around on social media. She did not strike me as a woman who indulged in inappropriate use of her work time.

Dr. Whitmore pulled the needle from beneath my skin with gentle hands, pressing a cotton ball to the small wound and securing it with a Band-Aid. It was clear he disapproved of my presence in Jacob's home, but at least he was being decent about it.

Maybe my concept of what was decent had been warped in my years living with the Jordans. I tried not to dwell on that thought as I led my visitors back to the front door.

Before they left I said, "Rachel, I ordered groceries, as Jacob suggested. They'll be delivered to the office." I trailed off, feeling badly about interrupting her day yet again for something as trivial as my groceries.

Rachel shook her head and said, "Jacob already filled me in, dear. It's not a problem. I'll bring them up as soon as they get here." She turned to the elevator, Dr. Whitmore trailing behind her.

I overheard him say, "Ms. Porter, Tell Mr. Winters I'm

not available for this kind of thing. I'll get the tests done, but . . ."

His voice trailed off. I couldn't hear Rachel's response, but the whole interaction left me feeling uneasy. Was this all a huge mistake? One more time, I tried to think of a way out of the trap I was in.

Without money and the power to protect myself, I'd be in deep trouble. I had no way to get the kind of money I'd need to take care of my mother and no access to the power to get Big John off my back. Not without Jacob. It didn't hurt that I was attracted to him.

If I could stop thinking so much, I could have my cake and eat it too. Or be the cake and let Jacob eat me.

Hearing those words in my head, I flushed. Jacob's no holds barred carnality was new to me. There was no denying that, with him, I loved it.

I spent the next few hours doing a lot of nothing and enjoying every second of it. Rachel delivered the food the same way she'd delivered the doctor, efficiently and politely. I enjoyed unpacking my selections and filling the barren refrigerator.

Based on the state of his kitchen, I was guessing that Jacob almost never ate at home. I loved to cook. It was one of the few places in my marriage that John and my interests had aligned.

My mother had been known throughout the county as the perfect hostess. She never had her parties catered, preferring to do all of the cooking herself, though if the guest count was too high, she'd bring in kitchen help.

I'd learned at her side when I was younger, and after my marriage, John had refused to let me work but had encouraged me to take cooking classes. College was out of the question.

He didn't feel his wife needed to be particularly well-educated, and I'd already completed two years at Georgia State.

To the Jordans, a woman with a college education, even one who'd never gotten her degree, was highly suspect.

They didn't want me giving the rest of the females in the family any ideas, and I think John hoped that by sending me to cooking classes, he could make an open declaration about how thoroughly he had domesticated me.

At the time, it had seemed like a fair trade-off. Maybe it was. My perspective on my marriage was too twisted up with grief and fear and tarnished dreams for me to make any judgments.

If I hadn't walked out of my marriage undamaged, I had left it with some serious skills in the kitchen.

I wasn't using all of them off the bat. Jacob had given me no hints as to what kind of food he liked, so I was guessing. Salmon with a Dijon sauce, herbed new potatoes, and green beans seemed like an easy place to start.

Unless he hated fish. Surely, if he hated fish, he would've said something. I put that thought out of my mind. It was too late to question my menu.

It was a fairly simple meal to prep, and it didn't take me very long to wrap the salmon in parchment paper and slide it in the oven along with the new potatoes, tossed with olive oil and herbs.

I was setting out the ingredients to my Dijon sauce when I heard the click of the front door opening. He was early.

My stomach clenched with nerves and need. At the sound of his footsteps coming down the hall, anticipation tingled down my spine. Jacob was home.

He stopped in the entry to the kitchen. I turned from

the counter, where I'd been measuring sour cream, and looked at him, my heart skipping a beat as I took in his tall form, devastating in a navy suit and crisp white shirt.

His dark hair fell over his forehead and his silver eyes gleamed. When he smiled, my knees went a little weak.

"I need to buy you an apron," he said, considering me. "I'd like to see you in my kitchen wearing nothing but an apron."

I had the vision of myself in a 50s style, full-skirted apron.

White with cherries and red trim, the bodice barely clinging to my full breasts, scraping my nipples as I cooked him dinner, my body almost covered from the front and completely naked from behind, my round ass exposed when I bent into the oven.

I felt my cheeks flush. Swallowing the sudden rush of lust, I said, "Would you like me to order one?"

Pacing closer, he said "Yes, I would."

"I'll do it tomorrow," I promised, my nipples tightening as he came to a stop right in front of me.

Taking the spoon out of my hand and dropping it into the container of sour cream, he said, "Is there anything in here that's going to burn in the next 10 minutes?"

"No," I whispered. "The salmon has another 20 minutes and—"

He cut me off with, "Take off your clothes."

CHAPTER TEN
ABIGAIL

My hands went to the hem of my cardigan, and I tugged it, along with the matching camisole, over my head. My breasts grew heavy. Heat bloomed between my thighs. I'd been a little wet all day.

Just being in Jacob's house seem to do that to me. But this—stripping my clothes off for him, knowing he was going to touch me—that was all it took.

Moisture gathered in my pussy. Feeling it as I shifted my weight to take off the clingy lounging pants only made me hotter.

I tossed my clothes on the end of the kitchen island and waited for my next order. Jacob didn't disappoint me.

"Turn around." I did, facing away from the stove. "Bend over."

I bent over the island, not exactly sure what he wanted. I leaned over the granite countertop on the island, bracing myself on my elbows.

Jacob corrected me, not with words but with light touches. He ran his fingertips down the outsides of my arms, gently lifting them from beneath me, raising me up and bringing them together behind my back, pressing my hands together until I caught the hint and locked my hands around my own wrists.

With soft pressure, he pressed me back down until my breasts flattened into the cool counter, my face turned to the side, my hot cheek against the hard surface.

"Beautiful," he said, his voice husky. His hand smoothed down my spine and over the curve of my ass. One long finger dipped lower to trace my pussy. "Spread your legs."

I did, more than happy to make room for his hand. I drew in a ragged breath, my body tense, ready, trying to guess what he would do next, wanting whatever it was.

He surprised me, yet again. His fingertip grazed the hot flesh between my legs just long enough to verify that I was wet before pulling away to drop a quick, impersonally affectionate smack on my rear end.

"Don't move," he said. "I'm going to change. I'll be back in a minute, and I expect to see you exactly like that when I return."

"Yes, sir," I said, the words slipping from between my lips as if I'd been saying them all my life.

I had been, but never, ever like this.

My mind raced as I listened to him walking away, his footsteps fading as he went down the hall toward the master bedroom. I couldn't believe he'd just left me like this, naked, arranged exactly as he wanted me.

Jacob Winters was a tease.

If I'd been in charge, I would have teased him back.

I knew, deep down, that I wouldn't be half as aroused by all this if I'd been in charge. If I'd been in charge, there would've been no spankings the night before, no nipple clamps, no naked dinner.

No Jacob eating dessert off my pussy and licking me until I came.

No, I didn't want to be in charge.

At the memory of his mouth on me the night before, I squirmed. My nipples were hard, tight points against the granite.

The edge of the countertop was uncomfortable against my hip bones, and my arms were getting tired. I didn't move. I waited, quietly, if not patiently.

My body was still, but my mind raced, thinking of all the things Jacob might do to me in this position.

It seemed like a year before he came back, though it was probably only a few minutes. I caught a glimpse of him in my peripheral vision, and a wave of lust and something else, something warm and sweet washed through me at the sight of him.

He'd shed his formal suit in favor of a pair of well-worn broadcloth pajama bottoms and an Emory T-shirt.

This wasn't Jacob, the billionaire playboy, or Jacob, the cutthroat real estate magnate. This was just Jacob Winters, at home, relaxed, and ready to play.

I could steel myself against all the other Jacobs, but this one was too real. He snuck under my guard, especially when he sent me an almost boyish grin, stopping beside me and resting a hand on my ass.

"You take direction very well. Now we'll see how well you can direct me."

Okay, then fuck me, I said in my head. I knew better than to say it out loud.

The hand on my ass dropped down, his fingers again tracing around my pussy, collecting the gathered moisture until they dropped further and circled my clit. I gasped, the shock of direct contact sharper than it would have been if he'd touched me before all the teasing.

"Do you know your recipe by heart?" He asked in a conversational tone as if he didn't have his hand between my legs, stroking my slick heat.

I tried to answer the same way, but I heard the tension in my voice, the need bleeding through as I said, "I do."

"Tell me what you were going to do next," he commanded. My brain scrambled to keep up.

"Make the Dijon sauce," I stuttered.

"Walk me through it." His fingertips left my clit as one long finger pressed inside me, slowly, as if he had all the time in the world. I resisted the urge to push back at him, knowing instinctively that wasn't the game.

The game was for me to let him tease me until he decided to fuck me. I really wanted to win. Forcing my mind back onto dinner, I said "See the red plastic bowl on the counter? You need to mix the sauce in there and then heat it up in the pan on the stove."

"And what goes in it?"

A second finger joined the first, stretching me, taunting me with the prospect of being truly filled. His knuckle grazed my clit, and I jumped.

His other hand came down on my ass with a quick swat, the flash of pain transmuting to pleasure, shooting straight between my legs.

"One third of a cup of sour cream, two tablespoons of Dijon mustard, two teaspoons of the chopped garlic, and two teaspoons of lemon juice. It should all be out there on the counter."

He repeated the recipe back to me, then said, "And what about these green beans? Are they done?"

Crap. I'd forgotten about the green beans. It was a good

thing I'd set a timer on the oven, or there was no chance the salmon and potatoes would come out in time.

"No," I said, my voice breathy with arousal. "Turn them on low. On medium," I corrected, "and put the lid back on, please."

I wanted to cry when his hands left my skin. After the heat of his touch, the cool air in the kitchen against the wet between my legs was freezing.

I heard sounds behind me, the clink of metal against glass, the slide of plastic on the counter, the click, click, whoosh of the gas stove turning on under the green beans.

"So I mix all these ingredients together in the bowl?" Jacob asked.

He was only a few feet away, but it felt like a mile. I wanted to tell him to forget about the sauce and come back over here and touch me. If I thought I had a chance in hell of getting it to work, I would've done it.

Instead, I said, "Yes, mix it all together with the whisk on the counter. When it's done, I'll tell you what's next."

It didn't take him long. I'd chosen a simple recipe on purpose for my first day in Jacob's kitchen, not sure what kind of equipment he might have.

I waited, trying to guess what each small sound was, feeling relief when I heard the whisk swirling against the plastic of the bowl. He rewarded me a second later by leaving the sauce and coming back to the island.

He pressed up behind me, the hard, thick ridge of his erect cock separated from me by only the thin cotton of his pajama bottoms.

My breath caught in my lungs. I wanted it inside me so badly. He leaned over, plastering his chest against my back until his lips grazed my ear. "What's next?"

"Turn on the medium-sized skillet," I said, my voice

shaking a little. "On low, and pour the sauce inside. You need to keep stirring it. You want it to warm up, but it shouldn't boil or it'll separate."

I almost wept at the realization that his attention to the sauce would mean he'd have to stop touching me until it was done. I wished I'd decided to make pot roast tonight instead of tomorrow, even though there hadn't been enough time.

Pot roast didn't need any attention. You could fuck all night with a pot roast in the oven.

Jacob peeled himself off me and stepped back, taking his lovely hard cock with him. I moaned at the loss. He'd barely touched me. Two quick smacks and a few strokes of his fingers had me shaking with need.

I heard the sound of another burner flicking on and the metallic scrape of the whisk against the stainless steel skillet. Conversationally, Jacob asked, "What's in the oven?"

"Salmon and herbed new potatoes," I whispered.

"And how long will this sauce take?" He asked so casually, I might have cried if I hadn't heard the steely thread of tension beneath his words.

"At least five minutes," I said, my voice so forlorn, I wanted to laugh at myself.

Jacob grunted in response. Was the tension getting to him, too? I hoped so. I'd imagined a lot of things when Jacob had proposed this deal, but I'd never guessed he would be such a tease.

The night before, he'd implied that the spanking hadn't been my punishment. The punishment had been sitting through dinner with the clamps tugging on my nipples while he watched, doing nothing to ease my need.

He was diabolical. An eternity passed, punctuated by

my uneven breaths, my racing heartbeat, and the quiet sounds of Jacob stirring the mustard sauce.

"How do I know when it's done?" he asked.

My brain trapped in a fog of lust, I managed to say, "Taste it. If the garlic is too sharp, it needs to cook longer."

"Mmm. Here, you try."

Jacob's finger appeared at my lips. I opened them, sucking at the offered fingertip, barely tasting the Dijon sauce, my tongue cleaning it from his skin, my tastebuds eager for the flavor of Jacob beneath the rich sauce.

"It's done," he spat out before yanking his finger from my mouth and shoving his pants down his legs. The head of his cock brushed my pussy, and I whimpered, unable to stop myself from rocking back against him.

He should have punished me. He must have been as lost as I was.

He leaned into my body, driving his thick, hard cock deep inside my pussy, not stopping until he was in to the hilt, his balls swinging forward to smack my clit.

I whimpered again, wanting more. Wanting him to fuck me hard and fast after I'd waited so long.

He did, driving into me. Fucking me hard, filling me. I wanted it, I wanted more. Our bodies shifted, and his hips drove mine straight into the edge of the granite countertop.

I let out a moan of surprise. It hurt, and not like the spankings. I wasn't sure what to do.

Should I tell him? Or was I just supposed to take it whether it hurt or not? I didn't know, and not knowing put a damper on my lust.

Jacob must have sensed something, or he was psychic, because he stopped and stepped back, his cock sliding out of me with a sucking pull that made me quiver.

Running his hands down my sides, he tugged back,

urging me to put space between my hips and the edge of the island.

His hands found mine, still clasped behind my back, and he released them, placing them on either side of my torso, skimming his hands up my front to cup my now exposed breasts.

Leaning over me, covering me with his body, he slid inside me again. I sighed in satisfaction.

"Always tell me if you're in pain," he whispered, his breath hot against my ear. "There's a difference between spanking and nipple clamps and when I'm actually hurting you. I'd never want to hurt you, Abigail. Not like that. Not ever. Promise me you'll talk to me. This won't work if you don't talk to me."

"I promise," I whispered, tears filling my eyes as he began to move, slamming his cock into me, kneading my breasts, pinching my nipples until all the sensations, in my body and my heart, collided in an orgasm so huge, I lost my breath and let it pull me under.

It took me a while to come back to myself. We stayed there, leaning over the island, his tall body covering mine like a warm, hard blanket, trying to catch our breath.

Just when I thought I might be able to move, Jacob drew back. For a moment, before I got myself under control, I missed his heat and strength with a fierce longing that took me by surprise.

He touched my back and said, "I'll take care of this. You can finish dinner."

By *this*, I knew he meant the condom. I wondered how long it would take for Dr. Whitmore's tests to come back.

"May I get dressed?" I asked, not sure I knew what I wanted him to say. As if he'd read my mind, he raised one eyebrow and said, "You decide."

It was a little chilly in the penthouse, or I might have left off clothes altogether. I wasn't above teasing Jacob back when I got the chance. However, I did not like to be cold.

As a compromise, I left the camisole, underwear, and lounge pants piled as they were on the countertop and slipped back into the cashmere cardigan.

By the time Jacob came back, I had dinner ready to serve.

He walked into the kitchen, his silver eyes taking in the elegantly arranged plates with salmon drizzled in a mustard sauce and fresh, crisp green beans and beautifully browned herbed new potatoes, served by me, wearing only an unzipped cardigan.

He grinned, the expression giving him that boyish look I loved and said, "I could get used to this, Abigail."

I was counting on it. The scary thing was that I could get used to it, too.

Chapter Eleven

Abigail

Another day alone in the penthouse. It had been two weeks since I'd shown up in Jacob's office, desperate for help. By now, I was settled in and almost used to living with Jacob.

If by 'used to' you meant I was less bothered by the fact that I had no idea what to expect from him. Jacob was unpredictable.

He hadn't been lying when he said he had a wide range of sexual interests. So far, all of them had worked out well for me, so I wasn't complaining.

Unfortunately, after two weeks, I was beginning to get just the tiniest bit stir crazy. I was safe here. Safe in a way that I hadn't been since my father had died.

For the first time in four years, I didn't have to worry about my mother. Not true. I always worried about my mother. She was sick, and there was nothing I could do to make her better.

The grief never mellowed. In my mind, I understood her disease. My heart only saw the mother I loved, alive but lost to me.

The only thing I could do was make sure she was cared for, and while I'd been doing that since my father had died, these last weeks with Jacob was the first time I felt good about it.

With John, I'd been free to leave our home, to see friends, to have a social life, and to visit my mother. Yet, for every second of our marriage, even the good ones, I'd felt horribly trapped.

Forced into a mold I didn't want to fill, forced to smile about the subversion of my life, terrified anyone would find out how much I resented the position I was in.

I'd been raised to be the wife of a man like John, or more truthfully, the wife of a man like Jacob, but it hadn't been what I'd wanted for myself.

I'd wanted to be a teacher. Those dreams seemed so innocent and far away. Some days, I felt ancient and far too defiled to teach children anything.

With Jacob, it was the opposite. Yes, I was constrained by my role as his pet. But so far, it was a role I didn't mind playing.

I enjoyed his company, and while he didn't treat me like a girlfriend, I wasn't sure I wanted him to anyway. In his own way, he was warm and affectionate, and he definitely appreciated my presence.

Other than making myself available to have sex with him and making dinner when he ate at home, he didn't expect that much from me. I certainly didn't mind having sex with him.

Understatement of the century. And I loved to cook. Especially for someone who didn't micro-manage every meal or criticize my choices.

I knew Jacob had grown up on an estate in Buckhead with a kitchen staff. While he enjoyed gourmet food and had probably been eating it since the cradle, he was just as happy with pot roast or spaghetti and meatballs.

He put in plenty of time in the gym on top of meeting his brothers and cousins for racquetball or a pickup game of basketball, so he wasn't worried about calories.

I had more orgasms than I could handle and free reign in the kitchen, and when Jacob wasn't home, I could do whatever I wanted. As long as I didn't leave the penthouse.

That was the sticking point.

Jacob's home was huge. I'd done some research on my shiny new laptop and had discovered that I was living in Winters House, a historic building Jacob had purchased almost 10 years ago—he must have still been in college—and renovated into luxury condos with office space and retail on the first floor.

I'd learned his younger brother and a cousin owned condos a few floors down, but Jacob's was the only one that occupied an entire floor to itself. It was massive. Still, it was starting to feel like a cage, and I was frustrated with myself for being so restless.

There was nothing I could do about it until the situation with Big John was resolved. According to Jacob, he'd been looking for me, but quietly. Unless Big John gave up or made a move overt enough to shut him down, we were stuck in a waiting game.

I was in the kitchen, putting together the ingredients for a chicken pot pie and wondering if Jacob would let me use the rooftop garden I'd read about, when I heard it.

At first, it was barely more than a whisper of noise. I'm not sure I heard footsteps so much as got a sense of something moving outside the penthouse door.

I froze, my stomach turning to ice in a heartbeat, reminding me that, as comfortable as I was with Jacob, danger was still far too close. It was mid-afternoon, far too early for Jacob to be home.

Carefully, silently, I set the rolling pin I was using for the piecrust down on the countertop and dusted my hands off on a dishtowel, my ears straining for the tiniest sound by the door.

Rustling. A thump. A scratching sound. Crinkling, like paper. Innocuous sounds. At least, not sounds that were overtly threatening. My lungs tight, almost lightheaded with fear, I knew that as subtle as they were, the sounds were wrong.

The only two people who should be at that door were Rachel or Jacob, and either of them would either ring the bell or let themselves in.

Someone was out there who shouldn't be. I forced myself to inch out of the kitchen and into the hallway leading to the foyer, where I'd have a view of the front door.

It looked normal. The handle wasn't twisting and turning as if someone was trying to get in. The deadbolt was still engaged. But, those sounds. More rustling, and that crinkling, scraping.

My terrified brain decided to get back in gear. I had to call Jacob.

Where was the phone? Where the hell had I left the phone? I almost never used it, and Jacob texted more than he called, so I didn't keep it right at my side.

I stood there, feet glued to the floor, eyes focused on the front door, racking my brain for the last place I'd had the phone.

Not the kitchen. My room. I'd had it in my room that morning.

I took a step away from the door and froze again. A brown shadow pushed under the door.

Every horror movie I'd ever seen of murderous ghosts and deadly phantoms oozing beneath closed doors flashed through my mind as I stared, transfixed with terror at the site of that dark shape sliding into the foyer of Jacob's penthouse.

It pushed further, slowly, twisting side to side as if struggling to pull itself beneath the door. Abruptly, its progress stopped. There was another rustle on the other side of the door.

Then nothing. Silence. Stillness. Whatever it was, it was gone, leaving the envelope behind.

The foyer lights were off, and without any windows in the space, it was dim even on a bright day. That was my excuse for imagining fantastical explanations for a plain brown envelope slipped under the door.

It took a few minutes, that felt like hours, before I summoned the courage to move forward and turn on the light in the foyer.

When I did, I felt like an idiot. It was just an envelope. It was unusual that someone had pushed an envelope beneath Jacob's door when the floor was supposed to be secure.

No one should be able to take the elevator to the penthouse level. But he did have a brother and a cousin living in the building. He hadn't said so, but I assumed they had access. Maybe they just didn't want to bother him in the office.

Or maybe, that envelope didn't have to do with Jacob at all. Maybe it had to do with me. I didn't want to believe Big John's people could infiltrate Jacob's security. I knew better than to think I was safe just because I felt safe.

Big John got what he wanted. When something fixed

itself in his mind, he could be relentless. He wasn't Jacob Winters, but he was powerful. Too powerful.

If he'd found me . . . I lurched forward, my limbs stiff with fear, forced into action as the terror of not knowing eclipsed my instinctive reluctance to touch that invading envelope, its plain brown paper so out of place against the rich colors of the hardwood floor and rug in the foyer of Jacob's penthouse.

I leaned forward to snatch it off the floor and retreated—scurried—back to the safety of the kitchen, berating myself for my cowardice the whole way.

Back in the kitchen, with bright sunlight streaming through the tall windows and the white cabinets gleaming, the brown 8.5 by 11 envelope, sealed with a single piece of transparent tape, didn't look as threatening. Before I could think twice about it, I slid a finger beneath the flap and opened it.

A picture slid out, floating between my fingers to land, face up, on the granite countertop. My eyes widened in confusion as I stared at it.

This had nothing to do with me. I didn't even know what I was looking at, only that it was horrible. It looked like a crime scene photograph, except that somehow, it didn't, but I couldn't put my finger on what was wrong with it.

Two figures lay sprawled on the floor, both obviously dead. I didn't recognize them.

The woman was the focus of the photograph, the man's body off to the side as if an afterthought. They both had bullet wounds, his a neat hole in his forehead, hers in the center of her chest.

She lay on a Persian carpet that reminded me of the carpets in Jacob's penthouse, her hand flung over her head, white blonde hair spread around her like spilled water.

I reached for the photograph to take a closer look, then snatched my hand back. I'd touched the envelope. Stupid. Now my fingerprints were on it. I hadn't touched the photograph though.

I didn't know what the picture was, didn't know who might've delivered it, or why. But looking at the photograph of those two dead bodies, I knew there was no good reason it should be here. Backing away, feeling a little sick, I went to get my phone.

I'd never called Jacob in the middle of the day. He answered on the second ring, his tone impatient. "What is it?"

"I–I think you should come up here. Something—" I realized I didn't know what to say.

"What happened? What's wrong?" he demanded.

"Something was delivered," I said. "I think you need to see it."

The phone slammed down, and I sat on the edge of my bed, staring down at the mobile phone in my hands, watching with blind eyes as the screen went dark. I had the feeling I'd handled everything the wrong way.

I should have called him the second I heard a sound. Except I hadn't wanted to bother him at work if it was nothing. I should've called him before I touched the envelope, but it hadn't occurred to me that it might be evidence of something. If that's even what it was.

I'd been so afraid it had to do with Big John and me that I hadn't thought further.

I rose slowly, reluctantly leaving the security of my bedroom, to meet Jacob when he came in. The door slammed open as I walked toward the foyer, Jacob's eyes shifting from alarm to relief at the sight of me, alone and in one piece. "You're all right?"

"I'm fine," I said, "but there's something in the kitchen. I don't know who delivered it. It was pushed under the door."

He turned and strode to the kitchen, me following in his wake, still trying to explain what I didn't really understand. He stopped at the edge of the island. I knew the moment he caught sight of the photograph because his body went still.

Standing beside him, studying his face as he took in the details of the obscene image, I knew that something was very, very wrong. His jaw tightened.

I thought I could actually see him grinding his teeth together. His silver eyes went hot with rage, then ice cold. I was alarmed to see his hands ball into fists at his side.

"What is it?" I whispered. Jacob didn't answer. "Jacob?"

He was a statue, only the rhythmic clench of his right fist and the twitch of his jaw muscle betraying any movement. I wish I knew what was going through his mind. Finally, he spoke.

"You touched this?" he asked, his voice low and dangerous. Instinctively, I took a step back.

"Just the envelope. Not the picture."

"When was it delivered?"

"Maybe twenty minutes ago," I said, not sure how much time had passed. "I was in the kitchen and I heard noises—"

I stopped talking when Jacob looked at me, the words drying up in my throat at the sheer rage in his eyes.

"You heard sounds at the door and you went to investigate?"

I swallowed hard, wanting to lie and knowing I couldn't. I couldn't seem to speak, my words frozen in my throat. I settled for a short nod. He turned toward me, the muscle in his jaw twitching, his fist clenching so hard I worried he would hurt himself.

Not me. In my gut, I knew that clenched fist wasn't the danger here. I wished I understood what was.

"What the fuck were you thinking? What the *fuck* were you thinking, Abigail?"

His voice rose to a shout as he loomed over me, two spots of red flushing his cheekbones. I took a step back. I'd never seen Jacob angry before. I wasn't afraid of him, not exactly.

I took another step back, which only seemed to enrage him further. He crossed the distance between us. "Stop fucking moving."

I stopped. I wanted to ask what about the picture had set him off. I wanted to demand he not yell at me. I didn't say anything.

His eyes narrowed on my face, his body vibrating with anger. He was a wild animal I didn't want to provoke. This man, his silver eyes liquid with fury, was not the Jacob I knew. Yet he was.

Here was the intensity he kept bottled up but let out with sex. Here, it was set free in anger.

"I never would have thought you could be so stupid. The next time you hear something you shouldn't, see something you shouldn't, you fucking call me. You fucking lock yourself in your room and you call me. You do not go check it out."

Finding my voice, I said, "What is it? I was afraid it might be about Big John. But it's not. What is it?"

I had to know what had upset him so badly. I didn't believe his anger was just about me, about worrying I'd put myself in danger. This was something else.

"It's none of your fucking business, Abigail. That's what it is. It doesn't have anything to do with Big John or you."

"I figured that out once I saw it," I said, keeping my voice as low and as soothing as I could manage, given his temper. "But what is it? Who are those people?"

His face went dark. Jacob closed his eyes, and when he opened them, they were blank of emotion. Moving mechanically, he used a dishtowel to pick up the photograph and slide it back into the envelope. The envelope, he put into a plastic bag.

"I'm going out," he said, ignoring my questions, his voice like ice. I didn't want to pry. I just wanted to help. He didn't care. "Don't go near the door, and keep your phone with you, for fuck's sake."

The door slammed behind him. A second later, the deadbolt clicked into place. My mind reeled, trying to catch up with what had happened.

I was trying not to feel hurt at the way he'd talked to me. He was right. I should have called him. I'd gotten complacent, so sure the penthouse was safe. The sounds at the door had scared me, but clearly, not enough. I wouldn't make that mistake again.

It still didn't explain the depth of Jacob's rage. I was fine. Nothing had happened. That outburst hadn't really been about me. He didn't care for me enough to get so angry over my safety.

I felt a little sick at the thought, but I knew it was true.

Jacob liked me, and he seemed pleased with the way our deal was working out. But I was his pet, not his girlfriend.

He wasn't in love with me, and he never would be.

I was a convenience. He should have been annoyed that I'd endangered myself, not furious, so why had he been so angry? Who were the people in that picture?

I was going to have to get over my curiosity. Jacob wasn't going to tell me, and it seemed smarter to stop asking. I wanted to take his anger away, to soothe the fury he'd felt.

That wasn't my job. Unless he wanted to fuck it out, his emotions were outside the scope of my duties. I still wanted to help. My chest was heavy with regret and a pain I didn't want to examine.

I'd made this deal. I knew what I was to Jacob, and he'd been more than clear about the limits of our relationship. I'd be the worst kind of fool to start looking for more.

With everything else I had to deal with, I didn't need to start having feelings for Jacob Winters. Gratitude. Lust. Those were okay. Anything more would be a disaster.

I looked at the counter, at the now warm pie crust. I could scrape it up and put it back in the fridge, then roll it out again, but the dough had already been handled too much.

Working it a second time would leave me with a heavy, dense crust. Heavy and dense, like the sick feeling inside me after the scene with Jacob. At that thought, I peeled up the dough and threw it away.

I had nothing else to do with my time. I might as well make a new one since that was all I was good for.

Pushing back the bitter, helpless pain in my heart, I emptied my mind of everything but the ingredients in front of me.

I couldn't help Jacob if he didn't want me to. I couldn't help myself any more than I already had.

All I could do was be here to fuck when he got home and cook his dinner. With a sigh, I started measuring flour, ignoring the hot tears rolling down my cheeks.

Chapter Twelve

Jacob

I called Cooper on the way to my car, the plain, brown envelope in my hands. My mind spun as I tried to register what I'd seen.

Who the fuck would send me a crime scene photo of my Aunt and Uncle's murder? They'd died twenty years ago. It was a cold case.

What was the point? I couldn't untangle the fury in my chest far enough to figure out what had me more pissed— the sight of their dead bodies, or the idea that Abigail had been just feet away from whatever sick fuck had delivered it.

She was supposed to be fucking safe. The whole point of her staying with me was to keep her safe.

She was not supposed to get the shit scared out of her by someone delivering a picture of dead bodies to the one place she was protected from the danger that had been stalking her ever since she'd married John.

I needed to get it together. Anger wasn't going to help anyone. Usually, that was my thing. Control. I didn't lose it, ever. I left the elevator and pulled out my phone, hitting the shortcut to the Sinclair Security office.

"This is Jacob Winters," I said when the receptionist answered, hearing the bark in my own voice. Toning it down, I said, "Put me through to Cooper."

"Sir, he's—"

"I don't care," I interrupted. "Put me through."

"Yes, sir," she said crisply. Seconds later, Cooper Sinclair picked up the line.

"Jacob, I'm in a meeting—" he said.

Talking over him, I interrupted. "Someone just slid an unmarked envelope with a crime scene picture of my Aunt and Uncle's murders under my door."

I gave Cooper a minute to filter through all the implications. He didn't disappoint me. Thirty seconds later, he said, "Are you on your way?"

"I'll be there in five," I said. He hung up the phone. I knew whoever he had in his office would be gone by the time I got there.

Not just because Cooper Sinclair and I had been friends since preschool. Not just because he'd known both my aunt and uncle and my parents before they died. This was about more than friendship and family connections.

Sinclair Security was responsible for designing and implementing the security protocols at Winters House. At every one of our residences and businesses.

If someone had gotten through their system far enough to slide an envelope beneath my door, Cooper would want answers almost as much as I did.

While I was the only one with access to the cameras located inside my penthouse, Sinclair Security had the recordings for all activity in the more public areas, including the elevators and the stairwells.

I wanted to see who had been at my door. I needed a face for my target.

I let myself in through the front door of the Sinclair offices, not seeing the gray walls, understated black leather furniture, and sedate charcoal carpet.

I'd been here too many times to notice my surroundings. All I was interested in was whatever Cooper had been able to find out in the five minutes since we'd spoken.

I opened the door to his office to find him sitting at his desk, his eyes trained on a monitor, his younger brother, Evers, beside him.

All four of the Sinclair brothers looked alike—tall, with dark hair and the same sharp cheekbones. Cooper and Evers shared their father's icy blue eyes, though Cooper's build was bulkier than his brother's since he'd started power lifting in college.

"Evers, I didn't know you were back," I said.

He looked up from the monitor and nodded to me, apparently too distracted by the hole in their security plan to be friendly. That was fine with me. We'd known each other too long to bother with that shit anyway.

"I finished up in Houston early," he said. "Since when do you have Abigail Jordan living with you?"

"Since she came to me asking for help. She said Big John wanted to use her as barter in one of his deals."

"Why didn't you just send her to us?" Evers asked, pinning me with his gaze. "We would've helped her. You know I've always had a soft spot for Abigail. She never should have ended up mixed up with the Jordans."

Under his breath, Cooper said, "Yeah, you have a soft spot, but Jacob has a hard one. He's been waiting years for a crack at Abigail."

Evers straightened, crossing his arms over his chest, his

eyes still intent on mine. "I know. That's why we're talking about it. Taking advantage of a woman in a desperate situation? That's low."

An unfamiliar mix of emotions tore through me, a crazy alchemy of jealousy and possessiveness and something else I didn't understand.

"Stay the fuck out of it, Evers," I said. "I need your help keeping her safe, not protecting her virtue. She knew what she was getting into with me. She's fine with it."

Evers raised an infuriating eyebrow, his disbelief clear in his eyes. "Is she? Or is she just doing what she has to? You're no prize, Jacob. Not for a woman like her. She had a shitty marriage. She deserves better. You're a step up from being stuck with Big John."

"Why do you care?" I demanded, offended by the comparison.

Maybe I wasn't offering Abigail a wedding ring, but that didn't make me an abusive sociopath like her father-in-law.

"You don't want Abigail. You've got a hard-on for my cousin." As I'd known it would, the mention of my cousin, Summer, was enough to derail Evers.

"She's a fucking pain in my ass," he complained. Summer had shown up months ago in the middle of a situation with Evers and Cooper's brother, Axel, and his now fiancée, Emma.

Summer was a mystery. Her last name was Winters, an unlikely coincidence, but we didn't know her and she acted like she didn't know us.

Evers had been discreetly keeping an eye on her ever since and had uncovered some interesting information, including her identity as a distant cousin to my branch of the Winters family.

But we'd had our hands full lately, and as long as

Summer kept to herself and didn't cause problems, for the moment, we were happy enough to let her be. Besides, she and Evers hadn't exactly gotten along.

Since the day they'd met, when he practically kidnapped her to bring her back to Atlanta so she could deliver evidence for Emma, they'd set sparks off each other whenever they collided.

With those two, it was either fight or fuck, and so far, they'd stuck with fighting.

"Have you seen her lately?" I asked. Evers glared at me, and Cooper hid a grin from his brother.

"No, I haven't, and stop trying to distract me. I'm keeping an eye on you and Abigail," he said. "She needs someone to look out for her."

"She has someone," I said, clenching my fist at my side for the second time that afternoon. "She has me. I'm not going to say it again, Evers. Back the fuck off Abigail. When she had trouble, she didn't come here. She came to me."

"Leave it, Evers," Cooper said. Rotating the monitor so I could see, Cooper pointed to the different segments of the screen, all of which showed specific areas of Winters House.

Some of the screens were frozen, as if Cooper had set them at pause, while some showed live-action.

"Whoever it was, they knew about the security. They didn't know the exact location of the cameras, but it's clear they knew they were being watched. Unfortunately, we don't have a good view of their face. Not good enough to run it for the facial recognition program."

"Can you tell how they got in?" I asked, frustrated. "Man or woman? General height, size, anything?"

"If it's a woman, she's tall. The intruder is about five ten, based on height relative to the elevator door. I'm inclined to think the hair is a wig."

He paused one of the screens and showed me the slightly blurred image of a figure in a long coat, face turned to the side, shaggy hair obscuring the line of the chin and forehead.

I understood what he was saying. Without the hair, it could've been a man or woman, but the style was the perfect choice to hide the intruder's features without being noticeable.

Cooper flipped through the screens, taking the figure back from crouching at my door to where he or she exited the elevator on my floor—a floor no intruder should have access to—to the lobby where they entered the elevator. He sat back in his chair and looked at me, an apology in his eyes.

"I lost him on the first floor. Retail at the entry level is good for business, but it's shit for security. I've told you before that you have too many entrances on the retail level and too many people going in and out of the offices to fully secure the upper floors."

I nodded. I knew this, and when I'd renovated the building, it hadn't been a major concern. Winters House was as secure—more secure—than most luxury condos. We hadn't designed it to be airtight.

There hadn't been a need. As long as we could keep out the paparazzi, we hadn't been worried about it. Now, my priorities had changed.

"Can you put someone on my door twenty-four seven?" I asked. "Until Big John turns his attention elsewhere, Abigail's not leaving my place, but this scared the hell out of her. I want to know she's safe when I'm not there."

"We'll take care of it," Evers said. "No one will get to Abigail."

I nodded again. We all gave each other a hard time. We've been friends too long not to, but as much as I knew Evers would give me shit when he had the chance, I also knew he'd have my back.

His face grim, Cooper raised his chin toward the plastic-wrapped envelope in my hand and asked, "Is that it?"

Pulling on a pair of thin plastic gloves he got from the top drawer of his desk, Cooper pulled the envelope from the plastic bag with a pair of long metal tweezers.

He laid the envelope over the plastic bag and teased it open with the tip of the tweezers. I looked away as he drew the photograph into view.

I knew what they were looking at. I didn't want to see it again myself. I barely remembered my aunt and uncle. A vague impression of cigar smoke and a bristly mustache, the scent of gardenias and the absolute security of tight hugs.

Losing them had been the first great shock of my life, of all of our lives. Their deaths had changed everything, in so many ways.

Looking back, knowing what had come after, James and Anna Winters' murders marked the beginning of the end for all of us. Echoing my thoughts, Cooper murmured, "What kind of sick fuck would send you this?"

I shook my head. "No fucking clue," I admitted. "The case is closed. It's been closed for nineteen years. What's the point in dragging it up now? If someone wanted to get a reaction out of me, they should've given it to me in a public place, not slid it under my door."

"Anything you're involved in that might lead back to this? New business deal? Someone you haven't worked with before? Anyone who owes you money?" Evers asked. I shook my head.

"I've already thought of that," I said. "The only thing new is Abigail. But this seems a little subtle for Big John."

"I agree," Cooper said. "Digging up a crime two decades old just to fuck with your head is not Big John's style. A rocket launcher into your living room, maybe. Running your car off the road and shooting you in the head, definitely. But this? I don't think this has anything to do with Abigail or Big John."

"Is it worth checking for fingerprints?" I asked.

Cooper busied himself putting the photograph away. None of us wanted to look at it any longer than we had to. Cooper and Evers had been young, but they'd known my aunt and uncle. Seeing that picture couldn't be easy for them either.

"We'll check and see if we find anything. I'll get it back to you when we're done."

"Fine," I said. Checking the time on my watch, I realized I had a conference call in twenty minutes that I didn't want to miss. "I have to get back to the office."

"I'm sending Griffen up to watch your door for now," Evers said. "We'll get a regular rotation on it starting tonight. I'll also increase security on the stairwell access and the lobby elevator."

Nothing was foolproof. I knew that, but increasing security was a start.

"Thanks," I said as I turned to leave. "Keep me posted."

I headed back to my office, trying to get my mind on my upcoming call. I was in the middle of negotiations for a plot of commercial real estate I was hoping to buy from the original investors at a steep discount after they'd completely fucked up the first stages of development.

I had to get my head back in the game. Since when was my personal life more distracting than business? Never.

Now that I'd dealt with the security issue, all I could see in my mind was the pain in Abigail's face when I'd yelled at her.

I'd yelled at her. I called her *stupid* and yelled at her. What the fuck was wrong with me?

She'd been scared enough by some fucked up intruder slipping stuff under the door without me losing my temper. She didn't need that kind of shit.

In the past two weeks, I'd seen her relax as the specter of Big John had faded. A steady diet of orgasms and safety had wiped away the pinched look in her eyes and the stiffness in her shoulders.

Despite the way we'd begun, I refused to accept Evers's implication that she was pretending to be happy because she had no other choice. Abigail wanted to be with me. She wasn't looking for more, and neither was I. Evers was completely off base.

Abigail and I were fine. Or we had been.

I'd taken pride in being the reason she was finally starting to be happy, and then I'd gone and fucked it all up. The sad thing was, I had no idea what to do about it.

Had I ever apologized to a woman before?

Maybe, over small stuff, but not like this. It had never mattered. I'd never cared if they accepted my apology, never really cared that they were pissed in the first place, except as it might inconvenience me.

With Abigail, the memory of that look in her eyes, that stomach turning combination of fear and sadness, pity and hurt . . . I had no idea how to fix it.

I thought about asking Rachel to order her flowers, then threw the idea away before it could fully form. Flowers wouldn't get the job done. Neither would jewelry or any other stupid clichéd gifts.

Abigail wasn't my girlfriend. She was supposed to be a pet. She was supposed to be uncomplicated and simple.

So what the fuck had happened?

I managed to banish Abigail from my mind for the rest of the day. I'll admit, though it makes me a prick, that when a minor crisis came up at five thirty, I opted to handle it myself rather than delegating it.

Call me a pussy, but I couldn't bring myself to go home and face Abigail. I texted her to let her know not to hold dinner, aware I was an asshole as I hit *Send*.

I should have tacked on an apology. Anything to let her know I was sorry for the way I'd behaved, but I couldn't get the words out, even in text form.

I was still trying to figure out how to make it up to her when I let myself in the penthouse just after midnight.

As the Sinclairs had promised, there'd been a guard outside my door—one who'd forced me to show ID and clear my palm print before he let me in.

I'd laughed about it with him, hiding my relief at one more layer of armed protection between Abigail and the rest of the world.

I didn't know what was going on with the picture, with Big John, or with Abigail. It meant more than it should have to know she was safe.

She was asleep, the lights out in the penthouse except for the foyer and the kitchen, which she left on but lowered, leaving me a dim trail to the note on the island.

Jacob,

Dinner in the refrigerator if you're hungry. Put it in the microwave for three minutes, 50% power.

A

A weight in my chest lifted, just a little. She might be pissed at me. She should be pissed at me, I'd been an asshole. But she couldn't be that mad if she'd left me dinner and a note.

I found her asleep in her bed, face down, one knee hitched up, the covers pushed down to her feet, leaving her body exposed.

She was alluring like that, revealed in sleep as she never was when she was awake. A part of Abigail was always on her guard.

I didn't mind. I respected that she was smart enough to try to protect herself. Tonight, I wanted her like this. Defenseless.

Stripping off my clothes, I climbed into bed beside her, sliding my hands beneath the silky nightgown, stroking the curve of her hip and the soft skin of her belly and cupping the weight of her breast.

She let out a moan and shifted against me, arching her back to press her breast into my hand. She whispered, "Jacob," and I was lost.

I needed this. I needed Abigail like this, soft and willing. Half-asleep, she let me open her to my touch, her warm brown eyes cracking a slit as I hooked her leg over mine and grazed her pussy with my fingertips.

My lips fell on her neck, tasting, closing my teeth on the tendons in a grip of possession. I couldn't stop myself. This body was mine. Abigail was mine.

She was wet after only a few strokes of my fingers. I could have fucked her like that, wrapping her in my arms and sliding into her from behind, but that wasn't what I wanted.

Not this time.

I needed to see her face. I had to look into her eyes,

languid and sleepy, as she came on my cock. I wanted her to know who was fucking her.

Untangling our limbs, I rolled her to her back, covering her with my body as I pushed my cock into her tight, sweet pussy.

Her arms came around me, fingers digging into my shoulders as I started to fuck her, slowly at first, then with rising urgency. Being inside her was too good to hold back.

"Jacob," she breathed in my ear. That was it. No begging, no words but my name. Jacob.

She knew who was fucking her. She knew who owned her body.

That should have been enough for me. If I doubted that her desire for me was an act, her sleepy welcome assured me. Abigail wanted me. Why couldn't that be enough?

It wasn't. I had her body. I shouldn't need more. But as I felt her come, her slick, perfect pussy clamping down on my cock so hard she tore my orgasm from my control, I knew her body would never be enough.

I wanted all of Abigail. She'd given me her body, but I wanted her soul.

Chapter Thirteen
Abigail

J acob was gone in the morning. I slept late and woke to find myself carefully tucked in, the covers nestled around my body, though I remembered shoving the duvet to my feet sometime after I'd fallen into a restless sleep.

Jacob hadn't bothered to come home for dinner, so the extra care I'd taken with the chicken pot pie had been a waste, though he'd sent a text to let me know instead of leaving me waiting.

I remembered him slipping into bed beside me in the middle of the night, his hands on my body, rolling me over and making love to me. For the first time, it had felt like making love, not just fucking.

I wondered if that part had been a dream. Not Jacob waking me to have sex. I could believe that. It was what came after.

I could swear I drifted awake at some point before dawn to find him still in my bed, asleep on his back, my head using his chest as a pillow, his arm wrapped securely around my shoulders.

Jacob never stayed in my bed. We'd never slept together. I might have thought the memory was wishful thinking if not for the dent in the pillow beside mine.

I took a shower and got dressed in a pretty lemon yellow sundress suited more for summer than spring, but I wasn't going outside, so what did it matter?

I tried to ignore my troublesome restlessness. With the delivery of the mysterious photograph the day before and the additional guard outside the door, I knew it was more important than ever that I stay inside where I was safe.

I could put up with it until we got this whole mess straightened out. Big John was dangerous, but he didn't have a long memory. Something else would come up, and he'd forget about me.

The picture was another story. Yesterday, in the shock of the intruder on Jacob's floor and then his angry reaction, I hadn't figured it out.

Sleep had a way of untangling the most complex of knots, and I'd remembered, while I was rinsing shampoo from my hair, where I'd seen those faces before. I'd been so young when they died, but I should've realized the second I saw the photographs.

Poor Jacob. He was an adult. He'd lived a lifetime since he lost his aunt and uncle, but it didn't excuse someone throwing it in his face. And for what purpose? The sheer malice of it made me shiver.

I left my bedroom to find the kitchen pristine except for a note on the counter and a dirty plate in the sink.

Abigail,

I'm sorry I missed dinner. I love chicken pot pie. It made for a good breakfast. I'll be home early.

Jacob

Still not a love note, but somehow closer. It *was* an apology, though he wasn't apologizing for the fight, just for missing dinner.

Jacob was not accustomed to explaining himself. If I wanted him to say he was sorry for raising his voice or for the things he'd said, I expected I would have a long wait.

This short note would have to be good enough. Oddly, it was.

Looking at the precise scrawl of his handwriting, his words were a caress. *I love chicken pot pie.*

I shook my head at myself. I was pathetic, imagining a connection that wasn't there. He'd thanked me for making dinner, that was all. I needed to be happy with what I had and stop looking for more.

Jacob was temporary. He wasn't interested in anything real. Not with me. Not with anyone. Someday, this thing between us would end, and I would be free to live my own life. To have a relationship, if that's what I wanted. It just wouldn't be with Jacob.

It's the circumstances, I told myself. *He saved you, and you're feeling a little too grateful, that's all. These aren't real feelings. It's Stockholm Syndrome or Florence Nightingale Syndrome or one of those syndromes. You're just grateful. You are not falling for him.*

For the rest of the day, I pretended I believed that. I was a sophisticated woman. I could handle an emotionally detached sexual relationship.

Of course I could.

The day unrolled, just as every day had since I'd come to live with Jacob. I slept late, did some yoga, read a book, and gave myself a mani-pedi in the same sunny yellow as my dress.

I tried to pretend I wasn't getting bored with being stuck inside, and eventually, I wandered to the kitchen to start dinner.

We had plenty of chicken pot pie left over, but I decided to save that for lunches, possibly another of Jacob's breakfasts, and make something new.

I was slicing chicken breasts into thin strips for a sesame stir fry when the unfamiliar jangle of the house phone startled me into dropping the knife.

I'd forgotten there was a house phone. Jacob rarely used it, preferring his mobile. I'd never touched it, since I wasn't supposed to make phone calls at all, and I had my own mobile if there was an emergency.

It seemed no one else used the house phone either, because in the two weeks I've been living in the penthouse, I'd never heard it ring.

It trilled again, the discordant sound making me uneasy. I was used to the electronic tones of a mobile phone. This phone was old-school, and the ringer sounded indignant, hoarse and off key as if it were rusty from lack of use.

Unsettled, I walked to the sink and began to wash my hands, wincing at the sting of the water on my skin. Blood dripped from my finger to stain the porcelain sink. I must have cut myself when I'd dropped the knife.

Wrapping a dish towel around my bleeding finger, I turned off the water, my ears strained for the sound of the next ring.

It never came.

Instead, I heard a click from the direction of Jacob's office and the sound of his voice inviting the caller to leave a message. I hadn't even known he had an answering machine. I didn't know anyone still had answering machines.

Holding the dishtowel around my finger, I dried the back of my other hand on its length and walked toward the sound of Jacob's voice as if drawn by the shadow of his presence in the forbidden room.

I'd seen his office. I'd never been inside. Usually, he left the door shut, making it easy to ignore. This afternoon, it was wide open. I had no difficulty hearing the content of the message as the caller spoke into the machine. Her words froze me in place.

"I'm calling for Jacob Winters. This is Nurse Hanford from Shaded Glenn. This message is in reference to Anne Louise Wainright. I'm afraid she's taken a bad turn and someone will have to come to the facility. Please let me know as soon as possible what arrangements you plan to make."

I didn't think. I snatched up the phone and croaked, "Hello, yes?"

"Who is this?" The woman's voice demanded. In the second it took for her to respond, I realized what I'd done. Maybe it was the thread of greedy excitement in her polite question. I'd made a mistake. I'd answered the phone, idiot that I was, at the first hint that something was wrong with my mother.

In my defense, I'd been growing increasingly bothered by our separation. I knew she was all right, and she was lucid so rarely, it was likely she didn't even miss me. That didn't make it easier. My mind raced, trying to think of a way to repair my error.

"This is Rachel Porter, Jacob Winters's assistant," I said, forcing my voice into a tone of genteel authority as close to Rachel's own as I could manage. "Why haven't you called his office line? You're lucky I was here to answer. Now, I need more detail on the situation."

There was a heavy pause. "I don't have a Rachel Porter listed on the account."

She was suspicious. Part of me desperately wanted to drop the pretense and beg for information about my mother.

Ruthlessly, I shoved that impulse aside. If something were truly wrong, Jacob would take care of it. The woman on the other end of the phone was probably not a nurse, and there was probably nothing wrong with my mom.

"I should be listed as an alternate point of contact. And you're wasting my time. If you're unable to disclose the details of the circumstances to me, then call Mr. Winters on his mobile line and tell him so that we can deal with it." I was shooting for efficient indifference, but I'm not sure I pulled it off. There was another heavy pause.

"Mrs. Wainright's situation is dire," the possibly fake nurse said. "I would feel most comfortable if I could speak with her daughter, Abigail. She hasn't been to see her mother in a few weeks, and if she wants to see Mrs. Wainright before . . . I need to let her know it's time."

Despair stole my breath. I wasn't ready. I wasn't ready for her to leave me. I knew it wouldn't be that much longer. The disease had progressed too quickly, and on top of that, she had a weak heart.

It was only a matter of time before she slipped away.

The child in me, the little girl still reeling at her father's death, refused to accept more loss. And the idea that this might be it, that my warm, gracious, full of love mother was close to dying, was too much.

The voice echoing in my ear startled me into the present moment.

"Excuse me. Do you know where Abigail is?"

"I do not," I lied, clearing my throat. "I'll speak to Mr.

Winters about this, and someone will be in. In the future, please restrict your calls to his office line. You're fortunate I happened to be here to answer this number."

I hung up the phone. Knowing Jacob wouldn't like me in his office, I left the room as I pulled my rarely used phone out of my pocket.

Jacob was going to be angry, and he'd be right. I shouldn't have answered the phone. I was no good at subterfuge.

Telling the caller I was Rachel was the best I'd been able to come up with, and I don't think she bought it. At least I hadn't been stupid enough to admit I was Abigail Jordan.

I hated the way that name sounded. As soon as I was clear of Big John, I was changing my name back to Wainright. I couldn't erase the last four years of my life, but I didn't have to carry them into the future.

I hit the button to dial Jacob and waited, my emotions careening from worry to fear and back again. Jacob would be right to be mad, and I wasn't sure I could handle it if he was pissed off at me.

As upset as I was about my mom, another furious lecture might roll right off me or crack me into pieces. I didn't want to find out, but I didn't have a choice.

"Abigail, are you all right?" he asked as soon as he answered.

"I am," I said cautiously, "but I think I did something really stupid."

"Are you safe?"

"As far as I know," I said. "I'm in the penthouse. No one's here, or trying to get in, but someone called on the house line, and I answered. I'm sorry. I didn't think—"

"Tell me what happened," he demanded.

I did, falling silent at the end of my explanation, terrified he was about to tell me he'd gotten a similar call there, that something really was badly wrong with my mother.

I wasn't ready. Not yet. Not when I hadn't seen her in weeks. I couldn't let her go. Not in the middle of this mess.

"Take a deep breath, sweetheart," Jacob said, his voice gentle and calm. He didn't sound angry.

Speaking slowly, he went on, "I haven't gotten a call here, and I never gave Shaded Glenn the house line, so I doubt that was really a nurse. I've got a guy with Sinclair, Griffen Sawyer, who's been visiting your mom every few days. He was there yesterday, and she was fine. I'll send him back right now. He'll put eyes on her and call me the second he knows she's fine."

"So she's probably okay," I said, relief and embarrassment warring inside me, "but I did something stupid. Again."

"Everything is going to be okay, Abigail," Jacob said, speaking slowly, still with that gentle tone, as if he was worried I wasn't registering what he said.

"If there was anything wrong with your mother, they would have called my mobile first. Those are their instructions. They would not have called the house. And you shouldn't have answered the phone, but it's not the end of the world.

"That was quick thinking, telling them you were Rachel. I'm sure they weren't expecting that. Still, don't answer that line again. No one uses it. I'm surprised the machine still works. Anyone important calls my mobile or the office. Big John was on a fishing expedition."

Miserably, I said, "He was fishing, and he caught something."

"Sweetheart, let it go. There's nothing you can do about it now. At least you didn't go rushing down there, which is probably what they were going for. At worst, you potentially confirmed that you might be with me. Big John could have figured that out if he got anyone at Shaded Glenn to talk about the change in contact information.

"We were considering prodding Big John a little to flush him out in the open. We'll see how this works out before we decide it was a mistake. I'll be home early. Don't worry."

Before I could respond, he hung up. I hadn't expected him to be so nice about it. I'd expected him to yell at me again for being stupid. He should have yelled at me. I was yelling at myself.

Why had I answered that phone?

Stupid question. I lost all reason when it came to my mom. My lack of judgment over her well-being was why I was in this disaster in the first place.

If I didn't learn, I was only going to make things worse. Except, in this case, being smart meant trusting someone else, trusting Jacob, to take care of my mother. I wasn't sure I could do that. I didn't have a choice.

All I had now was time. Time to wait for Jacob's guy to check on my mom and for Jacob to call me back. I slipped my phone back in my pocket and got a Band-Aid from the first aid kit in the pantry.

The cut on my finger wasn't bad. I washed my hands again and put on a little antiseptic and the Band-Aid before I returned to the kitchen to finish dinner.

When in doubt, cook something. Lately, it seemed to be my motto. I could either fuck Jacob or feed him.

I should have found those options offensive. Demeaning.

I didn't. If I could peel away the drama, get rid of Big

John and restore my mother to health, I'd be content to be exactly where I was.

Belonging to Jacob.

CHAPTER FOURTEEN
ABIGAIL

It was another two hours before I heard anything from Jacob. Dinner was prepped and stored neatly in plastic covered bowls in the refrigerator, waiting for me to start cooking.

I tried everything to distract myself—reading, online shopping, and researching potential schools to finally finish my degree, but I couldn't focus on anything, my mind glancing off every occupation and ricocheting back to worry over my mother.

I'd ended up in the home gym, trying to run off my nerves on the treadmill, something I almost never did. I hated the treadmill, which is why it worked so well to slow down the merry-go-round of fearful thoughts in my brain.

When I was occupied with hating the burn in my legs and the sweat trickling down my spine, I couldn't worry as much about my mother.

No news is good news. If anything were wrong, Jacob would have called right away.

Telling myself that didn't help.

Eventually, my thighs turned to jelly, and I left the gym

to take a quick shower. I was dressed again and pulling a comb through my wet hair when I heard the click of the lock on the front door. The comb fell from my hand, and I raced to meet Jacob.

Coming to a halt in the foyer, I searched his face for any sign that the caller had been telling the truth. He didn't make me wait.

"She's fine," he said. "Your mother's condition is unchanged. The call earlier was a fake. I'm sorry I didn't let you know right away, but it got a little crazy when Griffen went to check on her."

"But she's all right?" I asked.

Jacob stopped in front of me, looking down to meet my eyes. I couldn't read the expression on his face. His silver eyes were soft. A smile played over his lips. He cupped my chin in his hands and lowered his head.

What was he doing? Was he going to kiss me? As crazy as it might sound, Jacob had never kissed me. He'd touched every inch of my skin. We'd had our mouths all over each other, but we'd never kissed.

Kissing was for lovers.

I held my breath as his lips grazed mine, so gentle I wondered if I'd imagined it, before they were back, pressing harder this time.

He tasted like mint and some undefinable flavor I knew was simply Jacob, and when his tongue slid across my lower lip, I opened my mouth to him, helpless to resist. I let out a gasp as his hands dropped from my face to grip my hips, dragging me closer.

The thick cock I knew so well pressed into my belly through his suit and my thin robe.

Arms tightening around me, he pulled me flush to him, my breasts pillowed against his chest, my head tilting back as his mouth took me, the kiss flaring from sweet to hungry in a heartbeat.

The brush of his tongue against mine, the taste of him, made my head spin. He kissed me with his whole body, turning me to pin me to the wall of the foyer, to cage me with his body while he claimed my mouth.

My head spun. I thought I'd gotten used to Jacob's passion. This is something else, something new. This wasn't sex or lust. I raised my hands to his shoulders and held on for dear life, my lips moving under his, matching his need and his hunger.

He'd never kissed me before, and I didn't know if he'd ever kiss me again. I wanted this.

The kiss ended as quickly as it had begun. Jacob loosened his arms and stepped back, prying his lips from mine between one breath and the next.

His mouth beside my ear, he said, "I'm going to go change before I tell you the rest. I'll be right back."

Then he was gone.

I watched him disappear down the hall, still staring after him once he was out of sight, my knees shaking. Between the treadmill and that kiss, I didn't think I could walk.

I guess I didn't have to worry about Jacob being mad. No, now I had something new to worry about.

Why had he kissed me? I hadn't known how much I'd wanted it until I felt his lips on mine. That kiss had been less controlled, more Jacob, than anything he'd done with me.

I wanted that from him, but now that I'd had a taste, I wasn't sure I could bear it when he took it away.

Reminding myself, yet again, that we did not have a relationship and I could not, under any circumstances, fall for him, I peeled myself off the foyer wall and went to the kitchen to pour Jacob a glass of wine.

Deciding it was safer not to mention the kiss, I handed Jacob his wine when he got to the kitchen and asked, "So, what happened?"

I tried to ignore how appealing he looked in a pair of cut off sweatpants and a T-shirt with the logo of *Syndrome* from WGC, his family's gaming company. My head was still spinning, and I could taste him on my tongue.

It was too much. Being kissed senseless by devastatingly handsome, suited Jacob was bad enough. I might never recover from that.

I couldn't transition into drinking wine with casually magnetic down-time Jacob. I was too flustered to think.

Before he could start talking, I said, "Do you want dinner? Are you hungry?" I needed something to do.

Sending me an unreadable grin, he said, "I could eat."

Jacob was being odd. I ignored my uneasiness in favor of finding out what had happened.

Taking pity on me, Jacob said, "Griffen went to check on your mom to make sure she was all right, but also to see if anything was out of the ordinary there. Cooper put men on him to see if anyone was watching the facility or watching Griffen."

"And?" I asked, taking the chicken, vegetables, and sauce I'd prepared from the refrigerator so they could come to room temperature while I warmed up the wok.

For a man who didn't cook, Jacob had a lot of equipment in his kitchen. Even a rice maker, which looked like it had never been used before tonight. There was a lot about my current circumstances that made me uncomfortable, but I loved this kitchen.

"First," Jacob went on, "Griffen confirmed the call was a

fake. They don't have that number on file, they know who Rachel Porter is, and they know to call my office line or my mobile if there's any trouble. They did not call anyone today because your mother is fine."

Relief speared through me. I was delaying the inevitable, but every day I didn't have to face losing my mother was a good one, no matter what else might happen.

Embarrassed that I'd been taken in so easily, I said, "I'm sorry I—"

Jacob cut me off. "Don't be sorry," he said gently. His voice was kind, almost tender. I couldn't help looking at him in confusion.

Jacob could be a lot of things—bossy and commanding, mind-spinningly and panty-meltingly sexy, even dismissive and short-tempered. Gentle, kind, and tender were all new.

I wasn't sure I was equipped to handle this Jacob. This Jacob—casual, sweet Jacob—was way too close to dream-boyfriend Jacob for comfort.

Proving my point, he said, "You have one weak spot, Abigail. One. You don't seem to care at all about your own self-preservation, but anyone who knows you is aware that you'll sacrifice anything for your mother. It's how the Jordans trapped you in the first place. It's the only reason you're here."

He looked away from me when he said that, his silver eyes shifting to pewter.

"It's not," I started to say, then stopped.

It *was* the reason I was there. We both knew it. If it hadn't been for my mother, I never would have consented to an arrangement like this.

I was attracted to Jacob, even more so now that I knew what sex with him was like, but if it weren't for my mother, I would have demanded more from him than this.

I fell silent, willing him to continue his explanation, to get us past this incredibly awkward moment.

"Sweetheart," he said softly.

And what was with calling me sweetheart? He called me Abigail, sometimes Miss Jordan—never Mrs. Jordan—but *sweetheart* was new.

It sent a giddy flutter through my heart even as my head rejected it as a line or a meaningless endearment. I was not Jacob's sweetheart. Jacob didn't have sweethearts.

"You answered the phone because you were scared and you didn't think. You know it was dangerous, which is why you told them you were Rachel. That was quick thinking, by the way. They may *think* it was you who answered the phone, but they don't know."

"It was still foolish," I admitted.

Jacob shrugged. "Everyone does foolish things. Don't be so hard on yourself."

"You have someone going to visit my mom for me?"

I'd been wanting to ask him about that since he mentioned it on the phone. Yep, sweet Jacob was going to kill me. He shrugged again.

"It seemed like a good idea. I wanted someone who was used to the facility, and who they were used to visiting your mother. I also wanted first-hand reports—not from the staff —about your mother's condition and quality of care. Both of which are excellent, by the way, all things considered. I would have expected it, given what the place costs, but Griffen says they're taking very good care of her and the staff is top-notch."

"I know," I said. "They're the best. That's why my father put her there, and every place else I looked at after he died —" I shook my head. "I just couldn't bring myself to take her out."

"You played it off on the phone," Jacob said. "But they were definitely hoping you'd take the bait, because Cooper's guys clocked at least three of Big John's men waiting around the facility to grab you if you showed up. They noticed Griffen, but they didn't make a move on him. We're not sure if they know who he is and why he was there."

"Big John is losing patience, isn't he?" I asked, dumping vegetables into the sizzling wok, avoiding Jacob's eyes.

He came up behind me, wrapping his arms around me and resting his chin on the top of my head. My heart squeezed in my chest at his casual tenderness. We'd done plenty of touching, but he'd never held me like this.

I couldn't remember the last time anyone had held me like this. Tears gathered in my eyes. Horrified, I blinked them back.

Unaware of my internal struggle with his easy affection, Jacob said, "He's been searching for you since you disappeared. I've had Cooper and his team watching him. He was looking for you from the beginning, but now, his negotiations with the Raptors have stalled and he needs you to get them back online. He wasn't desperate before, but he's getting there."

"I'm part of the deal?" I asked, sick to my stomach at the memory of what Big John had said they would do to me.

"There's more to it than just you," Jacob said. "They can't agree on distribution. They can't agree on their cut—"

"Their cut of what?" I interrupted.

I was so clueless. Jacob gave me a squeeze. More affection. I was clueless in so many ways.

"Sales from heroin, mostly, and guns. Big John deals in more than that, but that's what he wants the Raptors for."

"Oh."

I didn't know what else to say. I couldn't believe John

had been involved in this part of his father's business, though I knew he probably had. But my John, the man I had married, had been soft.

Soft body, affable personality, there was nothing about him that would suggest he had the capacity to make deals with biker gangs or sell drugs and weapons.

Without realizing I was going to speak, I said, "The police told me John was the victim of a mugging. He was shot. But it wasn't a mugging, was it?"

Jacob's arms tightened around me. "No," he said. "I don't think it was."

"Do you know who killed him?" I asked, my voice small.

I wasn't sure I wanted to know, but I had to. Jacob gave me another squeeze. I turned off the wok and waited for his answer.

"I don't know, not definitely. From what Cooper has turned up, it looks like it was an inside job."

I stepped away from Jacob and went to get the plates for dinner, every muscle in my body stiff with shock and denial.

An inside job?

John had been killed by one of his own? I took the plates down from the shelves, my movements jerky, the china clattering as I tried to set it on the counter. Jacob edged me aside with a gentle nudge.

"I'll do this," he said, piling steaming rice on each plate before covering it with veggies and chicken in a sweet and savory sesame teriyaki sauce.

The scent of the food turned my stomach. *An inside job?* That possibility had occurred to me before, but I'd buried it.

I'd still been living in our house, surrounded by the Jordan clan. I couldn't afford to suspect them of something so awful. But what Jacob said made a sickening kind of sense. John had never fit in with the rest of them.

It wasn't his fault. His father had set him aside from the beginning, seeing John as a way for the family to carve out a presence in the legitimate world of business.

John had done as he was told—gone to all the right schools, where he made the right friendships. He'd gotten his business degree. He'd golfed, joined the country club, gotten tips on investments, and increased the Jordan family connections and wealth.

He'd even married me. I wasn't Atlanta royalty, but in our small but affluent suburb, I was considered a prize.

I'm not being conceited about it. I was pretty and reasonably smart, but I knew my appeal had far more to do with my parents' wealth and position in the community than it had to do with me.

My father had been a wealthy banker and my mother's family was old Atlanta. I'd been born with a silver spoon in my mouth and an impeccable pedigree, but had my father's failures become public knowledge, my tiara would have tarnished overnight.

Instead, John swooped in to save my mother and marry me. In retrospect, it was the beginning of the end for John. He'd accomplished everything his father had wanted. It had never been enough.

I recalled hushed arguments, John telling his father he wouldn't work for him and Big John telling him he was weak. A waste of effort. A regret.

Had Big John decided to cut his losses and wipe his hands of his oldest son in the most final way?

"Abigail." Jacob interrupted my thoughts. He stood in front of me, a plate in each hand. "Let's eat. What happened to John was set in motion long before you two got married.

You're lucky you got away. When this is over, you'll never have to think of the Jordans again."

That was oversimplifying things, of course. I couldn't just wash the last four years from my mind, couldn't forget John and our marriage, his family.

I wished I could. But Jacob was right. I *was* lucky to have gotten away. I didn't want to give Big John and his threats more of me than he'd already taken. Picking up the bottle of wine and our glasses, I followed Jacob into the dining room.

I had more to worry about than the Jordan family. Like what was going on with Jacob. Why had he changed so much?

Hugging me? Kissing me? Calling me sweetheart? He'd gone a whole day without ordering me to strip naked. That couldn't be good.

Maybe it was time for me to make a move. To put things back on even ground. Jacob was intimidating when he was ordering me around, but when he was being sweet, he terrified me.

I couldn't afford to fool myself into believing we were in love. I wouldn't survive it, not on top of everything else.

It was time to remind us both why I was there.

CHAPTER FIFTEEN
ABIGAIL

I don't remember eating dinner. Jacob cleaned his plate, so it must have been edible, but I merely picked at mine, distracted by thoughts of what to do next.

Jacob always made the first move. He'd tell me what he wanted, and I'd comply.

I liked it. I'd always bristled at being told what to do, until Jacob. So far, every order he'd given me had ended in mind blowing pleasure. I had no problem following his lead.

This time, I wanted to figure out how to take the lead on my own.

"Abigail?" I heard him say. I looked up, startled.

"Sorry," I said. "Just thinking."

"What about?" he asked, his eyes dark with concern.

Should I lie? I was still wearing my robe. I'd never gotten dressed after my shower.

Testing him, I ran one finger down the shawl collar of the light silk robe, trailing it over my skin to dip into my barely exposed cleavage. I tugged on the slippery fabric, exposing the inner curve of one breast.

Jacob's silver eyes heated, desire chasing away the dark.

The look sent a bolt of fire between my legs. Nothing turned me on more these days than Jacob looking at me as if he wanted to devour me.

Encouraged, I hooked my finger in the silk and pulled it back until the robe slipped off my shoulder, leaving me entirely bare on one side.

"What else were you thinking about?" he asked, his voice a little hoarse.

"That's what had me so distracted," I admitted. "I couldn't decide."

I stood slowly, letting the robe drift off my shoulders to puddle in the chair, and strode to him, feeling suddenly like the predator he so often resembled.

The unfamiliar sense of power was a rush. My breasts felt swollen, full and tipped with hard nipples that demanded his attention.

Between my legs, I was already slick with need for him. I wanted Jacob. I was going to take all my confusion, all my uncertainty about him and channel it into pleasure.

I was going to do what I was here for—use our bodies to make us both feel so good we'd forget everything else.

Coming to a stop in front of him, I stared him down.

Lounging in the dining chair, his silver eyes heavy lidded with desire, his dark hair a little messy, a bemused smile on his lips, he looked like a king in his court, waiting to be entertained.

Jacob was always in command, even when he let me take charge. The thought sent a shiver through me.

"Well?" he prompted.

"You're wearing too many clothes," I said.

"What are you going to do about it?" he challenged.

What was I going to do? I wished he were still wearing his suit. I'd always wanted to strip him naked, to peel away the armor of his daily life and lay his body bare.

Somehow, his t-shirt and cutoffs intimidated me more than his custom-made suits. I knew what to do with that Jacob.

This Jacob kissed me and called me sweetheart. This Jacob was a mystery. Feeling my way, I leaned forward, enjoying the way his eyes flared wide at the shift of my breasts, and slid my hands over his shoulders.

I tugged, pulling him to his feet, before I dropped my hands to the hem of his shirt and peeled it over his head.

I got lost for a moment in the sight of his neck and the beat of his pulse beneath stubbled skin. The scent of him, so warm and close.

All that bare chest and those cut abs. I knew now that he woke at five am every day to put in a punishing hour in his gym. I liked the results.

I was taking too long. I wanted him naked. Hooking my fingers in the waist of his loose shorts, I pushed them down, delighted to find he wore nothing beneath.

I'd begun stripping him uncertain of my path, but now I knew what I wanted. Without a second thought, I dropped to my knees on the soft carpet of the dining room.

His cock was ready for me, straining and hard. I opened my mouth and licked. Heat and the taste of Jacob.

Funny what could change in a few weeks. I'd always thought of oral sex as something a woman put up with. God knows, I'd never had the favor returned before Jacob.

The idea of wanting to do this, of needing a cock in my mouth, had been inconceivable. Why? But now I knew.

When it was this cock, Jacob's cock, I did want it. I had to have it. I wanted to make him come like this, using only my mouth.

I still couldn't swallow him all the way. I made up for it, running my tongue over his silky skin until he was slick and I'd tasted every inch of the gorgeous cock before I dropped my mouth over his length and took him inside.

I'd learned what he liked. With Jacob, I couldn't help myself. I loved the way he responded to my touch.

I was addicted to every hitch in his breath, every clench of his muscles.

I sucked him hard, drawing him as deeply into the heat of my mouth as I could, sliding my hand around the base of his cock in a tight grip I knew would make him catch his breath.

He didn't disappoint me.

"Abigail," he groaned, sinking his fingers into my hair, holding me where I was.

I had him exactly where I wanted him. I hadn't been able to entice him into finishing in my mouth since the first time.

I needed that. Teasing him, I sat back, releasing most of him, licking my tongue across the head of his cock to taste the fluid beading there.

Looking up, I met his eyes as I opened my lips and took him inside once more. His silver eyes were molten with lust—that I'd expected—but there was something else.

Something demanding, proprietary.

Something that said I was his and that I was precious. I dropped my eyes, unable to hold his gaze any longer. I was supposed to be taking control, reminding us what my place was in Jacob's life.

The way he was looking at me had me more off balance than ever.

His fingers stroked at my scalp, not holding me in place,

not tugging me closer. He was letting me lead, his hold on my hair a caress, not a command.

My heart squeezed in my chest. What was going on here? I tried to focus on his cock in my mouth. I'd make him come, and we'd be back on even ground.

It made sense in my head, but I was too far gone already, lost in the taste of Jacob, captured by his rough gasp when I sucked him hard, the low moan when the head of his cock hit the back of my throat.

I took every inch I could fit without choking, sucking hard, every nerve in my body on fire from the taste of him and his hands in my hair.

The tips of my hard nipples scraped his legs, and we both groaned. Every touch to my sensitized skin was too much. I was careening to overload, and he'd barely gotten his hands on me.

Between my legs, I could feel the swollen, wet heat of my pussy. I was ready for Jacob.

My mouth slid faster over Jacob's cock, my lips and tongue fucking him, tight and wet, setting a rhythm that had him unable to resist fucking me back.

A fierce joy exploded in my chest as his control slipped just a little. I needed to know I could do that to him, that I could push him until he needed me like I did him.

His fingers curled to grip my hair as he groaned, "Abigail, I'm so close."

He was giving me a chance to pull away. It wasn't going to happen. I wanted this as much as he did. I wanted him to come on my tongue. I had to taste him.

His orgasm was mine, and I'd earned every drop. My fist at the base of his cock milked him, my mouth sucking hard as his body stiffened and he came for me, his cock jerking on my tongue, his come filling my mouth.

I swallowed him down, triumph filling my chest. Whatever happened between us, this part of Jacob was mine.

We stayed like that, Jacob catching his breath, my head resting against his thigh, his thick cock still half-hard, not an inch from my mouth.

He'd just come, my tongue still coated in his taste, and I wanted to do it again.

Mine.

The thought kept running through my head. His long fingers stroked through my hair, and I reminded myself that he was not mine. I was his. Big difference.

He would never be mine.

The world flipped upside down as he bent over and picked me up, cradling my naked body to his chest. I wasn't surprised when he headed down the hall to the bedrooms. As we passed the door to the guest room, to my room, a jolt of shock hit me.

Jacob was taking me to his bedroom.

I'd been in there once, the first full day I'd lived in the penthouse, but I hadn't invaded his private space since then.

He came to me. Always.

I'd followed his lead and hadn't gone near his bedroom, sensing that he'd wanted that distance between us. As I'd drawn closer to him, I'd needed distance as much as he did. Maybe more.

I closed my eyes, hiding my face against his chest, suddenly afraid and completely unable to hide from him.

Jacob was everywhere. His arms around me, his scent pervading every breath, the sound of his heartbeat echoing in my ear. Carefully, he laid me on his bed, coming down beside me, nudging me until I was spread out in the center of his duvet like an offering.

His eyes locked on mine, and I couldn't look away. I was afraid to read him, afraid I was lying to myself when I saw tenderness there, tangled with desire.

I forced my eyes to close, catching my breath when his lips touched first one lid, then the other before taking my mouth in a deep, wet, claiming kiss.

I could hide my eyes, but I couldn't hide from that kiss. My body was out of my control.

My arms came up around Jacob, holding him to me, my mouth moving under his, matching him, falling into the kiss with my body as my heart tried to run. His body moved over mine, covering me with his heat as he settled between my legs.

His cock was hard again, thick and pressing against my slick pussy. No question that my body wanted him inside.

With a last, desperate wish, I wanted him to slam inside me, to fuck me hard, to take me with a rough detachment that would let me come with nothing more than a physical release.

Instead, a tight knot in the center of my soul began to unwind as Jacob slowly pressed that thick cock inside me, stroking me with his body, taking me with a thorough patience that left me with no doubt he knew exactly what he was doing and who he was with.

I couldn't pretend this was some anonymous fuck. That I was nothing more to him than a convenient pet. Not when his lips stroked my ear and he breathed, "Abigail, fuck, Abigail. You feel so good. Fucking made for me."

A sob hitched in my chest. It was too much. He felt too good. Too right. His cock filled me, stretched me open and made me into someone else.

This wasn't fucking. He was making love to me, his body singing to mine, stroking and touching me until I shook with it, desperate to come and wishing it would never end.

The orgasm broke over me in a wave of pleasure so sharp, I bit my tongue to keep from crying out. I was still trying to hide from him. I couldn't let him see me—he had split me open, stolen my defenses.

I'd given my heart to him, and I hadn't even known when it happened. I could pretend this was still a game, or a deal, but I knew. This agreement with Jacob was deadly serious, and I'd lost all control.

The pleasure built again, sharp and sweet. I couldn't fight it. With each steady, measured thrust in my body, Jacob claimed more of my heart.

He was stealing me, and I couldn't stop it.

My nails sank into his shoulders, my back arched, and I came again, my body claiming his in tight, fierce pulses of my pussy.

He groaned his own release into my neck, filling me with his heat, before collapsing and rolling us to the side so he didn't crush me with his bigger body.

I came back to myself slowly, his fingers stroking through my hair, soothing me, chasing away my thoughts before they could gather into coherent questions.

I felt tears drying on my face. I'd cried at the end as I'd come. I was still crying, silent tears trickling down my cheeks to land on Jacob's skin.

Why was I crying? What was going on with Jacob? With me?

Like a coward, I didn't sit up and demand he explain why he was behaving so differently. I stayed where I was, ignoring my own tears, treasuring the stroke of his fingers in my hair, the sound of his strong heartbeat beneath my cheek.

There would be time enough for explanations later. For now, I just wanted to pretend Jacob was mine, that this was real and I could have him for my own. I would deal with reality later.

I woke in the middle of the night to find myself still in Jacob's bed, my body draped over his and his arm clamped over my back, holding me to him, even in sleep.

I shouldn't be here. This was dangerous. Making love in his bed was bad enough. I couldn't start sleeping here too.

I'd tried to put us back on even ground, to remind us both what we were, and somehow, Jacob had flipped everything upside down anyway.

Now he was sleeping, and I was back in control. Holding my breath, I slid out from beneath his arm, carefully moving off the side of the bed.

My own sheets were cold and empty. I slid between them and turned on my side, gathering the spare pillow in my arms as if it could be some kind of replacement for Jacob.

Not likely.

There was no replacement for Jacob, just a chilly, empty bed and a heart that was beyond repair.

I lay there for hours, wishing for sleep, trying to fool myself into believing I was better off where I was. I drifted off as the first threads of dawn light came through the window, my cheeks again wet with tears.

CHAPTER SIXTEEN

JACOB

I woke up reaching for Abigail and found my arms empty. For a moment, my brain fogged with sleep, I panicked, nightmare images of Big John taking her flashing through my brain.

I bolted from the bed, heart thudding in my chest, before I skidded to a halt at her bedroom door at the sight of her curled up in her bed, fast asleep.

It was after dawn, and I would have been up already, but I'd turned off my alarm the night before. I hadn't wanted to wake Abigail. I had an early meeting, but I'd wanted to sleep as late as possible.

Now that I'd had her in my bed, I wanted to keep her there. Instead, she'd woken in the night and stolen away like a thief.

I didn't have to turn on the light to see the tracks of dried tears on her smooth cheeks. I didn't want to understand.

I'd be lying to myself if I didn't admit that I was disturbed by the changes between us. Abigail Jordan was supposed to be an experiment. A pet. A private indulgence.

I was not supposed to want to keep her. I'd planned to enjoy her until the danger from Big John had passed, then set up a trust to take care of her mother and send her on her way.

A few months of spectacular sex at a cost I could well afford. I'd always wanted a taste of Abigail, and this way, I could do a good deed and get my fill of her at the same time.

At its worst, the situation would soothe my conscience for all the time I'd spent lusting after another man's wife.

I should have known the plan would fall apart the first time she'd gone to her knees for me. The wave of possessiveness I'd felt should have been a warning.

I'd ignored it. I'd gorged myself on her, taking everything I wanted from Abigail, not caring that each day with her, my need had grown.

I hated the thought of her full name. Abigail Jordan. She didn't belong to them. John hadn't deserved her. She'd been wasted on him.

Abigail was mine.

It wasn't enough to own her body. At the start, I'd thought that would be more than enough. Her body and her willingness to give me anything I desired.

What more could any man possibly want from a woman?

What did I care what was in her heart, in her soul? The more I sated myself in her tight, slick pussy, the more her body alone wasn't enough.

I wanted her smiles, her laughter. I craved a soft look. Her casual affection. I knew she desired me. Abigail wasn't experienced enough to fake her body's reaction to me.

I was a greedy bastard, and I didn't care. I'd known what she was doing the night before with her strip tease.

Fucking hell, she'd been hot, peeling open her silk robe and sucking my cock like she'd been dreaming of it all day.

By the time I got inside her, she'd been soaked, so turned on from sucking me off that the moisture from her pussy had slicked down her legs.

Abigail was a treasure, and she was terrified of me. Of what was happening between us.

I wanted to pretend I didn't get it, wanted to tell myself this was simple. I knew it wasn't. She'd been victimized by her husband. He might have married her, while I'd tried to make her my pet, but John had used her love for her mother to enslave her.

And how is that different from what you did? A sly voice in the back of my head demanded.

But it *was* different. Maybe not at the very beginning. But I'd planned to set her free.

And now? Are you going to set her free now?

No, I was not going to set her free. I couldn't.

What if she actually left? First, she wasn't safe. I'd hid from her the details of Big John's intentions. He wasn't just planning to use her to convince the Raptors to work with him. She'd become part of the deal. If he got her, he'd give her to them.

What they'd do with her didn't bear thinking about. There were gangs out there who weren't that bad. Not all criminals were animals.

I knew a few legitimate businessmen who were far worse than some of the men and women on the wrong side of the law. The Raptors were every ugly cliché made worse. Abigail would be better off dead than with them.

And when that problem is taken care of? Will you let her go then?

The sneaky voice sounded a lot like my conscience. I wished it would shut the hell up.

I was taking better care of Abigail than John ever had. And no, I was not going to fucking let her go. I wouldn't chain her to the bed. I wasn't an animal. I wasn't Big John.

I'd just have to make sure she didn't want to leave me. She hadn't cried the night before because she *didn't* want me. I wasn't a mind reader, but I knew Abigail wasn't that good of an actress.

When she was hiding her thoughts, she got all proper and dignified. She didn't drop to her knees and suck my cock like she'd been dreaming of nothing else for her entire life. She didn't cling to my arms and cry out her orgasm.

I'd felt her shock when I'd kissed her. I'd shocked myself. I'd avoided kissing Abigail for weeks. Now that I'd done it, I had to wonder what the fuck had been wrong with me.

Kissing her was like tasting her soul. All her sweetness, everything that made her Abigail, was right there in her lips, in the way her mouth opened for me, in the little gasps and hitches of her breath as I claimed her.

Now that I'd kissed her, I was going to do it every day. Every hour.

She needed to tell herself that we were just sex. I understood. She'd been stripped of too much in the last few years. She couldn't take the risk of losing more. Of losing her heart.

Was that what I wanted? Her heart? Stop being such a pussy, that irritatingly knowing voice said. *Man up and admit what this is about.*

Fuck. *Love.*

Was it about love? Is that what I wanted from her?

I'd never wanted it from a woman before. I knew what

156

love was. Knew what it looked like. I'd grown up in a home filled with love before it had been stolen from us.

A memory of the picture some asshole had sent of my Aunt and Uncle's deaths flashed through my mind, carrying with it a bolt of nausea.

I remembered that I still hadn't apologized for being such a bastard to Abigail. Fuck. If I wanted her to stay, I was doing a shit job of convincing her I was a good bet.

I had to do better. She was scared, and she should be. I'd been an ass from the start, wanting everything on my terms.

If I was really going to be honest with myself, that wasn't going to change. I still wanted everything on my terms. It's just that now, I wanted what was best for Abigail.

If I was going to give her my best, I had to make sure she wanted the same thing I did. I wanted Abigail to stay with me. I needed her to be mine. All I had to do was convince her she wanted the same.

I was already more than halfway there. She might have convinced herself otherwise, but I knew she never would have come to me in the first place, never would have let me touch her body the way I had, if she hadn't already been half in love with me to start.

She could have told herself that she was exploring her sexuality, or whatever bullshit she'd used to justify giving me control of her body, but the base fact was that Abigail would never have accepted my offer if she hadn't already had feelings for me.

At the very least, she trusted me. I could work with that.

My mind occupied with Abigail, I got dressed for my meeting and left the penthouse. I'd get coffee and breakfast there. Maybe I'd even leave work early. The building was quiet at this hour, the parking garage well-lit but silent.

That was probably why the scuff of the shoe on

concrete caught my attention so easily. I couldn't see anyone else between the rows of cars. No engines were running, and no headlights flashed.

I slowed, looking around. We had security down here, at the entrances from the street, on top of cameras and hand scanners on the stairwell and the elevator.

No one should be able to get into the garage who didn't belong, but it wouldn't be the first time someone had managed to slip through the guards.

Cooper was right. If I'd wanted a truly secure building, I would have left off the retail and the office space. Once I decided to give the public access to Winters House, I'd made it far more complicated to keep the building safe from intruders.

At the time, that hadn't been a concern. Now that it was, I was starting to wonder if we shouldn't relocate to the real Winters House.

Our family home didn't have a formal name, but all of us had always called it Winters House, and my giving this building the same name had been an inside family joke.

The real Winters House, where my oldest brother, Aiden, and my younger sister, Charlotte, still lived, was a ten-acre estate in the heart of Buckhead.

Surrounded by a high wall, protected by motion detectors and armed guards twenty-four seven, Aiden's home, my home, was close to impenetrable. But I didn't want to move in with my brother.

I didn't think he knew what I'd been up to with Abigail. If he did, I'm sure I would've had a phone call or a visit already. Aiden loved his siblings and his cousins, but he was a nosy bastard. He took his position as the head of the family seriously. Too seriously.

I wasn't sure I was satisfied with my explanations to my

own conscience. I already knew they wouldn't be good enough for Aiden's.

It was the best indication I could have that I needed to get myself together where Abigail was concerned. As my mother always used to tell us, "If you're too embarrassed to tell the people you love about something you're doing, either you're doing wrong, or you need more confidence in your choices."

I missed my mother.

Nearing my car, I heard it again. The scuff of the shoe on concrete. Not a dress shoe like mine. A sneaker. Maybe a work boot. Something softer, rubber, but the sound was there.

Investigate? Or get in the car and call Cooper? I wasn't stupid. I was in good shape, and I was fast. I knew how to use a gun, but I wasn't carrying.

If I thought there was trouble, I was better off getting the hell out of there than trying to deal with it on my own.

Walking faster, I clicked the button to unlock my car and swung my briefcase to my right hand. It wasn't the best weapon, but it was all I had.

Possibly sensing that his quarry was going to escape, whoever else was in the garage stopped trying to hide.

Footsteps came toward me, shuffling then pounding at the concrete. I was less than a yard from my car. Diving for the driver's side door, I wrenched it open and slung myself inside, losing my briefcase on the concrete.

The engine turned over, and I jammed the car into reverse when the rear window exploded in a shower of glass.

Where the fuck was the Sinclair team? At that thought, I heard shouts from behind my car. More gunshots. Hitting the gas, I reversed out of the parking space, then jammed on the brakes when I felt the thud of impact. I hoped it wasn't one of Cooper's guys.

I looked around the parking garage wildly, trying to figure out my next move. I could hear the shouts of 'security', then my name.

"Jacob Winters. I'm with Sinclair security. I've got two guys in here, and Cooper's on his way. Don't move your vehicle. The shooter's down behind your rear wheels."

"Is it all right if I get out of the car?" I asked.

"Not yet," the nameless voice answered, drawing closer to my car. "Let us get the shooter secured and clear the garage. Keep your head down to minimize the target until we give you the all clear."

"Got it," I said. I didn't want to sit in the car while the action was going on around me, but I wasn't stupid.

The Sinclair team were the best. If they told me to stay put, I'd stay put. Sliding down, I reclined the driver seat so my upper body was out of view of the windows.

It burned a little to hide. I didn't hide from my problems. But this wasn't my normal style of problem. This wasn't a business deal gone sideways. This was someone with a gun trying to shoot me.

I had no doubt the shooter was connected to Big John. He wanted Abigail, and if the Raptors were putting on the pressure, he'd be getting desperate. Desperate enough to try to take me out of the equation. I'd held off on locking down the garage, not wanting to inconvenience the residents and employees who had to use it. That was over. My phone beeped with a text. I eased it out of my back pocket and checked the display.

On my way. Team clearing the garage. Sending an extra man to your floor. Stay put.

Cooper. I texted back,

Got it. I'm in my car waiting for the all clear. Everything all right upstairs?

What if the shooter in the garage had been a diversion? What if someone was going after Abigail right now while the security team was all over the garage? But that was why Cooper was sending an extra guy upstairs.

He's on it, I reminded myself. Cooper knows what he's doing, and Abigail is fine.

Unable to help myself, I pulled up the security app on my phone and logged into the cameras in my penthouse. I hadn't spied on Abigail since that first day.

I'd wanted to, but invading her privacy repeatedly was dehumanizing. After what she'd been through in her marriage, I couldn't do that to her.

This time, I wasn't trying to catch her in anything. All I wanted to see was her sleeping peacefully in her bed, exactly the way I'd left her.

I hadn't been nervous when I heard the footsteps in the garage. Not even when the window had exploded behind me. I'd felt a rush of adrenaline, my senses had sharpened, and I'd been ready to act, but I hadn't been afraid.

Waiting for the cameras to come online, I felt a cold, deep fear. The garage had never felt so far from the penthouse. I might as well have been a mile away for all I could do to help her. Knowing there was security upstairs didn't help.

The camera on the front door flashed to life, showing part of the hall and both of the men Cooper had put on my door. Their posture was alert, but at ease.

Flicking through the camera views on my phone, I let out a breath when I found Abigail's room and saw her, now stretched out on her stomach, one arm wrapped around her pillow, her hair loose and spread over her shoulders.

The tight band of fear around my chest loosened. I could handle whatever was going on here as long as Abigail was all right.

In the distance, the wail of sirens bled through the quiet morning. Shit. Of course, we'd have to call the police.

Sinclair Security had a good relationship with Atlanta PD. They even did jobs for them at a reduced rate when needed, and they maintained that relationship by playing by the book. Most of the time.

An intruder had shot out my window and I'd hit him with my car. Explanations were in order. I'd have to file a police report.

Shit.

The press would be right behind the police, and my quiet morning was about to turn into a total cluster fuck.

I texted Rachel and told her to cancel my morning meeting. Frustrated at being stuck in the car while the security team cleared the garage, I contented myself with watching Abigail sleep.

As long as she was safe, everything else would work out.

CHAPTER SEVENTEEN
ABIGAIL

I slept late and woke with the scratch of dried tears on my cheeks. Stupid.

Crying over Jacob was a waste of time. I'd made my bed. Literally. The least I could do was sleep in it without getting weepy.

Annoyed with myself, I dragged my tired body out of bed and took a long, hot shower. When I stepped out, feeling more together, if not quite awake, I pulled on a matching pair of yoga pants and hoodie.

Though I never left the penthouse, I usually dressed with a little more formality. Loungewear was comfy, but it wasn't really me.

That morning, I'd woken with a dull headache, my body feeling heavy as if I hadn't slept. I wanted comfortable clothes and a mug of tea. As I zipped up the lightweight hoodie, my mobile phone rang.

Jacob.

My stomach tightened with nerves. He never called during the day. Something was wrong.

"Jacob?" I said when I answered.

Immediately, he responded, "Everything is fine."

No, it wasn't. Not if he'd bypassed 'hello' for reassurance.

"What happened? Is it my mother?" I asked, suddenly dizzy. I sat on the edge of the bed, the pounding in my head worse.

"No. Your mother is fine. Griffen already checked. We had an intruder in the garage. He shot at my car."

I gasped. "Are you okay? Jacob—" He cut me off.

"I'm fine. He didn't hit me, just my window. I backed into him, and he's in police custody. The building is secure, I've got eyes on every entrance to the penthouse level, and the guards are on the floor below, blocking the stairwell.

"Elevators above the office level are locked down to hand prints only. No one is getting upstairs. I moved the guard from directly outside the door—between the police and the press, it's a mess down here, but you're completely safe. I didn't want you to see the building on the news and worry."

"I never watch the news. I read the paper," I said absently, my mind racing over what he'd told me.

I wasn't worried for myself. Jacob had reassured me he had this level covered. I was worried for him.

"Big John is coming after you, isn't he?"

"It looks like it," Jacob admitted. "The shooter was a mid-level guy with the Jordans. He already had a record, so they IDed him right away."

"I should leave," I said, panic arcing through me. When I'd come here, I'd been thinking of my mother. And myself. Jacob had seemed invincible. I never thought Big John would come directly for him. Not like this.

"Abigail," Jacob's hard voice cut through my rising panic. "Don't do anything. Stay in the penthouse."

"But—"

I couldn't stand the idea that Jacob would be hurt because of me. I'd been selfish enough asking him for help. I couldn't let him get hurt.

"No, listen to me," he commanded. "Even if you leave, he'll come after me. At this point, I'm his best lead. The only way to stop that is for you to turn yourself over, and that is not going to happen. Understand?

"I'm covered. I have the best security all over me. I'm locking down the building. I was avoiding going that far—I didn't want to draw Big John's attention by changing things at Winters House too much. Now that he's come after us, there's no reason not to get serious about security.

"Before, we were trying to keep it low-key. Now, it's going to get very visible. No one is getting in the building who doesn't belong here. No one."

"Okay," I said.

He had a point. The only way to pull Big John off Jacob was to turn myself in. If I did that, I was as good as dead. Worse than dead.

"I'm sorry," I whispered.

"Don't be, sweetheart. I'm starting to think the day you came to my office might have been the luckiest day of my life. We'll figure out a way to handle the Jordans, and then you'll be free again. Trust me."

"I do. You promise you're all right?"

"I promise. I have to go down to talk to the police and make some arrangements with Cooper and Evers. I'll be back around lunch time. Don't worry."

"Okay," I said again.

He hung up the phone. I was a liar. Of course I was going to worry. Big John had sent someone to shoot at Jacob.

I felt sick to my stomach. My head pounded. I dragged myself to the kitchen and made a cup of tea.

In a movie, I'd sneak out of the penthouse and confront Big John. I'd figure out some clever way to get myself out of this mess and save the day.

I was no action movie heroine. This penthouse was the one place in the city I knew I was safe. I'd do as Jacob said and sit tight, as much as I hated being useless.

I finished my tea and took something for the headache that wouldn't go away. It helped a little, but I still felt slow and draggy. I thought I'd slept well, but maybe I hadn't. I drifted off on the couch, waiting for Jacob to come home.

The sound of pounding on the penthouse door startled me awake. I rolled to my feet, fighting off a wave of dizziness, and stumbled to the kitchen, grabbing the house phone off the counter.

I'd left my mobile somewhere. I couldn't remember. I'd been good about carrying it with me since the picture had been delivered, but somehow, I'd misplaced it that morning after I'd talked to Jacob.

I started to dial his number when I heard the key in the lock. It couldn't be Jacob. He wouldn't have knocked. But he'd assured me an intruder couldn't get to the penthouse level. And an intruder wouldn't have the key.

Clutching the phone in my hand, I waited for whoever it was to come down the hall.

A man rounded the corner, dark hair falling in his eyes, his face determined and pissed off. The expression was familiar.

Not sure what to do, I said, "Leave, or I'm calling security."

"Who the hell are you?" the stranger demanded. "And what are you doing in my cousin's penthouse?"

I relaxed a little. One of Jacob's cousins. I knew he had one who lived a few floors down and worked in the building.

That would explain how the stranger had gotten on the penthouse level without anyone raising an alarm. And how he had a key. Studying his face, the family resemblance was clear.

"You're one of Jacob's cousins, I presume? Which one? You're too young to be Gage or Vance, so you must be Tate."

"Good call," he said, his eyes narrowed on my face. "When will Jacob be back?"

"You'd better come in," I said, turning back to the kitchen. I set the phone down in its charger, finally spotting my mobile beside the single-serve coffee machine.

"Who are you?" he asked again.

"I think it's better if Jacob answers that question," I said.

If Jacob hadn't told his family what was going on, I wasn't going to do it. "But I have his permission to be here, if that's what you're worried about. Would you like some coffee? Tea? It's a little early for lunch, but I can probably throw something together."

"Coffee, and something to eat if you have it. It's been a long morning," he said, sitting down at the counter facing the rest of the kitchen.

I started a cup of coffee and decided to make him a sandwich. We had turkey and some leftover pesto sauce. I'd made bread the day before. Unless Jacob ate at the precinct, he'd be hungry when he got back.

Making lunch would keep me busy. I snuck glances at Tate while I worked. He didn't bother sneaking, his deep blue eyes openly studying me as I moved around the kitchen.

He looked so much like Jacob it was a little scary.

Except for the eyes, a warm blue to Jacob's cool silver, and his youth, he was almost a carbon copy.

They had the same thick, dark hair, though Tate's was worn longer, showing its wave. The same aristocratic face and lean frame. Tate wasn't that much younger than Jacob, I didn't think, but he had a lightness to him that I didn't see in Jacob.

Maybe it had nothing to do with age. I could imagine Jacob as a serious toddler, barking orders and concentrating intently as he built a Lego empire.

"Do I know you?" he asked.

"Wouldn't you know if you did?" I countered. "Cream? Sugar?"

I held up a steaming mug of coffee. Normally, I loved the smell, but this morning, it turned my stomach. I needed more tea. With honey. My throat was starting to prickle when I swallowed.

"Black is fine," he said, taking the coffee. "Did the mess in the parking garage this morning have anything to do with you?"

I couldn't help my flinch, but I settled my expression to hide my nerves before I answered him.

"You really need to ask Jacob," I said. Checking the clock, I saw it was close to noon. "He should be home soon."

Tate drank his coffee in silence as I finished making his sandwich and slid it in front of him. He ate it in big bites, as if he were starving. Part of me wanted to ask what he knew about the 'mess' in the garage, but I didn't want to betray my own ignorance.

I knew I was safe with Jacob's family, but I wasn't going to tell Tate anything Jacob didn't want him to know.

Feeling off balance wearing such casual clothes in front of a stranger, I excused myself and went to my bedroom.

My wet hair was still up in a simple twist, so I left it. Despite the medicine, my head hurt. I didn't want to touch my hair.

Shedding the yoga pants and hoodie, I pulled on a loose but tailored shift and shoved my feet into matching sandals.

Comfortable, but more appropriate. I added some make-up, alarmed to see how pale my skin was, with two bright spots of color on my cheeks.

I never got sick. I was one of those people who escaped unscathed when everyone else caught a cold, but I was beginning to think I might have picked something up.

How, I had no idea, since I never left the penthouse and Jacob was vibrantly healthy. I hoped he didn't catch whatever I had. It was bad enough I'd gotten him shot at. I didn't want to get him sick on top of that.

A short laugh escaped me as the idiocy of my thought caught up to me. A cold wasn't exactly the same as dodging bullets. Jacob had almost been shot because of me.

Just the idea of someone trying to kill him sent a fresh wave of nausea through me. Every time I tried to make things better, I ended up creating a bigger disaster.

People used to say I was smart, back when I was in school and had my whole life in front of me. My current circumstances were proof that having good grades didn't mean I had any common sense.

I left my room, wishing the day were already over and I could crawl back into bed and sleep for a year. Maybe by then, this would all be over. Voices filtered down the hall from Jacob's office. Jacob, sounding cold. Tate, angry and frustrated.

Moving closer, I heard Tate demand, "Why do you have a crime scene picture of my parents' murder? What the fuck is going on? Does this have anything to do with what happened downstairs? And why do you have a woman living with you that none of us have ever seen?"

The picture. I hadn't realized Jacob had left it out. Tate shouldn't have seen it. He'd only been a child when he'd lost his parents.

"Would you relax?" Jacob asked, his voice icy and unyielding.

He'd sounded the same way when he'd walked out on me after I'd shown it to him. It hurt him to look at it. The idea that he hadn't protected Tate from it would make him furious.

"No, I will not relax," Tate shot back. "I want to know what's fucking going on. My girlfriend just broke up with me over that bullshit in the garage."

"Your girlfriend? Since when do you have a girlfriend?" Jacob asked, sounding as if he were laughing at Tate. I eased away and went back into the kitchen to make Jacob something to eat.

I didn't want to get caught listening to their conversation. With the office door open, I could hear them easily. They weren't making much of an effort to be quiet.

I tried not to smile at the sulk in Tate's voice when he said, "Since this morning, but it didn't last very long, thanks to you."

I heard the sound of a drawer slamming shut, then Jacob say, "I'm not going to talk about the picture. Not yet. Come back in the kitchen. It's been a long fucking morning, and I'm starving."

They came into the kitchen, Tate sitting back down at the island in front of his empty plate. Jacob came around the island to stand beside me as Tate asked, "Are you going to introduce us?"

Jacob slid his arm around my waist, the woodsy scent of

him making me lightheaded. He dropped a gentle kiss on my neck just below my ear.

"Are you all right?" he asked, nuzzling me, his arm pulling me against him.

Tate seemed nice enough, but at that moment, I wished he were anywhere else. I wanted to stay exactly where I was, leaning on Jacob, his lips warm on my skin.

"I'm fine," I said. "Did you get everything straightened out?"

"Yes. Everything is locked up tight. They won't get that close again."

He stepped back from me, leaving me cold without his arm around me, and said, "Abigail, you've met my cousin, Tate. Tate, this is Abigail Jordan. She's my guest, and while she's here, security has been tightened."

"It's nice to meet you, Abigail," Tate said, sending me a charming smile I imagined got him his way more often than not. To Jacob, without a smile, he said, "Where have you been all morning? What happened in the garage?"

Jacob took the coffee I handed him and sipped before he said, "Abigail has an unfortunate situation that is none of your business. As part of that situation, someone tried to shoot me in the garage this morning. We're still not sure exactly how he got in, but he's in police custody and I'm fine. When she got here, I increased security, but I did it quietly because we didn't want to broadcast her location. After this morning, that's no longer a concern."

"The Sinclairs are on it?" Tate asked.

Jacob nodded. I was grateful for his discretion. I was ashamed enough about my situation. I didn't want to stand there while Jacob laid out my dirty laundry for his cousin. He went on.

"You, Holden, and the other residents will get a briefing

this afternoon. Traffic in and out of the garage will be personally checked. It's going to be slow, but it should prevent the kind of scene you dealt with this morning."

"And you're not going to tell me why someone was shooting at you?" Tate asked.

I started to speak, feeling like he deserved some kind of explanation, but Jacob flashed me a glance that clearly ordered me to stay silent.

"It's not your business," Jacob repeated. "Despite what happened this morning, I don't want anyone to know Abigail is here, so don't tell Holden or your brothers."

With a mischievous grin on his face, Tate said, "What about *your* brothers?"

Jacob's spine went straight and he glared at Tate. "Don't fucking tell Aiden anything."

I didn't want Tate to goad Jacob into a fight. Interrupting, I asked, "Your girlfriend broke up with you because of what happened in the garage?"

"Because of the reporters," Tate explained. "They were like a pack of wolves, shouting and taking pictures. Emily has problems with anxiety and panic attacks, and it was too much. She freaked out, and then she broke up with me."

Jacob didn't say anything, just narrowed his eyes, but I frowned and considered. I knew a little bit about anxiety issues. My freshman year roommate had social anxiety disorder and panic attacks.

I asked, "Did she freak out or did she have a panic attack?"

"She had a panic attack," Tate admitted. "It was pretty bad."

I could imagine. I'd seen Christine suffer through several, and they'd been miserable.

"I had a friend in college who had panic attacks," I said quietly. "I always felt terrible for her when they happened."

Tate said, "Emily was a victim, in a mass shooting, when she was a kid, the only survivor, and the media was relentless. She said the panic attacks started because of that."

"We know what that's like," Jacob said, his annoyance with Tate softening. The Winters family knew too much about how bad the media could get. I could imagine the rabid excitement of the press at the prospect of a new Winters scandal to chew on.

Poor Emily. I felt a fresh wave of guilt. I'd brought this on them when I'd come to Jacob.

"Walking into that garage this morning must have been horrible for her," I said. "Is she all right?"

Tate shook his head. "I don't know. She told me she couldn't deal with me anymore and kicked me out."

"She kicked you out? And you just left?" Jacob demanded.

"You don't understand," Tate said, sounding lost and miserable.

"So what are you going to do?" Jacob asked. "Or is this going to be the shortest relationship in the history of relationships?"

"What am I supposed to do?" Tate asked, sounding irritated.

"I don't know," Jacob said, sarcasm dripping from his words. "Go apologize? Beg her forgiveness and tell her you can work things out? Or is her condition too much and you don't want to deal with it?"

"It's not too much," Tate protested. "But I can't force her to want to be with me. And she's right, we do have to deal with the media. I can try to keep her safe from that, but I can't make any promises. I won't lie to her."

"Do you love her? Or are you just having fun?" Jacob's eyes were hard, and he looked angry, surprising me.

It wasn't like Jacob was all about love and happiness. He'd taken me on as his sexual pet, though he'd been oddly sweet lately. But it wasn't like he was the king of commitment.

He, himself, had admitted that he didn't do love or dating. Who was he to make Tate feel worse?

"We haven't been together that long," Tate said. "I've never been in love before. I know I don't want to lose her. I've never felt like this about any woman. I just don't know how to fix this."

Wanting them to stop sniping at each other so I could go lie down, and wishing I could help Tate, I said, "Tell her how you feel. Be honest with her and tell her how you feel. She had a shock this morning, and she probably regrets breaking up with you. I'd give her a little space to get over the panic attack, but not too much, and then go talk to her."

If I were Emily, that's what I'd want. A little time to get over my shock, and then honesty. Especially if the honesty came with a confession of love from the man I wanted.

I shook my head at myself and turned to make myself some tea. I wasn't getting a confession like that from any man. Especially not from the one I wanted.

But I hoped Emily did. Someone should get a happy ending around here. I knew better than to think it might be me.

After all the mistakes I'd made, I didn't deserve one.

Tate pushed his chair back. Saying to me, "Stay here," Jacob put down his sandwich and walked Tate to the door of the penthouse.

This time, their conversation was nearly silent. All I

caught were low murmurs. My tea finished brewing, and I poured in a generous dose of honey, stirring slowly.

The familiar scent of Earl Grey teased my senses. It was still early, barely lunch, but it felt like midnight. All I wanted was to go back to bed.

Cradling the mug in both hands, I sipped, letting the honey tinged hot fluid soothe my throat.

Jacob's footsteps sounded on the floor behind me. "When were you going to tell me you have a fever?"

CHAPTER EIGHTEEN
ABIGAIL

"I don't know," I said honestly. I'd only just realized that I was sick, though a fever would explain the headache. The truth was, I'd felt nervous about admitting to Jacob that I wasn't well.

He wasn't my roommate or my boyfriend. Technically, I was there to do a job, and we hadn't negotiated for sick days.

He stood in front of me and raised both hands to my face, pressing them against my cheeks. I leaned into his touch. Jacob's body was normally hot, but just then, his hands felt blessedly cool against my skin.

"You definitely have a fever," he said. "What are your other symptoms?"

"I'm all right," I protested. "My throat is a little sore, and I have a headache, that's all."

"Tired? Achy?"

I nodded. All of it. I felt all of it. Jacob took the mug of tea from my hands and set it on the counter. Sliding an arm around my back, he led me out of the kitchen and down the hall to the bedrooms.

I followed, too tired, my head hurting too much, to bother arguing.

"I'm going to get something for your headache," he said, but I interrupted.

"I took something a while ago. It's on the bathroom counter. It helped a little."

Jacob swore under his breath and said, "How long ago? If you took something for the headache, it should've brought your fever down."

He unzipped my dress and slid it off my shoulders, leaving me standing beside my bed in my underwear. For the first time, being mostly naked in front of Jacob didn't leave me aroused.

A minute later, he was guiding my arms into a cotton T-shirt. He urged me beneath the covers, asking again, "How long ago did you take it, Abigail?"

I curled on my side, nestling into the cool sheets, and said, "An hour? Maybe two? I didn't look at the clock."

Jacob swore again. "I'm going to get your tea and a glass of water. I want you to go to sleep."

I nodded, unable to fight the pull of sleep, but my head hurt a little too much to let me succumb completely.

His footsteps echoed down the hall, then gradually got louder as he returned. The clunk of my mug on the bedside table and the scent of tea with honey.

I heard movement in the hallway outside my door, and Jacob's voice, low, talking to someone. He sounded worried.

I wanted to tell him everything would be fine, but I couldn't seem to find the energy to open my eyes.

Time passed. I might have slept.

A cool, wet cloth was on my forehead. It was delicious. My skin was baking, hot and dry. The cloth swept over my cheeks and forehead, smoothed across my collarbone, and down my arms, bringing icy cold relief.

I moaned with pleasure. My head was thick and heavy, my throat a ball of prickles when I tried to swallow. An arm went around my back, pulling me into a sitting position as a familiar voice said,

"Fuck, you're hot. Dammit."

I wanted to laugh at his turn of phrase. He usually said things like that when I was naked. Given how I felt, I imagined I looked even worse.

I could feel the fever burning me from the inside out. Something hard pressed to my forehead and beeped.

"104.3," Jacob said. "I need you to sit up a little more, sweetheart. I talked to the doctor, and he said it sounds like a cold, maybe the flu, but he'll come back to see you if we can't get the fever down. He said I could give you more Tylenol."

Tablets at my lips, and a straw. I sipped the cool water, washing down the pills, wincing as I swallowed.

As soon as the pills were down, Jacob switched the cups and urged me to drink the tea.

I took a few swallows, the honey easing the prickles in my throat, before it was too much and I turned my head to the side.

"No doctor," I murmured, remembering the disdain and judgment in the doctor's eyes at his last visit. I didn't want that again, not when my defenses were down and I felt so horrible.

Jacob settled me back into the pillows, smoothing the cool washcloth over my face, cooling my skin before he held it against the back of my neck. I don't think anything had ever felt so good in my entire life.

"We'll see," Jacob said. "If that fever doesn't come down, either he's coming here or I'm taking you to the ER."

I shook my head in denial. He ignored me and continued to run the damp washcloth over my hot skin, saying nothing. He got up once.

I thought he was leaving, but he returned after the brief sound of water running in the bathroom with a freshly dampened cloth. I must've fallen asleep, because I opened my eyes later to find the room empty and dark.

A glance at the window showed light leaking from behind the blinds. Still daytime, but later. My head was foggy, and my throat felt like it was on fire, but my head didn't hurt as badly, which was something.

Sitting up, I realized I'd woken because I desperately had to go to the bathroom. I remembered Jacob urging me to drink the water, then the tea, and I wasn't surprised.

I swung my feet to the floor slowly, my head spinning a little as I moved. Feet sounded on the carpet, and then Jacob was there, standing in front of me, his hands on my shoulders keeping me on the bed.

"Slow down, sweetheart. What do you need?"

"Bathroom," I whispered, heat flooding my cheeks beneath the fever.

I didn't know how I could be embarrassed about telling Jacob I had to pee after all the things we'd done together, but I was. He leaned down, wrapping an arm around my back, and helped me to my feet.

I let him lead me to the bathroom door but stopped once I was inside and carefully turned to say, "I can go to the bathroom by myself."

His silver eyes narrowed doubtfully on my face, but he gave in. Good. I didn't want to pitch a fit, as sick as I was, but there was no way Jacob was supervising while I emptied my bladder.

Not going to happen, not if I had to crawl across the tile by myself.

I closed the door and made my way to the toilet, leaning heavily on the counter. I was weaker than I wanted to admit, but I didn't want to give Jacob a reason to break down the door.

I peed, flushed, and washed my hands. My long hair was a hopeless tangle around my pale yet flushed face. My eyes were glassy, and my hands shook just a little. I was almost at the end of my strength, and I hadn't walked more than a few feet.

The door opened, making me jump. "Jacob!"

What was he doing?

"You were too quiet," he said.

I was too sick to be annoyed. Correction, I was plenty annoyed. I was too sick to waste the energy yelling at him for invading my privacy.

"What do you need?" he asked

"I want to brush my hair," I said.

I'd fallen asleep with it damp, fastened in a twist, and now it hung loose, pins everywhere, strands stuck to my cheek and down my neck.

I looked on the bathroom counter for an elastic band and my comb, finding them neatly lined up behind the sink where I'd left them, the elastic wound around the handle of the comb.

I picked it up and lifted my arm to pull it through my hair, appalled to find my muscles trembling from the strain.

Tears sprung to my eyes in frustration and helplessness. I hated being sick, especially in front of Jacob. I was supposed to be taking care of him, not the other way around.

"I'll do it," he said, taking the comb from my hand and winding his arm around my waist, supporting me as he led me back to the bed.

I sat, Jacob behind me as he ran his fingers through my damp hair, methodically searching for and removing every pin. He set them on the bedside table, one by one. I counted the tiny clicks they made as he lined them up.

One, two, all the way to six. I used a type of corkscrew pin that was much more effective than traditional straight hair pins, but I still needed six of them. I have a lot of hair. At the moment, it felt like a wet tangled blanket on my hot skin.

As if he'd done it before, Jacob combed away the tangles, starting at the bottom and working his way up to my scalp, getting out every knot without causing me any pain.

The tug of the comb through my hair was soothing, reminding me of my mother and the way she'd combed and braided my hair before bed when I was a little girl.

I was so tired, my limbs heavy, my eyelids drifting closed. Without asking what I wanted, Jacob gathered the mass of hair into three chunks and braided it just as I would have asked him to.

He fastened the elastic at the bottom and tucked me back beneath the covers. He left for a few minutes. Or maybe I fell asleep, and it was an hour.

When he came back, he urged me into a sitting position and put a straw to my lips.

Icy juice.

He pulled the straw away and replaced it with two tablets. I swallowed them when he gave me back the straw.

My throat hurt, but the juice was so cold and sweet, I wanted more.

When I was done, he lowered me back down, pulling my braid out from under my back so it wouldn't tug on my scalp.

My eyelids weighed a ton. I couldn't bring myself to open them, so I couldn't see his face as he stroked the wet washcloth across my forehead, but his voice was gentle as he said,

"Your fever is down, so no doctor. Not yet. You need to sleep, and we'll see how you feel tomorrow."

I thought I nodded. I meant to nod. I probably just fell asleep to the cool strokes of the washcloth on my skin and the soothing murmurs of Jacob's voice telling me everything was all right.

The next time I woke up, the room was dark. Jacob was beside me, and something was beeping. A red light flashed in the room.

He murmured, "A little over 103."

Two more of the tablets at my lips, and the straw, the juice now warm but still sweet.

I swallowed the tablets and drank as much juice as he would let me, wincing at the painful stabbing prickle in my throat with each swallow.

Struggling to sit up, I became aware of the pounding in my head and the uncomfortable sensation of being cold and hot at the same time.

I was shivering, could feel myself shaking, could feel how hot the sheets were beneath my skin, and I knew my skin was equally warm, but none of it seemed to touch me.

I was so, so cold. Surrounded by heat and shaking with cold. Jacob's weight shifted on the mattress, and he pulled me into his lap, bracketing my body with his legs and wrapping his arms around me.

For a moment, I sank into his warmth, letting the touch of his skin chase away the cold, before I started to struggle.

"Shh, Shh, Abigail, settle down," he said, holding me tighter.

"No, Jacob, no. I don't want to get you sick," I protested, too weak to break his hold with my feeble struggles.

"Sweetheart, stop."

His arms tightened like iron bands around me, holding me still.

"If you haven't already gotten me sick, I'm not going to get sick. Understand? I'm not going anywhere. I'm right here, and I'm fine. Don't worry about me."

"But, what if—"

"I'm not going to get sick. I promise. I've been around you since this first hit, and I feel fine. I'm getting plenty of sleep and taking my vitamins. You're not going to get me sick. Just relax."

"Promise?" I whispered.

I couldn't stand the thought of Jacob feeling this miserable. It was bad enough that he had to take care of me, bad enough that Big John's guys had shot at him and he had to lock his building down.

I'd caused enough trouble already.

I wondered if it would be too much. If he was just waiting for me to get better and then he'd send me on my way.

Jacob didn't do complications.

I was supposed to be easy. A regular check to Shaded Glenn, and sex whenever he wanted it. This—the juice, braiding my hair, holding me while I shook with fever—was so far outside our agreement, I didn't know how to make sense of it.

Maybe I was hallucinating. That would make more sense than Jacob's solicitous care of his sick mistress.

So tired. My cheek fell onto his shoulder as I relaxed into his solid strength. He seemed very sure I wouldn't get him sick, and I didn't have it in me to argue anymore.

Thoughts flitted through my mind and drifted away, the worries and pains and anxieties momentary until they circled back to haunt me again.

Eventually, I drifted off as the chills slipped away. I woke once in the night to take more pills, drink more juice, and use the bathroom again.

This time, Jacob followed me all the way in before I waved him away, mulishly refusing—even mostly asleep—to sit on the toilet while he was in the room.

The next day, I drifted in and out of sleep, my brief periods of wakefulness dreamlike and blurry.

Jacob was there, always there with the ever present tablets and juice. With warm tea thick with honey, so soothing on my raw throat. I woke more than once to find him stretched out in the bed beside me, his computer open on his lap.

I was never aware of being alone. The fever went in and out, always better after the pills. The chills came one more time, leaving me so cold I was in tears, only the heat of Jacob's body able to chase them off.

I heard him once, out in the hallway, his footsteps pacing, his voice barking into the phone. A while later, vaguely familiar sounds, a voice I knew, strange hands, cold metal on my chest and my back, before I was alone again.

It didn't register until after they were gone that Jacob had called the doctor.

How sick was I?

I couldn't be that sick, because they left me in bed on the same regimen of pills—I thought Tylenol—juice, and tea. At some point, on the third day or the fourth, Jacob brought me salty, rich broth.

Warm, but not hot. He'd asked a few times, but I denied all interest in food.

My throat hurt so badly that the thought of chewing and swallowing anything solid was revolting. Honeyed tea and juice were bad enough.

The broth was delicious. I drank the whole mug in greedy but pained swallows before handing it back, then immediately realized I had to pee again.

I hated being sick. I hated for Jacob to see me like this. That time, he let me go by myself, but I sensed his eyes on me, alert for any indication that I wasn't steady on my feet.

I made it to the bathroom and back, even managing to wash my hands and brush my teeth without falling over. Progress. When I got back to the bed, Jacob was waiting with my comb and a fresh T-shirt.

Arranging my limbs like a child, he changed my clothes and sat me on the edge of the bed while he unfastened my now loose braid, combed my hair, and re-braided it. By then, I was exhausted.

My head was pounding less than it had been, and I didn't feel quite as hot, but every muscle in my body was weak. I let Jacob tuck me back under the covers after swallowing two more tablets.

He stretched out beside me and tucked me into his body, pulling my head to rest on his chest. The thump of his heart beneath my ear lulled me to sleep almost immediately.

It was another day before I was well enough to get up

on my own. Jacob found me standing in the bathroom, testing the water of the shower.

"What do you think you're doing?" he barked, crowding into me and glaring down. I raised my chin and met his silver gaze with my own stubborn one.

"I'm taking a shower," I said. "I'm filthy. I feel disgusting."

Disgusting didn't even cover it. My fever had broken the night before, leaving me soaked in sweat.

I vaguely recalled Jacob picking me up and putting me in the arm chair in the corner of the room, then carrying me back to bed and tucking me into clean sheets sometime later.

I'd been grateful that I hadn't slept in the damp, sweaty bed linens, but the T-shirt I was wearing felt stuck to my skin and I was afraid the ripe scent wafting to my nose was me.

"You are in no shape to take a shower by yourself," Jacob said.

I raised my chin a little higher and didn't say anything. I didn't have the energy to argue with him, and I was taking a goddamn shower. If I had to sit on the floor, I would, but I was not going to smell bad for a second longer.

Jacob gritted his teeth and stuck his hand under the spray. He adjusted the temperature before he set his hands on his hips and said, "Fine. We'll take a shower, but then, you're going back to bed."

"Fine," I said.

I had no illusions that I would be in any shape to do much but sleep once I got myself through a shower, but at least I'd be clean.

Jacob stripped off his clothes with brisk efficiency, barely giving me time to admire the cut lines of his torso and the perfect curve of his tight ass before he was pulling the shirt over my head and ushering me beneath the warm spray of the shower.

I did little more than stand there. I was alarmingly weak. Jacob squirted my body wash onto a shower pouf and scrubbed every inch of me.

When I reached for the razor to shave my armpits, he plucked it from my hand and did it himself, ignoring my eyes squeezed shut with embarrassment. No way would I ask him to shave anything else.

His hands lingered on my body, gentle and arousing in a distant way. He smoothed soap over my breasts, lingering for only a moment on my nipples, cleaned me between my legs, touching but not trying to turn me on.

My brain struggled to adjust. I wanted his hands on me, felt the jut of his hard cock against my back as he stroked his hands over my breasts and down my stomach, but I couldn't seem to muster the will to do anything about it.

Sex and orgasm were a distant dream. Reality was my legs shaking after holding me up for an entire fifteen minutes after days in bed.

Done cleaning my body, Jacob sat me on the bench in the shower and stood beside me to wash my hair, using the hand-held shower head to rinse the shampoo and then the conditioner.

I sat there, acquiescent and deeply grateful he'd thought to wash my hair. I rested my head against his hipbone as he worked, my eyes fixed on his thick cock shifting in front of me, close enough to touch with my mouth if I moved only a little.

I wanted it, but I didn't have the energy to do anything about it. He hung up the sprayer and looked down at me, a wry smile on his face.

"You're killing me, sweetheart," he said. "You're looking at my cock like it's a lollipop."

Involuntarily, I licked my lips.

Realizing what I'd done, I blushed and turned my face into his hip, hiding my eyes.

I had been.

I'd been staring at his cock like it was a lollipop. I'd been thinking how much I wanted to lick it.

How did he always know what I was thinking?

Pulling me to my feet, he wrapped a fluffy towel around me and said, "Later. Maybe when you can stand for more than a few minutes without your knees knocking together."

I knew I was getting better when the thought of licking that magnificent cock stirred a wisp of desire between my legs, the most alive my body had felt in days.

CHAPTER NINETEEN
ABIGAIL

I thought about touching him, then abandoned the idea. I could barely stand up. If I tried to seduce him, I'd pass out from the exertion.

Instead, I stood there as Jacob dried my body and used the towel to squeeze water from my hair. I was wonderfully clean, but exhausted again.

Jacob led me back to the bed and sat me down on the side, dropping yet another T-shirt over my head. I fed my arms through the holes and looked down to see the words, *Emory Athletics*.

There was something intimate about sleeping in his shirts, so much more personal than the decadent lingerie he'd purchased for me. I loved silk and lace, but not as much as I loved wearing his T-shirt.

He sat beside me and squeezed water from my hair a second time before gently combing it straight and braiding it.

"How do you do that so well?" I asked.

"You know I have a little sister, right?"

I did know that. Charlotte, though he often referred to

her as Charlie. She'd gone to business school at Emory and worked for his older brother, Aiden, at Winters Incorporated.

Still, a lot of men had sisters, but I didn't think most of them knew how to braid hair. My father had had a daughter, and he would have had no clue.

"Did you braid Charlotte's hair?" I asked.

"Sometimes," he said. "My mother had her hands full with all of us. She didn't work outside the home, but she was very active in the community on top of trying to run herd on her own kids, plus my cousins after my aunt and uncle died."

"You didn't have a nanny?" Most families of their social class would have had a nanny. My own family had been a few rungs below the Winters clan in terms of wealth, if not social standing, and I'd had a nanny when I was a child.

"We did," he admitted. "But she was only one woman, and there were eight of us. Plus, my mother loved being a mom. She didn't want any of us raised by staff, so she had some help, but she mostly did it on her own, which meant those of us who were older chipped in some with the younger ones.

"I was tight with Charlotte. Aiden and Gage thought she was a pest, and Vance teased her, so she always asked me to braid her hair."

"You are sweet, Jacob Winters," I accused, smiling as he fastened the elastic on my braid and urged me to lie down again.

"Shh, don't tell. See if you can get some sleep. If you feel up to it, Rachel made you chicken and dumplings for dinner."

My stomach rumbled at the thought of solid food. It

wasn't enough to stop me from drifting to sleep. The shower had wiped me out.

Sleep now. Eat later.

I'm not sure how long I slept. Time had been fuzzy since I'd been sick. I woke up feeling better than I had in days, with no fever and only a mild headache, with clean hair and a clean body lying between clean sheets.

The only problem was my growling stomach. Slowly, I sat up and swung my legs over the edge of the bed.

Dizziness swamped me for a few seconds, but that was normal after so much time spent lying down. I waited until my head cleared to stand up. I thought about changing clothes, but I was loath to take off Jacob's T-shirt.

Once I was better, things would go back to normal. I doubted Jacob would be lending me any more of his T-shirts. They didn't fit my job description.

I found my silk robe and pulled it on over the shirt before I went in search of Jacob.

He looked up when I came to a stop in the open doorway of his office, his eyes concerned as they studied me. "Are you ready to be out of bed?"

"I'm hungry," I confessed.

He stood, closing his laptop, and rounded the desk toward me.

"So am I," he said, taking my arm and leading me to the dining room. As we neared that side of the penthouse, I became aware of a rich, salty scent in the air, warm, comforting, and delicious.

Explaining before I could ask, he said, "Rachel made you chicken and dumplings. It's heating on the stove."

He led me to my usual seat in the dining room, pulling out my chair and helping me sit as if I were fragile, ready to crumble at any but the gentlest touch.

I sat, concentrating on pulling my chair into the table after he left, still not sure how to respond. He returned a few minutes later with two white stoneware bowls brimming with thick, creamy chicken and dumplings.

Chicken and dumplings is one of those meals, like gumbo or lasagna, that can be made a thousand different ways.

Some people favor a clear broth with flat hand-rolled noodles. On the other side of the spectrum, cooks like myself preferred a creamy soup base with big chunks of chicken and dumplings that resembled small biscuits.

With a rush of grateful pleasure, I saw that Rachel and I were on the same page when it came to chicken and dumplings. Just the scent, familiar and soothing, brought tears to my eyes. And a little confusion.

Chicken and dumplings wasn't the most complex meal, but it did take time. Especially if it had been made from scratch, as this looked like it had.

I should know. I'd made the meal often enough myself.

Before I took the first bite, I asked, "Rachel made this? Why?"

Taking a bite, I hummed in the back of my throat. It was perfect. Exactly what I would have wanted, hearty yet gentle on my throat and stomach. Jacob chewed slowly and swallowed his own bite before answering.

"I'm sure you don't remember, but she was here when you were sick. She brought me more Tylenol and the thermometer, plus she brought work back and forth so I didn't have to leave you alone. She felt terrible because, apparently, her granddaughter had the same virus last week.

"Since you haven't left the penthouse and Rachel is one of the few people you've had contact with, no matter how slight, she probably passed it to you."

"You told her it wasn't her fault, right? She couldn't have known I'd get sick. She didn't have to make me soup."

Jacob shrugged, his silver eyes glinting with amusement.

"I told her not to feel badly about it. And she didn't make you soup because she thought she had to. She could have just ordered in. That's what she usually does if I need food and I don't have time to go out. She made you chicken and dumplings because she likes you."

My jaw dropped in astonishment. Of all the people in Jacob's life, Rachel was one of the few who knew who I was and what I was doing there. She'd witnessed the humiliating scene with the doctor. She'd bought me clothes and toiletries.

I would have thought she despised me but was professional enough to keep her opinion to herself. Unable to let it go, I asked, "What do you mean, she likes me?"

Jacob shrugged again, this time the amusement taking over his face as his lips curled up in a grin.

"She said you have manners and class and I could do worse. Actually, she said I have done worse. She may have suggested it was possible you could do better."

I didn't think my eyes could get any wider. Rachel liked me? I'm sure she was teasing Jacob when she said I could do better, because it wasn't possible to do better than Jacob Winters.

I had no idea what to say, so I concentrated on eating my dinner. It had been a few days since I'd had a solid meal, and though it hurt my throat, I ate eagerly.

Rachel's recipe wasn't exactly like mine. She used less black pepper and more thyme, but it was close enough to be immensely comforting. I only made it halfway through the bowl before I was forced to stop, my stomach uncomfortably full.

"Have you given any thought to what you want to do once you're clear of Big John?" Jacob asked, his voice oddly neutral.

I had given it thought. A lot of thought. I had not, however, come to any conclusions.

"I don't know," I admitted. "When I left school, I was halfway through a degree in education. I wanted to be a kindergarten teacher."

"And now?" Jacob asked.

I shook my head. That girl, with her dreams of small children at her feet and a classroom of her own, seemed so very far away.

"I don't want to teach anymore. I don't know why. It just doesn't feel right. And anyway, the salary is too small. I have to find a way to take care of my mother, and a teacher's salary would barely cover her expenses, much less my own."

"You don't have to worry about that, Abigail," he said, sounding annoyed.

I couldn't help scowling at him. Most of the time, Jacob was brilliant, but sometimes, he could be ridiculously stupid.

"Of course I have to worry about that, Jacob. I didn't do all of this to walk away from her. She's only getting worse, I can't move her somewhere else, and I'm not qualified for the kind of job that can pay for her care."

An ugly thought occurred to me, and I lifted my hands helplessly. "Except for this one. And mistressing has a limited shelf-life."

Jacob scowled, his silver eyes flashing with anger. "You are not my mistress, and this is not a job."

I stared back at him, confused. Maybe I wasn't his mistress. Mistresses were generally allowed to leave the house. But it was the closest description appropriate for polite conversation.

Sex slave sounded funny at the dinner table. And he might not like the word, but this *was* a job. I didn't like it either.

I'd give anything to pretend that what we had together was more than an arrangement where I provided service and he compensated me. But I'd be the greatest kind of fool if I let myself think anything else. I didn't understand his anger at the turn of the conversation.

Jacob knew better than anyone what we were to each other. He was the one who'd made the proposal in the first place, though I'd gone to him looking for something just like it.

I watched as he took a deep breath and visibly got his temper under control. When he spoke again, his voice was calm and inviting.

"Pretend you don't have to worry about your mother's care. Pretend you could do anything. What would you do?"

I didn't want to play this game. Pretending with Jacob was dangerous. But I did need to figure out what I was going to do with my life, and Jacob could be a helpful sounding board.

When it came to things like school and jobs and work experience, he had a far better grasp of the possibilities than I did.

Marshalling the thoughts I'd had over the past few weeks, I said, "I think if I could do anything, I would go back to school and study something to do with business. I don't know how I would go about it, but the one thing I always liked were the charity events I helped with. I was very good at raising money. I know there are a lot of organizations out there that need help with funding, but I don't understand the finance side of it, and I think I would need to if I wanted to do it as a job instead of a hobby."

Jacob studied me for a moment, the look in his eyes both relieved and approving.

"Emory's business school has a concentration in non-profit management. You'd have to finish your undergraduate, but you only had two years left, correct?"

"A year and a half. I'd finished my sophomore year when my father died, but I went to school over the summer, so my credits put me halfway through my junior year."

An unfamiliar lightness spread through my chest, a sense of anticipation and potential I hadn't known in years. Since my father had died, I'd felt essentially useless, unable to take care of both my mother and myself, as if all my life skills had no point.

I'd married John out of desperation and taken up the role my mother had held as a society wife, mostly feeling trapped and unhappy.

I'd dreamed of being a teacher, not one of the ladies who lunched. But I'd loved volunteering for the charity events we put together.

Many of the women saw them as nothing more than an opportunity to see and be seen at prime social events, but I'd enjoyed throwing parties whose sole purpose, in truth, was to separate wealthy donors from their money and use that money to help the less fortunate.

The art was to do it all in a way that made everybody happy.

Interrupting my thoughts, Jacob said, "I'm sure you would've made an excellent teacher, but I think this is a much better plan for you. I remember the events you put together when you were married to John. You managed to raise an obscene amount of money. You have a knack for it, and that's a valuable resource to organizations in need of funding. We'll look into what you need to do to transfer your credits over from State and finish your undergrad."

My head was spinning, both from his compliments and his assumption that I would be pursuing this plan. Jacob was paying for my mother's care and had given me a credit card, but I didn't have any money.

Finishing college and going to graduate school were expensive. There was no way I was applying for student loans. I had enough financial obligation on my shoulders without adding more.

I was fairly sure the kind of job Jacob was talking about didn't pay a huge salary. Probably better than a kindergarten teacher, but I doubted it would be enough to cover my mother's fees, not to mention my living expenses and tuition while I finished my education.

This was why pretending was dangerous. I'd given Jacob my ideal situation, but my reality left me with no path from here to there.

"Jacob, I can't afford to—"

He cut me off with a shake of his head and a slash of his hand. I closed my mouth, knowing better than to argue with him when he was like this.

"Is this what you want to do?" he asked." If you could do anything, you said this is what you want."

I nodded. It was. It was also completely impractical and out of my reach.

"Then we'll do it," he said as if it were that simple. For Jacob Winters, it probably was. Part of me wanted to argue, to force him to admit that our situation was far more complicated and short-term than this conversation implied.

If I'd been feeling better, I would have.

I think. I don't know.

It was very hard to argue with Jacob when he was set on a course. It was a moot point because my stomach was full, my head was starting to hurt again, and I was exhausted from sitting up for the first time in days.

We could fight later. Now, I just wanted to go back to sleep for a while.

Jacob, satisfied he'd gotten his way, was more than happy to end the conversation, at least for the moment. He walked me back down the hall, leading me past my room and to his own.

"What—"

He interrupted me again. "The housekeeper is coming, and she hasn't been in your room in days. Take a nap here."

I was too tired to argue. I was well enough that I was sure I wouldn't get him sick, and his bed filled my vision, wide and tall and inviting. I let him peel the robe down my arms and usher me beneath the covers.

He stroked a loose strand of hair from my cheek and laid a soft kiss to the side of my mouth, saying, "Sleep tight."

He joined me in bed later, wrapping his warm body around mine, one arm tucked around my waist. I had the half-formed thought that I should go back to my own room, but it slipped away beneath the comfort of Jacob's body beside me and the weight of my exhaustion.

I slept late the next morning and awoke to a bowl of oatmeal on a tray in the living room.

I didn't like oatmeal that much, but I was hungry, and when Jacob shrugged and said, "I'm sorry it's instant. It's all I had," I ate it without complaint, touched that he'd made me breakfast himself.

The housekeeper showed up while I was eating, which was curious, because I'd thought Jacob had said she was coming the day before. That was his reason for moving me into his bedroom.

I didn't ask. He pressed the remote into my hand and said, "Why don't you watch TV for a while and see how you feel?"

I was bored with being sick, but not up for anything more energetic than lying on the couch. A few hours of mindless TV sounded perfect.

It was crazy how doing nothing more taxing than sitting upright and binge-watching do-it-yourself home improvement shows could tire me out, but by the time Jacob brought me a lunch tray with a bowl of chicken and dumplings and I'd eaten it, I was ready to go back to sleep.

Again, he directed me to his room. The housekeeper was long gone. I was in no shape to confront Jacob. I thought about just climbing into his bed and letting it work itself out later, but I didn't like the sense of confusion on top of being weak from sickness.

"I should sleep in my room," I said, coming to a stop outside my bedroom door.

Jacob's hand tightened on my arm, not enough to hurt, but in a strong grip that made it clear he wasn't planning to let go.

His jaw set, he glared at me, then said, "No. I've had your things moved to my room. From now on, you're staying with me."

"Jacob," I said, my voice too loud and too sharp. "I can't stay in your room."

Jacob swept me off my feet, settling me in his arms. Before I could struggle, he tightened his hold, keeping me still.

"Do you want to sleep alone?" he asked, his voice low and dangerous.

I wanted to lie.

I didn't.

"No, but it's inappropriate."

He laughed, surprisingly, and dropped a kiss on the top of my head. "It's too bad you're still sick, because it turns me on when you get all proper and dignified."

Mute with surprise and annoyance, I said nothing. Just before he tucked me into his bed, I mumbled under my breath, "It's not right, Jacob, and you know it."

He pressed his lips to mine and kissed me, one hand tucked beneath my jaw, lifting my face to his. I kissed him back, falling into his touch as I always did.

I'd missed his kisses while I was sick. I'd worried that after I was well, we would revert to our more formal arrangement of no kissing. Relief speared through me as I realize this would not be the case.

Then again, the fact that he'd moved me into his bedroom changed everything.

He pulled away slowly and whispered, "Abigail, whatever we want is right. I want you in my bed and my room. If you want to be here too, that's where you'll be."

With that, he left. I tried to examine his words, picking at them like a teenager with her first crush, trying to understand what he really meant and getting nowhere before sleep claimed me and my mind shut off.

I don't think I slept very long. No more than a few hours.

The sounds of voices woke me, low male voices talking over one another, at least one of them strident with anger. The thread of aggression in the muffled words sent adrenaline spiking through me, and I sat up in a rush, fighting off a wave of dizziness.

I looked at the clock. Just after four in the afternoon. I

sat there for a minute, trying to decide what to do. I could hide in the bedroom, but I doubted Jacob would have let anyone dangerous into the penthouse.

I was tired of hiding. If Jacob wanted me to stay in his room, he'd come tell me. But if he didn't, I wasn't going to greet our company wearing my pajamas.

CHAPTER TWENTY
JACOB

Family could be a royal pain in the ass. I have no idea who let it slip about Abigail—had to be either Tate or Rachel—but that afternoon, they arrived on my doorstep en masse.

My brother, Holden, and my cousins, Vance and Tate, were more than welcome. I stuck them in the kitchen to make coffee while I dealt with the more complicated of my arrivals—my older brother, Aiden, and William Davis.

William had been best friends with all of our parents since college. In the case of our fathers, they'd been friends practically since birth. He'd been like a second father to me most of my life, and I loved him like family.

But much like my older brother, he thought his main purpose in life was to tell the rest of us what to do and how to do it. I hadn't liked it when I was a kid, and now that I was in my 30s, it was unacceptable.

Part of me wanted to throw them all out. I was tempted, but they were my family, and I hadn't seen them much since Abigail had come to live with me. Since I've never had a woman living in my house before, I'm sure Tate found the gossip irresistible.

He probably kept it from Aiden but told Holden. Those two were almost the same age. They'd literally shared a cradle, and I think they were constitutionally incapable of keeping secrets from each other, especially one as juicy as Abigail Jordan living with me.

It was easier to deal with whatever they wanted and send them on their way than try to kick them out now that I'd let them in the door.

I was grateful Abigail was safely asleep down the hall in my bedroom. She'd put up a fight about sharing my room, but as I'd hoped, she'd given in. I was mostly certain she wanted to be there.

Mostly.

Aiden and William followed me into my office and took the chairs opposite my desk, both of them making themselves comfortable. They'd been there often enough in the past to feel at home.

"Jacob, what is this I hear about Abigail Jordan living in your home?" William asked, spearing me with his most paternal gaze.

I looked at Aiden, whose face was completely neutral, before I answered.

"I don't know," I deflected. "What did you hear? And from whom?"

William ignored me. "So it's true then?" He shook his head, giving me his best disappointed father look. "Jacob, I know that she's a beautiful woman, but this is completely inappropriate."

I couldn't help but smile at the way his words and tone mimicked Abigail herself. I was getting the impression

William wanted her out of my house, so he probably wouldn't be amused to know he reminded me of her.

Knowing it would irritate him, I shrugged and shoved my hands in my pockets.

"Maybe," I said. "Right now, very few people know she's here. I'd like to keep it that way until her situation stabilizes."

"And then?" Aiden asked, cutting in. His dark eyes betrayed nothing of his feelings on the matter of Abigail and myself.

Aiden was tricky like that. William gave everything away from the start, but Aiden would let me hang myself before he'd tell me what he planned to do with me. Usually, a one-on-one confrontation with Aiden put me on edge.

I love my brother, and I've never doubted for a moment that he loves me, but that didn't mean he was easy.

I wasn't going to hide my intentions for Abigail. Meeting his eyes, I said, "Once her situation stabilizes, I hope I can convince her to stay on a more permanent basis."

"And you think that's wise?" Aiden asked. "Taking on the Jordans is no joke. You've already been shot at. Is she worth it?"

"Of course she's not," William said, impatient. "She's damaged goods. Maybe if you'd gotten to her before the Jordans. Maybe. Your grandfather was friends with hers, and her mother was a good woman before she got sick. But even before John Jordan ruined her, her father became a disgrace."

"It's not common knowledge," I protested.

"Common enough among the people who matter. She's tainted. She was tainted before she married John Jordan, and she's lucky a single person received her afterward. The ones who did so did it out of respect for her mother and her grandparents, but she's hardly an appropriate match for a Winters, Jacob. Be realistic."

I crossed my arms over my chest and scowled at William.

Sometimes, he sounded like his own father, stuck in the past, nattering over bloodlines and who people's people were.

That kind of thing was less important than it used to be, and not at all important to me. I heard what he was getting at.

He was worried I planned to marry Abigail. I could end this whole aggravating conversation by telling him the truth about our arrangement.

I opened my mouth, then shut it.

I couldn't do it.

I would never humiliate Abigail that way, for one thing. And for another, at this point, I didn't know exactly what my arrangement with Abigail *was*.

I still planned to keep her safe and take care of her mother, but the idea of keeping her as a pet had gone out the window. How had I ever thought that was a good idea?

Abigail was no man's pet.

She was a woman. A smart, beautiful, passionate, intriguing woman.

William was wrong. There was nothing damaged about Abigail. Just the idea that her association with her father and her husband somehow made her less worthy pissed me off.

Her father's choices were not her fault. If he were still alive, I might be tempted to kill him for the situation he'd left his wife and daughter in.

Marrying John Jordan had been a mistake. I wouldn't argue with William about that. But she'd been young, frightened, and in a terrible position. She'd done the best she could.

No one should fault her for that. The more I thought about what William had said, the angrier I became.

Reading my face and sensing my temper nearing the breaking point, Aiden cut into my thoughts.

In a level, almost disinterested tone, he asked, "Is she a potential match, Jacob? Is that what this is? Or are you just helping out a friend?"

Was Aiden giving me an out? I could go through door number two, claim I was just being a good guy, and shut the whole conversation down.

Why wasn't there a choice in between? Why did Abigail have to be either a future mate of a Winters male, or just a friend?

I already knew the answer. Because Abigail, despite William's claim that she was damaged goods, was not a woman you fucked around with.

This wasn't the 1800s. Plenty of respectable women had affairs. But Abigail Jordan had never been that kind of woman, and neither had her mother.

I knew more about Abigail than she'd like. Cooper had conducted a thorough investigation in the name of finding out everything that might help us keep her safe from Big John.

No serious boyfriends before her marriage. A 3.8 GPA in college. A few newspaper mentions in high school related to charity events her mother had sponsored.

She joined a sorority in college, but based on her GPA, I didn't think she'd done much partying. I had no doubt she'd been a virgin on her wedding night.

Abigail was a throwback. That was part of the allure of

trapping her here, of having the elusive Abigail Jordan all to myself.

Now that I had her, it turned out I was the one who was trapped.

Aiden studied my face, patiently waiting for a response, while William tapped his foot on the carpet and shook his head at me as if I were a recalcitrant schoolboy who owed him an apology.

I would not apologize for Abigail. Not for having her here, and not for her circumstances. Neither of us had anything to be ashamed of.

"Frankly, it's none of your business," I said to both of them. A copout, but I didn't know the answer myself. This was far more than helping out a friend. Abigail was not my friend.

Did I want to marry her? I hadn't thought about marrying anyone. Not seriously. I didn't need a wife.

Between Rachel and my housekeeper, my life was well organized. I never had trouble finding a companion for social events.

Ditto for sex. If I'd been disinclined to have a girlfriend because of the demands on my time and attention, a wife . . . a wife was a girlfriend times ten. Or worse.

Why would I want that?

That sneaky voice in the back of my brain woke up again and whispered, *But what if that wife were Abigail? What if she were here every day? What if all of that loyalty and devotion and passion were yours forever?*

Unbidden, an image of what that might be like sprang into my head fully-formed. Both of us coming home from work, discussing our days over dinner, and Abigail eating naked because I'd teased her into it.

I shook my head as if to chase the picture away. I'd only

just gotten her to agree to sleep in my bedroom, and that was under protest.

Until we dealt with Big John, she couldn't even leave home safely. We could worry about the future later.

Suddenly annoyed at being put on the spot like a child, I said, "This discussion is over. Abigail isn't going anywhere. If we make any decisions that impact the family, we'll be sure to let you know. Until then, you can both butt out."

William surged to his feet, his eyes hard, voice approaching a yell. "Jacob Winters, stop acting like a horny teenager. There are more important things at stake here than your cock. Find some other woman. Abigail Jordan is already reflecting on this family. People are talking, and it's unacceptable—"

As if the rise in William's tone didn't bother him in the slightest, Aiden leaned back in his chair and studied the older man with deceptive calm.

His voice, however, held an edge when he said, "William. That's enough."

William spun to face him. "Aiden, you should know better. After the debacle with Elizabeth—"

Aiden's face went cold. We didn't talk about his brief marriage or his former wife. No one mentioned Elizabeth, ever. When we ran into her socially, we were polite, but that was it.

For William to bring her up now—if he'd wanted Aiden on his side, he'd just lost his shot. I was getting ready to intervene, not liking the deadly look in Aiden's eyes, when the door to my office opened and Tate stepped inside, his dark blue eyes narrowed and his jaw set.

Closing the door carefully behind him, he said in a low voice, "Just so you know, your shouting woke Abigail up, and she's in the kitchen. We can hear everything you're saying."

God dammit.

Fuck.

She would be appalled and humiliated. I was going to kill William. And I was pissed at myself. I should have realized she might have woken up, should have thought before we raised our voices.

Ignoring Aiden and William, I looked at Tate. "Is she all right?"

Tate shrugged. "She seems to be fine, but I get the feeling that Abigail could pull off dignified and collected in the middle of a tornado, so I don't really know. Holden invited Emily and Jo up, and Vance is charming her, so she's distracted."

Changing the subject before I could respond, he said, "Did you show them the picture?"

Fuck.

Why could my fucking family never keep their noses in their own business?

Except a photograph of Tate's mother and father's murder *was* his business.

I still didn't know what to make of it, and Cooper had come up blank. I'd tried to write it off as an isolated incident, some sick asshole getting his jollies, but that didn't sit right.

I went around to the other side of my desk and opened the top drawer, withdrawing the envelope that contained the photograph.

"Someone we haven't been able to identify got through security and slid this under my door a few days ago."

I opened the envelope and slid the photograph out, glancing at Tate as the image was revealed. His eyes went dark with the same shock and pain I'd seen the first time he'd been confronted with the picture of his parents' bodies.

It wasn't easy for me to look at it either, and I remembered them better than he did. But, they weren't my parents. Almost as good as, since we'd all grown up together, but I knew if I were looking at a picture of my own parents' murder, I'd feel even more torn up than I did right now.

"Tate, you don't have to—"

With a jerk of his shoulder, he said, "It's fine."

It wasn't fine, but Tate was a grown man and it wasn't my job to tell him what he could handle. I nodded and laid the picture down on my desk.

Aiden reached out to flick on my desk lamp, aiming the bulb directly at the photograph. His face, as I would've expected, was unreadable. Also, as I would have expected, William's was an open book.

His eyes were comically wide, his face pale. Voice shaking, he demanded, "How did you get this? Who gave this to you?"

Ignoring William's questions, Aiden asked, "Fingerprints?"

I shook my head. "Nothing. Whoever delivered it didn't know exactly where the cameras were in the hallways, but they must have known they were there, somewhere, because they wore a long coat and a wig. We've got photos, but it's impossible to tell much more than general height and build, though even that could be part of the disguise."

"And you've received nothing else? No other communication? No threats?" Aiden asked, his eyes probing mine, demanding truth.

I might hedge with my brother about Abigail, but I wouldn't about this. I shook my head again.

"Nothing. It doesn't make any sense."

Unable to look at the picture any longer, I picked it up and slid it back into the envelope. Tate, standing beside me, his posture stiff and his shoulders tight, visibly relaxed as the image of his dead parents slid out of sight.

If I didn't worry we'd need it, I'd burn the damn thing. But until we understood who had delivered it and why, and what they might want from us, it seemed smarter to keep it around.

"Bizarre," Aiden said. I could see the gears turning in his brain as he considered the problem.

William said nothing. He stood there between Tate and Aiden, his eyes still wide with shock, his face white as if he'd seen a ghost. Which, in a way, he had.

Abruptly, he blinked and said, "I have to go."

He turned on his heel and rushed out of my office, almost as if he were being chased. Odd. William lecturing me on appropriate behavior was to be expected, but his reaction to the photograph was weird.

By the confused expressions on their faces, Aiden and Tate agreed with me. Something to deal with later.

"We need to tell everyone else about the picture," Tate said.

"No." Aiden's face was hard and uncompromising. "No one needs to see that."

"They have a right to know," Tate insisted.

"Not Charlotte or Annalise."

Aiden crossed his arms over his chest and glared at Tate. Tate threw his hands in the air in exasperation.

"Newsflash, Aiden. The girls aren't children, and they don't need you to protect them from life."

I could hear Aiden grinding his teeth as Tate went on, "I know you want to handle everything, and you still think of Holden and me and the girls as children, but we're not.

We're all adults, and this is part of our life. Holden and I run two successful companies, Charlotte works for you, and Annalise travels the globe with her camera. We deserve to be treated as equals. Don't shut us out."

Aiden shook his head in resignation. "Fine. But not today. I want to talk to Cooper, and I want to think about this before we discuss it with everyone else."

Probably surprised Aiden had caved so quickly, Tate said, "All right."

"Are we good here?" I asked, impatient to get to Abigail and make sure she was holding up. She was still weak, and my family could be overwhelming.

"I'm good," Tate said, "Especially if you're not planning to kick us out before dinner is ready."

I hadn't noticed until he'd mentioned it, but the scent of garlic and tomatoes had wafted into my office when William had opened the door.

Was Abigail cooking? She was supposed to be resting, not cooking for the horde of Winters and girlfriends who'd descended on her.

I didn't wait for Aiden to respond to my question before heading out to Abigail.

Aiden would make up his own mind, and unlike William, I could trust him to treat Abigail graciously, even if he sided with William and wanted her gone.

I didn't think that was going to happen. Oddly, Abigail had more in common with Aiden than almost anyone else I knew.

They both hid their feelings behind a mask of dignity and reserve, relying on manners in difficult situations. They both loved nothing so much as their family and would sacrifice anything to keep the people they loved safe.

William was distracted by meaningless gossip and old

scandal. He was family, but he wasn't a Winters. We'd lived through scandal and gossip and come out the other side, not once, but twice.

We could survive it a third time if it came to that. I sure as hell wasn't going to sacrifice Abigail because I was afraid of what people would say.

If I were that weak, I didn't deserve her.

Chapter Twenty-One
Abigail

I was stirring a huge pot of Bolognese sauce when Jacob's office door opened and an older man stormed out, sending me an icy glare as he half-stalked and half-fled through the penthouse and out the front door.

The other occupants of the kitchen looked startled at his rushed exit but didn't comment. We were all trying to ignore the awkward conversation we'd overheard.

I had no doubt the older man was the source of the most scathing accusations about me, mostly because the other voice had been too young and too calm to belong to that harried, angry man.

I couldn't quite believe I was cooking dinner for Jacob's family. I'd woken to the sound of their voices, and after cracking the door to make sure there wasn't an emergency, I'd ducked back into Jacob's room to change into something more appropriate for guests.

My clothes had been hung in Jacob's expansive walk-in closet opposite his own so that we each had our own side.

It looked too cute, the shared closet, and I might have

stopped to absorb the strangeness of it, but I felt as if I needed to know who was in the penthouse.

Quickly, I'd brushed the tangles from my hair and twisted it into a simple spiral bun, a style I loved because it was easy, once I got the hang of it, but it looked somewhat ornate.

A little makeup and a simple linen sundress in poppy red with matching patent leather flip-flops, and I was ready.

It was casual enough to wear around the house, yet tailored enough that it provided me with armor to face whoever had invaded our sanctuary.

I emerged in time to hear Jacob's office door close. Three men were in the kitchen, and I was relieved to see I knew at least one of them.

Tate. The other could have been Tate's twin, except for his dark brown eyes. The third man shared Tate's vibrant blue eyes and bone structure—definitely another Winters male—but he had dark blond hair, cut close on the sides and messy on top, and had a heavier build than the other two.

He wasn't so much taller as packed with muscle. Well-developed shoulders and biceps strained the fabric of his worn T-shirt, and I couldn't miss the colorful tattoo sleeve on his right arm.

Not the normal type of Winters, then. This must be Vance, the artist. I couldn't see this man in a board room. There was something a little wild about him, though maybe that was just the tattoos.

Straightening my spine and pasting a serene expression on my face, I entered the kitchen with a smile and said, "Tate, it's so nice to see you again. How are you?"

He knew what I was asking and grinned at me, breaking away from the other men to come forward and take my outstretched hand, tugging me into a quick hug and dropping a kiss on my cheek. "I'm great, thanks in part to you."

"Really?" I asked. "You worked things out with Emily?"

"I did. Actually, she's downstairs with Holden's girl, Jo. We thought we'd see what you were up to before we dragged them along with us."

The Tate clone stepped forward, his hand outstretched, and said, "Tate has no manners, but I'm Holden, his cousin and Jacob's brother. This is Vance, Tate's older brother. Don't let the tattoos scare you off."

I shook Holden's hand and turned to Vance to take his, surprised when he lifted my fingers to his lips and kissed them in lieu of shaking.

Blushing a little, I said, "It's nice to meet you, Holden, and Vance, I've seen your work. You're very talented, but I'm sure you know that. I particularly like the piece on the terrace at La Mystere. It anchors their whole aesthetic. Did you make it on commission or did they design around it?"

Not releasing my fingers, Vance turned to his brother and cousin and said, "I like her. Maybe I'll steal her away from Jacob."

Tate winked at me and said, "I would *love* to see you try."

Gently, I extracted my fingers from Vance's grip and took a discrete step away, raising my eyebrow to let him know I was waiting for him to answer my question.

He gave me an almost imperceptible nod and said, "They designed around it. The owner had purchased it a few years before he planned the restaurant and moved it from his own garden to the dining terrace."

"I'd always wondered," I said.

The French bistro was one of my favorite restaurants in the city. Their outdoor eating space had an overgrown, wild quality that formed the perfect counterpoint to the almost muscular, oversized metal sculpture at its center.

I knew Vance's name, but I'd never seen him up close. Now that I had, I could imagine this man—with his powerful arms and colorful tattoos—creating the piece.

He reminded me of a debonair Viking, if such a thing were possible.

I looked at the clock and realized we were nearing dinnertime. I didn't know what Jacob had planned, but if everyone would be happy with a simple meal of pasta with Bolognese sauce, I'd stocked the ingredients in the pantry and freezer, just in case we needed an emergency meal.

"Do you all have plans for dinner?" I asked, not sure if I wanted them to stay or go.

"We do now," Vance said. "Can we help?"

I shook my head. I was still a little wobbly, but I could make pasta with Bolognese sauce in my sleep.

I even had a loaf of bread in the freezer from the week before when I'd made too much and realized it would go stale before we could use it.

"I'm calling the girls," Holden said, pulling his phone from his pocket. I was taking the defrosted meat from the microwave when a knock sounded on Jacob's door.

Tate went to answer it and returned, followed by two women. They were a few years younger than me, one dressed casually with long, dark blonde hair and pretty blue eyes.

She was curvy, though her t-shirt and jeans didn't show off her figure as well as they could have. Holden grabbed her arm and pulled her into him, sliding his hand over her hip in possession as he kissed her. She must be Jo.

That meant that the brunette tucked into Tate's side

was Emily. She gave me a shy smile, her shiny, dark hair falling into her unusually clear gray eyes.

Like Jo, and like me, she was all curves, her figure soft and well-rounded. It seemed the Winters men had a type.

We were in the midst of greeting each other when an older man's voice cut through from Jacob's office. We couldn't hear every word, but the sounds of my name and 'damaged goods' were clear, as was the word 'tainted', repeated twice.

I swallowed and pretended not to hear, saying, "Holden, there's a loaf of bread in the freezer. Would you get it out and defrost it in the microwave?"

"For garlic bread?" Jo asked. "I'll make it, if you don't mind."

"Jo makes fantastic garlic bread," Emily said, smiling at me to cover the awkwardness left by the words we'd all overheard.

"Thank you, that would be great," I said, hanging on to my smile and their friendliness as we heard a younger voice cut in, too low for the words to be distinct, then Jacob, again too low to make out.

I let out a breath I hadn't realized I'd been holding.

We fell into a rhythm of cooking, me putting together the sauce as Jo and Emily poked in the fridge and set the bread to defrost, when the first voice shouted, "Jacob, stop acting like a horny teenager. There are more important things at stake here than your cock. Find some other woman. Abigail Jordan is already reflecting on this family. People are talking, and it's unacceptable—"

Tate swore and whirled out of the kitchen. I started to tell him not to bother when Holden's hand landed on my shoulder.

"Let him go. That's uncalled-for." Holden's dark eyes

were thunderous.

Vance leaned against the counter, thick arms crossed over his chest, his expression just as pissed as Holden's. He shook his head.

"Fucking William. He's like family, but he can be an ass. Ignore him."

I looked from Holden to Vance. "Are people talking?" I asked.

Both men shared an uncomfortable glance. Vance shook his head at me, less in denial than in commiseration.

"A little, but it's not bad, and it's nothing we can't handle. Don't let William bother you."

"Do you know who I am?" I asked.

If he knew who I was, he might agree with William and wish me gone, my tainted past far away from his cousin.

Without a flinch, Vance met my eyes and said, "I do. I know exactly who you are, Abigail Jordan, born Abigail Wainright to Gerald and Anne Louise Wainright. I don't give a shit about gossip, but I do pay attention to my family. I also trust Jacob's judgment. I'm sure he knows everything about you. He probably knows things you've forgotten."

"Cooper," Holden cut in. "Jacob would've had Cooper Sinclair run a report. Don't take offense. It's habit. Aiden's probably already run one on Jo and Emily."

"What?" echoed from both women on the other side of the kitchen. "He ran a report on us?" Jo said.

Holden gave a sheepish shrug and said, "Just let it go, love. Both of them are control freaks. It's easier to let them invade your privacy a little so they feel better and back off."

Emily shook her head, and Jo let out an irritated huff, but they both dropped it. I looked back to Vance, waiting for him to finish making his point.

"If Jacob has you living with him, when no other woman

has been invited to do more than spend the night, and that only rarely, then he must have a good reason. I trust his judgment. Besides, you recognize my talent, so clearly, you're intelligent."

Not sure how to thank him for his reassurance, I said, "It's good to see that you're not plagued by insecurity like so many artists."

Vance winked at me—definitely a debonair Viking—and Tate said with a laugh, "Insecurity? If Vance didn't have Magnolia around, his ego would blow up so big it would carry the entire city away."

"Magnolia?" Jo asked. "I didn't know Vance had a girlfriend."

Vance let out a scoffing grunt and ignored his brother, going to the refrigerator for a beer and saying, "I'll put water on for the pasta."

"Vance doesn't have a girlfriend," Holden said. "He has a string of girls who think they're his friends. With benefits. Magnolia is his long-suffering assistant. She's way too good for him, and I have no idea why she puts up with him. We've all tried to hire her away, but for some reason, she's loyal to the charming bastard."

Vance must have known his way around Jacob's kitchen, because he pulled the oversized spaghetti pot out from the cabinet and set it in the sink to fill.

I expected a snappy comeback to Holden's taunts, but instead, his shoulders looked tight and his jaw was set. Interesting.

That was when Jacob's door swung open and the angry older man stormed out, ignoring the rest of us in his rush to leave. As the door slammed behind him, Jacob left his office and headed straight for me, his silver eyes sharp with concern as he scanned the room, taking in the mood.

He grabbed my hand and pulled me to him as he turned and headed out of the kitchen, past another man who could only be the mysterious brother, Aiden.

"Jacob, the sauce," I said, looking over my shoulder at the pot of meat sauce simmering on the stove.

"Holden will get it," he said.

Holden was already moving to the stove when we disappeared down the hall to the bedrooms. Jacob crowded me into his room and shut the door behind us with a slam.

"Are you okay?" he asked, cupping my face in his hands and tilting my chin up so he could meet my eyes.

My throat tight, I nodded, unable to lie to him when he was looking at me so closely. Instead, I said, "Your family is very nice."

"They are," he said, dropping his hands from my face and pulling me into his arms. "But don't listen to a thing Vance says. He's charming, but he's an asshole. I'm a much better bet."

I giggled, a silly, light sound that surprised me.

"Jacob," I started. He squeezed me in his arms.

"You heard what William said?"

I nodded against his chest.

"Some of it," I admitted. "Enough."

"Forget about it," he ordered. "He's old school, and he thinks if we all have pristine reputations, we can erase the past and restore the Winters name to glory. It's bullshit. The only person who cares about that is William."

"But I don't want to be the reason people are talking about you. This was supposed to be a secret. I didn't want to taint you with—"

"Don't fucking say that word." Jacob's arms tightened until I could barely breathe.

His head dropped until his breath washed hot over my

ear. "Don't ever refer to yourself as tainted. Ever. You are perfect. Nothing will ever change that. Do you understand? Tell me you understand, or so help me, I will beat the ever living shit out of William Davis. I don't care if he is an old man."

This time, I wanted to giggle, but I couldn't quite find it in me. My emotions swung from shame to wonder to confusion.

I settled for letting out a sigh and melting into Jacob's steely embrace. He rubbed his hands soothingly up and down my spine.

"I don't want you on your feet, cooking this crowd dinner," he said.

"It's too late," I said. "I already invited them."

"Then they can finish cooking. You can sit at the counter and supervise with a mug of tea."

"Bossy," I said into his shirt.

"Damn straight. I'm always going to be bossy. You should just get used to it and prepare to let me have my way."

"Not likely," I mumbled under my breath.

"I heard that, sweetheart."

His arms loosened from around me, and he leaned back to kiss me, first on one cheekbone, then the other, butterfly kisses, before dropping his lips to mine for a kiss that was as ardent and possessive as the first two had been sweet.

My knees were weak with more than fatigue when he pulled away.

"Let's go eat," Jacob said, his hand clasping mine. "Did Tate and Holden bring their new girlfriends?"

"They did," I said. "They seem very nice."

"I think they are," he said, "which makes me wonder what they're doing with Holden and Tate."

He spoke loudly enough for the occupants of the kitchen to hear him, and I said under my breath, "Jacob!"

Both Emily and Jo had clearly overheard and were grinning at Jacob.

Holden said, "I thought you'd be less of an asshole once you got your own girl."

To my surprise, Jacob pulled me into his side and dropped a kiss on the top of my head before he said, "Now that I have a woman as amazing as Abigail, I'll probably be more of an asshole."

"Smug," Vance said.

"Absolutely," agreed Jacob.

Jacob sat me at the counter and, true to his promise, made me a mug of tea and wouldn't let me do more than supervise the preparation of the meal.

He took a stool on one side and Vance the stool on the other, as if standing guard. The guys all ribbed each other, and in between, I managed to get to know both Jo and Emily.

They were younger than me, graduate students at Georgia Tech. Both were also brilliant, which was a little intimidating, but they were too nice to rub it in.

They invited me out for drinks, and I started to demur, when Jacob said, "Not until this situation is resolved, sweetheart."

"I know," I said, elbowing him in the side in annoyance. To Jo and Emily, I said, "I'm having some problems with my former father-in-law, and I can't really go out until they're resolved. But once they are, I'd love to get a drink with you."

Holden cut in to say, "Not without us. Not unless you go to Manna. I don't think my heart can take the stress of the three of you let loose on Atlanta."

Jo slapped his chest with a potholder and said, "I think

it's cute the way you think we're in constant danger of men hitting on us."

Tate crossed his arms over his chest and shook his head at both Jo and Emily. "We don't think it's cute the way you two are completely clueless. If you had any idea what men are thinking when they're talking to you—"

"He's right," Vance cut in. "If either of you ever left the lab, you'd know. Those geek boys you work with have their heads too buried in their projects to know what to do with a woman. If I'd run into one of you before these two clowns—"

He ducked to the side, dodging the apple Holden lobbed at his head, catching it easily out of the air and taking a bite, an amused grin stretching across his handsome face.

"You need your own woman," Holden muttered, "so you can stop flirting with ours."

"He should just go out with Magnolia," Tate said. "She's the only woman who can put up with him for more than a night."

"Magnolia is too good for him," Holden said. "And anyway, she's engaged."

"Whatever," Tate said. "Maggie's been engaged for two years, and there's no ring and no wedding."

Vance mumbled something into his apple, catching Jacob's attention. He straightened and pinned his cousin with his silver eyes, demanding, "What did you say?"

Vance swallowed the bite of apple and let out a sigh. "They broke up. Don't tell her I told you, because she feels like shit. But the fucking bastard broke up with her."

"I thought you didn't like him," Jacob asked evenly.

Vance braced his elbows on the counter and shook his head, all the charm drained from his expression, his eyes dark and serious.

"I didn't. He was a tool and a user, proven by the fact that not only did he never get her a ring or set a date, but he lived with her without covering a single one of the bills, and the second he finished his residency and got accepted into a good practice, he dumped her for the daughter of the lead surgeon in his new office."

"That's a mistake," a deep voice said.

Aiden had been so quiet that I'd almost forgotten he was there. He stood off to the side of the kitchen, leaning against a wall, arms crossed over his chest, drinking a beer and observing his family in silence. I'd felt his eyes on me, steady and curious, more than once, but he hadn't spoken until now.

He went on, "Magnolia Henry is a catch. She's wasted on Vance, professionally speaking. But he'd be a moron if he didn't take advantage now that she's available."

"None of your business, Aiden," Vance said between gritted teeth.

Aiden flashed him a surprisingly lighthearted grin and shot back, "Vance, you should know better. Everything is my business."

His eyes settled on me as he said the last, neither accusing nor approving. So, the jury was still out on me. That was fine. I understood.

Despite Jacob's words of comfort in his bedroom, I knew I didn't belong there. Maybe once, I would have. Before my life went to hell. Before my father died and I'd made so many foolish decisions.

Not now, not as John Jordan's widow.

Jacob could reassure me that they didn't care about gossip, but that wasn't the world we'd been raised in.

Society was built on gossip, innuendo, and reputation. As ugly as his words had been, William was right.

I was tainted.

And Jacob was a Winters. Whatever we had between us, it couldn't last.

Dinner was finally ready, and we sat at the long dining room table, everyone passing plates and serving themselves, talking over one another and laughing while Aiden watched us all in silence.

I watched him back, too tired by then to jump into the lively conversation. His face bore the Winters stamp, but there was something austere about his features. He watched his family like a guard dog, ready to jump at any threat.

I wondered what would happen when he decided *I* was a threat.

I'd deal with it later. By the time Jacob brought out a container of cookies I'd made before I got sick, my eyes were drooping. I didn't resist when Jacob plucked me out of my chair and settled me in his lap, tucking my head under his chin.

I heard him say, "This is the first time she's been up and around in days. She had the flu so badly, I almost took her to the ER."

I struggled to open my eyes, but the combination of so many hours out of bed and a stomach full of pasta was too much.

Time passed before I was aware of Jacob carrying me to bed, stripping me of my dress, and removing the pins from my hair with a gentle efficiency.

He had my hair in a loose braid and another of his T-shirts over my head before I knew it and was pushing me down to the pillow, tucking me in moments before sleep pulled me under.

CHAPTER
TWENTY-TWO

ABIGAIL

I woke alone the next morning, a note on the pillow beside me in Jacob's handwriting that read,
At the office, home early. REST.

I could do that. The evening before, meeting Jacob's family had been fun and educational—except for William Davis's brief presence—but it had wiped me out.

I wasn't sick any longer, just exhausted and weak. I lay in Jacob's big bed and tried to catch up with the events of the past week.

Everything had changed between Jacob and myself, and I didn't understand how or why. For a man who didn't do relationships, Jacob was treating me an awful lot like a girlfriend.

Maybe he couldn't help himself. As autocratic and commanding as he could be, as used to getting his way as he was, at his core, Jacob was a good man.

He'd helped me when he didn't have to, and this whole arrangement could have gone completely differently. With any other man, it would have.

I suspected that while Jacob had initially liked the idea

of my being no more than a pet, over the long term, he couldn't sustain that kind of distance. Especially with me living in his house.

Just because he was starting to treat me like his girlfriend didn't make it true. I needed to remember that. We still had an arrangement.

We were not equals.

I remembered the conversation the night before about Vance's assistant, Magnolia, and her former fiancé.

Things like that happened to women all the time. I'm sure at some point, he'd asked her formally to be his wife, or maybe just said 'we should get married', and then started acting like they were a permanent couple.

She had probably responded to that vague promise and fallen into the role of future wife because he put her there, but Tate was right. No ring and no date made the assumption of engagement pretty weak.

Jacob could treat me like his girlfriend. He might be sweet and he might have moved me into his room, but I'd be an idiot if I read too much into that. He'd never said our deal had changed.

No matter what small things were different, as long as the arrangement hadn't been withdrawn or altered, I had to remember it stood between us.

If I hadn't had my mother to worry about, I would've ended it myself. I wasn't made for this. I couldn't keep my heart safe. Every day that passed, I longed for Jacob. I wanted more from him.

If I had to keep reminding myself about the way things stood between us, I was already in too deep. But I did have my mother to worry about, or I never would have approached Jacob in the first place. I couldn't reconcile my feelings.

A part of me bitterly regretted the position I'd put myself in, and another part was gleefully thrilled I'd finally had an excuse to get naked with Jacob Winters.

I needed to focus. I had no control over my relationship with Jacob. I could try to protect my heart, but that was pretty much a lost cause. I couldn't walk away while my mother needed me.

Jacob's talk about my going back to college was enticing, but it wasn't today's reality. In my future, I might have options. In my present day, I had no money and my mother to support.

I missed her. I missed her so much. There was a hollow ache in my chest every time I thought of her. The mother I remembered, the woman who'd raised me and loved me, was already gone.

Even a year ago, I still got brief glimpses of her, though they'd been getting fewer and further between no matter how often I visited. By the time John died, I was there every day, and she only remembered me a few times a month.

Worse, her mobility had declined, and she'd been having trouble communicating. I hadn't needed her doctor to tell me she was progressing to the final stages of her condition.

We'd been apart for weeks. I'd seen her a few days before I'd fled Big John's house. Since then, it hadn't been safe.

Now that Big John knew where I was, I wanted to go and see my mother. I knew it wouldn't be without danger. We'd already determined he had people watching Shaded Glenn. But surely, the Sinclairs could figure something out.

I wasn't worried about any risk to myself. I'd been worried about leading Big John to Jacob, but that was already done, and I couldn't stand going one more day without seeing my mother.

I'd been dreaming of her. Memories from when I was younger, before she got sick. Nightmares that she slipped away before I could see her again.

I couldn't stand the thought of losing her at all, but the idea that she might die without me there, before I could hold her hand one more time, was too much.

I got out of bed and took a quick shower. The kitchen was clean, only the container of leftover pasta in the refrigerator a clue that we'd had Jacob's family over the night before.

I was still tired, so I followed Jacob's orders, making tea and toast and taking them to the couch, where I settled in to watch more home improvement shows and maybe take a nap.

True to his word, Jacob came home early, letting himself in the penthouse in time for a late lunch. The sound of the door closing woke me and I sat bolt upright, my heart pounding before I realized no one but Jacob or his family could have let themselves in.

I moved to get up to make him lunch, but he said, "Stay there."

I obeyed, mostly because I didn't want to piss him off before I started making demands.

"Are you hungry?" he called from the kitchen.

I realized I was and called back, "A little."

My stomach still wasn't used to solid food, but I wanted something more than toast. At least my throat felt better. It was still the slightest bit tender, but not really sore. Jacob returned a few minutes later with two bowls of pasta.

Before I could stand, he waved me back and said, "Stay there. We'll eat on the couch."

Again, I didn't argue. At the first bite, my stomach roared to life, and I realized I wasn't just a little hungry. I was starving. I forgot about talking to Jacob and focused on inhaling my lunch.

Swallowing the last bite, I looked up to find Jacob watching me, a sexy quirk to his lips. Not quite a grin, but almost.

I wiped the sauce from my mouth and said, "What?"

He shook his head, the quirk blooming into a smile, and said, "Nothing. It's just nice to see you eating again. You had me worried for a while."

I didn't respond to that. Sweet Jacob still set me off balance, especially now that I was better.

Instead, I said, "We need to talk."

Jacob's eyes narrowed on me in suspicion and, I thought, maybe worry.

"What do we need to talk about?"

Taking a deep breath for courage, I said, "I want to see my mother. I know it's dangerous, but it's been weeks. I've never gone this long without seeing her. Not since she got sick, and I can't—"

Tears welled in my eyes and spilled over, dripping down my cheeks. I reached for the mask of dignity I used to protect myself when I felt threatened, but I couldn't find it.

I was raw and open in front of Jacob, without defenses, and I hated it, hated being so dependent on anyone, hated the fear for my mother.

Suspicion washed away under what looked like relief before his eyes went wide with alarm. There was a note of panic in his voice when he said, "Sweetheart, don't cry. Don't cry. We'll figure something out."

I put my hands over my face, blocking my view of him, but more importantly, hiding my tears. He reached for me, and I tried to lean away, but he ignored me, pulling me into his arms and stroking my back. I was tired of feeling like a mess.

My breath hitched in my chest as I wiped the tears from my cheeks, trying to get myself together. Sitting back, I said, "I don't know how much time she has left, Jacob. I don't want to be reckless, but I need to see her before it's too late."

Jacob nodded. "I came home early to check on you, but also because I have a meeting with Cooper and Evers, and I wanted to see if you'd like to come with me."

"Yes, please. Can we ask them about visiting my mother?"

"I'll make a deal with you," Jacob said. "We'll ask. If they think they can get you in with an acceptable degree of safety, we'll do it. But Cooper is a risk taker. If he says no, he's got a damn good reason, and we're going to listen to him, okay?"

"Okay," I agreed.

I wasn't completely irrational, even if I was feeling emotional. I wanted to see my mother. I needed to see my mother. I also knew she would be furious if I got myself killed in the process.

At least, she would have been when she still remembered who I was. But, of all the things I'd done in the last few years of which I knew she would *not* approve, getting myself killed would be at the top of the list.

I had just enough time to change and put on some makeup before the Sinclair security vehicle would arrive in the garage to transport us to their offices.

I pinned up my hair and put on a little more makeup than I'd been using lately in celebration of my first foray outside the penthouse since I'd arrived weeks before.

I debated over what to wear, then settled for the most

businesslike outfit I had, a pale pink Chanel suit, more suited to a ladies' lunch than an office, but still more appropriate for a meeting than a sundress or one of my yoga pants & hoodie outfits.

The suit, composed of an A-line dress with a somewhat short skirt and fitted jacket, flattered my curvy figure without showing too much leg or cleavage.

I liked my body, most of the time. When I wasn't at a social event surrounded by bony women in tiny black dresses, I loved my body. I was fuller figured then most of the women I knew, but I had a nice curve to my waist and my full breasts were fairly perky for their size.

I looked like a 1940s pinup, and the flare in the suit skirt emphasized the comparison. I couldn't resist the cream leather spike heels on the floor of my closet.

I didn't know where they'd come from. I hadn't ordered them. I recognized the designer, and I knew the shoes cost hundreds of dollars.

My wardrobe at Jacob's had started with the few items Rachel had purchased for me and been augmented by my own online shopping, but a few pieces here and there, mostly lingerie and shoes, had shown up out of nowhere.

It was hard to imagine Jacob shopping, but I couldn't see him asking Rachel to buy me lingerie. Shoes, maybe.

I sincerely hoped she had not purchased some of the lingerie. I'd never be able to look her in the eye again if she'd been the one to select any of the wispy, lacy collection of La Perla in the drawer.

I wasn't even going to consider the thought of Rachel choosing the black satin bustier with silver buckles and matching thong from Agent Provocateur.

I left the bedroom on time and met Jacob at the door,

gratified to see his eyes go dark as he scanned me from head to toe.

"Maybe I can move our appointment," he murmured against my lips as he pulled me in for a kiss. "It's been days."

"Poor baby," I teased. My body had been half-dead while I was sick, sex the last thing on my mind. At the touch of Jacob's lips to mine and the heat of his fingers pulling up the hem of my skirt to skim over my hip, every nerve in my body roared back to life.

Without meaning to, I shifted my stance, spreading my legs just a little, making room for his hand as it slid around my hip to skim the thin lace of my panties.

Abruptly, Jacob dropped his hand and stepped back, leaving me cold, my knees shaky. Before I could speak, he opened the door and said, "Let's go."

I stood beside him in the elevator, painfully aware of the emptiness between us, my nipples hard, my breasts full and ready for his touch, wishing his hand were back between my legs.

CHAPTER TWENTY-THREE

ABIGAIL

"Jacob," I started to say. He shook his head, silencing me.

"Taking you out of the building is dangerous," he said. "We have to pay attention. As much as I want to peel that suit off you and play, now's not the time."

I nodded, my cheeks flashing red. He was right, and I was an idiot. The second he got his hands on me, my brain leaked right out my ears.

The elevator arrived at the garage level, but the doors stayed shut. Jacob pulled his phone from his pocket and checked the screen. I glanced over but couldn't see anything.

A few seconds later, a green box popped up.

Jacob slid his phone in his pocket before I could read what it said, but it must've been what he was waiting for because he hit the button to open the doors and we entered the garage level to see a huge black SUV pulled up directly in front of us.

A man with sandy blonde hair and clear green eyes

jumped out, nodded to us, and opened the rear passenger door.

Jacob nodded back, said, "Griffen," and helped me in. I slid across the smooth bench seat, glad I'd worn a full skirt. If the fit had been any tighter, he would have had to pick me up to get me in the tall SUV.

Minutes later, we were pulling into an underground parking garage. Griffen jumped out as soon as we were parked and opened Jacob's door, waiting for us to get out before taking the rear of our little procession.

As we got in the elevator, he said, "You look exactly like your mother."

I looked at him in surprise, then remembered Jacob said he had someone visiting my mother. This must be the guy.

I smiled at him and said, "Thank you. How is she?"

His eyes flicked away from mine and settled on Jacob for a second before returning to me. "Her condition hasn't changed much in the last few weeks," he said finally. His voice had a hint of an accent. Almost Southern, maybe Texas.

My head dropped, and I studied my feet.

I knew what he wanted me to read into that. She wasn't doing well.

Not a surprise, but I must have had the faint hope that he would grin and say she was a fantastic card player and he loved hanging out with her, or something equally absurd.

Anything but the truth—that she was in the final stages of Alzheimer's and was dying.

I was lost in thought as I followed Jacob from the elevator to Cooper's office, my hand tucked securely in Jacob's. I got the impression of spare modernity—lots of chrome and gray and black—the opposite of Jacob's offices.

Jacob dropped a quick knock on a door and opened it,

leading us inside. Griffen followed and closed the door behind us.

I didn't know the Sinclairs very well. Socially, we'd intersected on occasion, but their business had never crossed over to either my family or the Jordans.

Sinclair Security had a reputation for getting the job done, and while I knew they worked with both the police and federal law enforcement, they were also known to take clients of a less legitimate variety.

However, they didn't work for criminals, which meant they'd never worked with Big John. For all of that, we'd been introduced more than a few times, and I recognized both Cooper and Evers Sinclair on sight.

Like the Winters men, the Sinclair brothers all looked alike. Evers and Cooper shared the same icy blue eyes, but Evers wore his dark hair military short, while Cooper's was longer and casually messy.

I extended my hand to Cooper. "Cooper, thank you for including me in the meeting."

His fingers tightened around mine as he smiled.

"Of course. We've been trying to spare you the details, but at this point, I think it makes more sense for you to chip in any ideas."

Evers took my hand in his and gave it an affectionate squeeze. "Abigail, how are you holding up? Do you need anything?"

"Abigail has everything she needs, Evers, but thanks," Jacob said.

He slid his arm around my shoulder and pulled me into his side, glaring at Evers. If I hadn't known better, I never would've guessed the two of them were lifelong friends. I looked between them, Jacob furious and Evers annoyed and also possibly amused.

I was deciding how to handle them when Griffen said, "Abigail, I have some pictures of your mother, if you'd like to see them. It's nothing exciting. There really haven't been any changes, but I thought you might want them anyway."

I did. I didn't care if there hadn't been any change to my mother's condition. I was desperate to see her, even in a picture. I stepped away from Jacob, pulling free of his arm and leaving him to deal with Evers on his own. Griffen pointed me to a chair opposite Cooper's desk, and I sat, gratefully accepting the file folder of photographs.

There weren't many, all of them showing my mother asleep in her bed, the quilt my grandmother had sewn for her tucked securely around her thin frame.

She was too young to be so ill, and in a picture like this, she didn't look sick. She just looked like she was sleeping. Tears threatened, and I bit my lip hard to push them back.

I was not going to start crying in this office filled with testosterone. I would probably have an argument on my hands if I wanted to go see my mother, and the last thing I needed was for these guys to think I was too emotional to handle it.

I knew well enough that while none of them were overtly sexist, their base instinct when it came to females was to sleep with them or protect them. Crying in front of them would not help my case.

I blinked away the moisture in my eyes and re-settled the pictures in the file, closing it carefully and laying my hands on top. I wouldn't dwell on the photographs, and I wouldn't cry, but I couldn't bear to give them back. Not yet.

Jacob took the seat beside me, Griffen leaned against the wall beside the desk, and Evers took a position half-sitting on the corner of Cooper's desk.

Before the meeting could start, I said, "I'd like to see my

mother. I know it's dangerous, but it's been three weeks, and I appreciate Griffen visiting her, but—"

"It's not the same," Cooper finished for me.

"No, it's not. I know it's dangerous—"

"Is there a way we can get her in and minimize the risk?" Jacob asked.

Cooper stared at us both for a long moment before answering.

"The short answer is yes. Now that he knows where she is, it's not as much of a risk if she gets tailed back to Winters House, but we shouldn't make a habit of exposing her."

Before I could get annoyed that Cooper was discussing me in the third person when I was sitting right in front of him, he looked at me and said, "Abigail, I suggested Jacob include you in this meeting because whatever we decide will affect you more than anyone else."

"What do you mean?" I asked.

What were they deciding?

Cooper sat back and crossed his arms over his chest.

"We're at a stalemate with Big John right now," he said. "His talks with the Raptors have stalled, but they're not dead. That keeps you in play. We don't know definitely, but our feeling is that the second you pop back up on the game board, everything will shift back into high gear."

"That keeps her trapped indefinitely," Jacob commented. Cooper nodded.

"It does. Which means either you ride it out and wait, hoping the situation resolves itself, or we make some moves to push this to a head. Either way, if you want to see your mother, soon is as good a time as any. If we decide to escalate things, we won't want you out on the street."

"What does that mean?" I asked "*Escalate things?*"

Cooper looked up at Evers, who explained.

"Big John heads his own organization, but he doesn't handle distribution or sales of product out of this region. In that sense, he's a cog in a machine, albeit a dangerous and powerful cog. Making a visible member of Atlanta society a key point in a distribution deal with a biker gang is not good business.

"You are not some homeless junkie or hooker. You're a Wainwright. Your grandmother was president of the fucking garden society for a decade. Big John's bosses may not know who your people are, but if someone tells them what he plans to do with you, they will not be happy."

My eyes widened as the implications of Evers's words sank in. I'd been subject to Big John's will for so many years that I'd forgotten where I belonged in the bigger picture.

Evers was right. Big John couldn't just make me disappear and hope no one would notice. In the short term, my prominence wouldn't help me.

If Big John got his hands on me, by the time law enforcement came rushing in to save the day, I would have already disappeared. But I could see how that kind of attention would be bad for the entire organization.

"Especially now that Jacob has claimed you," Griffen cut in. "These guys won't be happy to hear that Big John wants to kidnap the woman of a guy who golfs with the governor."

Jacob golfed with the governor? I looked at him, and he shook his head. "I try to avoid golf when I can, sweetheart. It's not my game."

"But you've golfed with the governor?" I asked, curious.

"We usually settle for lunch at the club," he said. That was enough to make their point.

"What happens if you escalate the situation? What does that mean, exactly?" I asked.

"It means," Cooper said, picking up a pen from his desk

and flipping it over his fingers, "that I get a message to the people who pull Big John's strings and let them know he's showing signs of instability that will draw the wrong kinds of attention. It may come to nothing, and it may make things worse."

"But you think it will get him off my back," I said. Cooper leveled his eyes on me and said nothing for a long moment.

"I think it's a risk. A rational man will respond to threats from his superiors by toeing the line. If Big John Jordan were rational, he never would've dragged you into a negotiation with the Raptors in the first place. If he were rational, he wouldn't have had your husband assassinated. These are not the actions of a rational person. That makes him dangerous."

I flinched when he stated so boldly that John had been murdered by his own father. I thought I'd made my peace with that, but I guess I was wrong. And Cooper was right. Big John was not rational. He was unpredictable.

But what were my options? Let things continue as they were and remain a prisoner in Jacob's penthouse? For so many reasons, that situation was temporary.

One way or another, the threat of Big John had to be resolved.

"It's your call, sweetheart," Jacob said, taking my hand in his and intertwining his fingers with mine.

"What do you think I should do?" I asked.

"Don't ask me," he warned. "I'm not rational either."

Under his breath, Evers mumbled, "No kidding," loud enough for all of us to hear.

Jacob sent him a livid glare before turning his eyes back to me.

"I can't stand the thought of you in danger," he said. "If it were up to me, I'd pack you up and ship you off to a hunting cabin in Montana until Big John was permanently out of the picture."

I couldn't help smiling at the thought of Jacob trying to dump me in a rustic cabin in the middle of nowhere. I was not the outdoorsy type.

"No," I said. "That's not going to happen, Jacob."

He returned my smile and shrugged. "I know. I haven't done it, have I? I'm just saying, I'm not going to stand by and let you put your life in danger, but you have the right to make your own decisions. If you want to stay holed up at my place and see how this plays out, then let's do that. I'm in no hurry to shake things up, especially if it means putting you in more danger. But it's your call, Abigail."

I'm in no hurry to shake things up, he'd said.

And that was our problem in a nutshell. I was trapped by circumstances and the threat of Big John. Meanwhile, Jacob had me exactly where he wanted me, tucked away and convenient.

Even better for him, I didn't really want to leave. I could easily see our circumstances stretching out for months.

Or longer.

With me falling deeper and deeper in love with a man for whom I was little more than convenient sex and disposable companionship.

I didn't know what would be left of me by the end. There wasn't really a decision to make.

"Escalate things," I said. "I don't think we have a choice."

Cooper nodded once, his face expressionless. Griffen crossed his arms over his chest and looked at the floor, but I couldn't read whether he thought my decision was a good one or not. Evers stood, shoved his hands in his pockets, and shook his head.

"What?" I asked. "You think I should just keep hiding?"

Evers scowled at Jacob, then turned a gentle smile my way.

"No, Abigail. I think all of your choices suck. I think this is a terrible situation, and I wish I had a better, safer answer for you. Jacob's going to beat the shit out of me for asking, but I don't care. Do you want to stay with him? I would feel better about this if you could look me in the eyes and tell me —all other concerns aside, if you knew your mother and Big John were not an issue—would you want to stay with Jacob?"

I realized, with a flood of embarrassment, that Evers knew exactly what my arrangement with Jacob was, and he did not approve.

My face burned, the flush of humiliation spreading down my neck over my collarbones until I was pretty sure every inch of my skin was blushing.

It was bad enough that Rachel and the doctor knew. Bad enough that there was already gossip that connected me to Jacob only months after John's death. But to have Evers Sinclair stare at me with pity and ask me if I was okay with being Jacob's whore—that was too much.

"Evers," Jacob growled, "I swear to fucking God, I will tear you to pieces if you say another word to her."

Evers took a step back, then held his ground. His voice low and unbearably gentle, he said to me, "Abigail, honey, I'm not trying to embarrass you. I just want you to know you have options if you want them. We have safe houses. We can get you out of Atlanta until this is resolved."

"Am I safe with Jacob?" I asked.

Jacob's fingers, still intertwined with mine, tightened painfully. I shied away from the thought that I had to consider Evers's offer.

Even though I was sure he wouldn't bill me for a stay in their safe house, there was still the issue of my mother's care to consider. I'd accepted Jacob's deal partly for protection, but mostly for her. If I ran out on Jacob, who would take care of my mother?

It was one thing to accept the Sinclairs' protection without paying, but her fees were too much to lump in with a favor for a friend, and a distant friend at that.

Be honest, I told myself. *This isn't entirely about the money.*

The truth was, I didn't want to leave Jacob. Not yet.

"Am I safe with Jacob?" I prompted.

"Yes," Evers admitted after Cooper rumbled his name under his breath. "We've got Winters House locked up tight. There's going to be a risk getting you in and out of Shaded Glenn, but that would be true no matter where you were staying. You're as safe as we can make you with Jacob."

"If I left, would Jacob be any safer from Big John?" I asked.

Jacob let go of my hand and turned to face me.

"Abigail, that's not an issue."

"It is an issue," I insisted. "When I came to you, I was scared, and I wasn't thinking clearly about what could happen to you if you took me in. I was selfish, worried about myself. But he shot at you. You could've been killed, and it would've been my fault. Don't ask me to forget about that."

"I don't care," he said, his voice rising to a shout.

"Well, I do," I shouted back. Taking a deep breath and searching for calm, I looked at the three other men in the room and repeated my question. "If I leave, will Jacob be safer?"

I expected Evers or Cooper to answer, but Griffen cut in. "Possibly, marginally safer. But again, Big John isn't being rational. He's pissed, and Jacob hid you from him. If this makes a difference in your decision, if you leave him, I wouldn't recommend making any changes to his security."

"So you're saying he would still need the same level of protection whether I'm with him or not?" I asked.

Griffen gave a single nod. "That would be my assessment, yes."

He shifted his lazy stance leaning against the door and stepped forward to stand beside Evers. "And just so you know, the nurses at Shaded Glenn have a lot to say about you. And the woman they talk about? She didn't have any good choices in this situation. You did the best you could. Jacob knew exactly the threat involved when he took you in, and you were looking out for your family. Don't ever feel badly about that."

I nodded and looked down at my lap. They were all watching me, waiting for my decision. Jacob leaned forward, taking both of my hands in his, and squeezed my fingers until I raised my eyes.

His voice was soft, free of anger, when he said, "Stay with me, Abigail. Please."

I searched his eyes, so familiar and yet often impenetrable to me. Maybe, if I had more self-respect, I would have taken Evers up on his offer. Jacob had a reputation for being tough in business, but he wouldn't throw my mother out on the street. He might present me with a bill when this was over, but he wouldn't have her thrown out of Shaded Glenn.

If I was going to stay with him instead of going into a safe house, I should at least be honest with myself and stop hiding behind my mother as an excuse. This may have started because I was trying to take care of her, but it wasn't about her anymore, and I was lying to myself if I thought I was sitting here trying to make a decision.

There was no decision to make.

"I won't leave," I said, wishing with all my heart that his request had included more.

Stay with me because I love you.

Stay with me because I can't live without you.

I was terribly afraid that what he really meant was *stay with me because I like fucking you and you're a pretty good cook.*

The truth was, I wasn't staying because he'd asked me to. I was staying because I was in love with him and I wasn't ready to give him up.

I looked across the desk to Cooper and said, "When can I see my mother?"

CHAPTER
TWENTY-FOUR
JACOB

Getting Abigail out of Winters House and into Shaded Glenn turned out to be less complicated than I thought. Griffen picked us up in a generic white van with a cleaning service logo on the side.

He drove through the city long enough for the team following us to determine we'd lost any tails before picking up his speed and driving to Shaded Glenn.

A combination of assisted living and twenty-four-hour nursing care, Shaded Glenn was located on several attractively landscaped acres north of the city.

The buildings were laid out in a traditional Georgian-style red brick, with black shutters and white columns. At night, even the back entrances were well-lit. We passed the wide gated drive of the main entry and turned the corner to the narrower but still gated service entry.

Cooper had sent two men ahead to check over the facility and supervise our entry and exit. As far as any threat from Big John went, the whole operation was clean and simple.

I wish the rest of it had been as easy. Abigail was under

too much strain, tension coiled inside her like an overwound watch.

The confrontation in Cooper's office earlier in the afternoon hadn't helped.

I was still ready to fucking kill Evers. It wasn't just that he'd tried to take her away from me. But Evers didn't even want her, not the way I did.

The way he'd thrown our arrangement in her face, seeing how humiliated she'd been—just thinking about it made me sick with anger.

And whose fault is that? My conscience prodded. *Evers's, or yours?*

I was really starting to hate my conscience. I refused to regret my arrangement with Abigail. Offering safety for Abigail and her mother in exchange for Abigail in my bed was not my most noble moment.

Neither of us had been thinking clearly when she'd shown up in my office. She'd been scared, and I'd been greedy. I could admit that, but it wasn't any of Evers's fucking business, and if he cared so much about Abigail, he wouldn't have made her feel like shit in front of everyone.

Blaming Evers was so much simpler than dwelling on what I could've done to make the situation easier. I was taking care of Abigail, wasn't I?

I'd given her everything she needed. The best sex of her life—the way she lit up for me, I knew she'd never had better—free reign to buy whatever she wanted, I was taking care of her mother, I'd given her a spectacular place to live, and I was even helping her figure out college.

What fucking more did everybody want from me?

Before my conscience could pipe up again, I dragged my attention back to the situation at hand. It was no wonder my mind had wandered.

As nice as Shaded Glenn was, with its hyper-attentive staff and beautiful facilities, this was not a happy place. The people here were not going home. And in Mrs. Wainwright's building, most of them were nearing the end.

I hadn't known Anne Louise Wainwright before she fell ill. Seeing her lying in the bed, eyes closed, a brightly patterned but clearly worn hand-stitched quilt tucked carefully around her frail body, it was hard to accept that she was in her late fifties.

She looked at least a decade older, but still beautiful, with the same thick, dark hair as Abigail, the same cheekbones, and the same nose.

I was looking at a vision of Abigail twenty-five years from now, and she would still be just as beautiful as she was today. At the same time, the most basic part of my soul revolted at the sight of Mrs. Wainwright in that bed, looking so much like her daughter, the beep of machines a soundtrack to her slowly declining health.

I never wanted to see Abigail like this. Never. I was watching the end of a life, come far too soon, and seeing it happen to the image of Abigail made me sick.

I led Abigail to a chair that had been placed beside her mother's bed. She sat, her eyes glued to her mother, and took her mother's hand, silent tears streaming down her face. I stood behind her, rubbing the back of her neck, at a loss for what else I could do.

I would fix anything for Abigail. Right any wrong. Save her from any threat. It was killing me that the only thing I could do now was write a check.

The most wrenching pain she'd ever experienced, the loss she feared more than any other, and I was helpless before it.

Eventually, I stepped out in the hall to check in with

Cooper and make some calls. We weren't going anywhere. Now that Abigail was with her mother after so long apart, I couldn't drag her home until she was ready.

It was a long night.

We stayed until Abigail started nodding off. When she was asleep, I gently untangled her fingers from her mother's and lifted her from the chair. Her eyes fluttered open.

I said, "It's time to go home, sweetheart. Okay?"

She registered what I was saying and her eyes filled with tears, but she nodded her head against my chest and whispered back, "Okay." She took a breath to steady herself. "I can walk. Put me down, please."

I didn't want to let her go, but I did as she asked. My arm around her shoulders, I held her tight to my side as we waited just inside the exit door for the all clear to leave. The same white van we'd arrived in was waiting.

Pearly dawn light gave the small parking lot an other-worldly look. In the still, quiet air, I wanted to hold my breath. The only sounds were the scuffle of our feet on the pavement and the low murmur of the Sinclair Security team talking through almost invisible microphones.

I was braced for an attack that never came. I helped Abigail into the van and climbed in beside her. The driver and another guard jumped in, waited until we finished fastening our seat belts, and took off.

Abigail's eyes started to close as we headed down the long, narrow drive back to the main road. She looked so lost, sitting on the other side of the bench seat.

I reached out and took her hand in mine, and the startled expression on her face told me she didn't expect comfort from my direction.

Was I doing such a bad job at taking care of her? I thought not, but after the confrontation with Evers and her hesitance as she held my hand, I had to wonder if my take on this whole situation was off.

I hated being wrong, probably because I had so little practice with it. Not being arrogant, it's just the truth. Still, taking in the defeated, anguished expression on Abigail's face, I had to wonder if this might be one of those very rare times I was completely fucking up.

The squeal of tires broke into my thoughts. I barely had time to straighten and look out the front windshield before metal crunched and the van spun sideways, throwing us hard to the left.

I heard the crack of Abigail's head against the side of the van, gunshots, then the pounding of feet on pavement, muffled through the metal of the van.

"Don't move," the driver of the van said, sounding disturbingly calm considering the fact that we were now stopped in the middle of the road, straddling both lanes, and apparently under attack.

Both he and the other guard jumped from the van, slamming the doors behind them. I heard the beep of a lock, then nothing.

I'd never imagined I'd wish for Cooper's commando skills. I could shoot a gun, and I was fit, but I was not stupid enough to think that I had any option other than to stay exactly where I was and wait for them to sort this out.

Abigail's hand had been torn from mine when we'd been hit. I found it on the seat beside me and grabbed it again, squeezing tightly.

"What just happened?" she asked, her voice thready and terrified. Her eyes were wide, and I caught the dark gleam of blood on her left temple in the early morning light suffusing the van, but it didn't seem to be flowing.

I didn't think she was badly hurt. I hoped she wasn't.

Her left hand went to her seatbelt, and I said, "No. Leave your seatbelt on. I don't know if they have another vehicle, but I think we should stay strapped in until the Sinclair team tells us otherwise."

She blinked and said, "You're right. Of course, you're right." Lifting her hand, she briefly touched the side of her head, then stared at the stain of blood on her fingers. I loosened my tie and pulled it from my collar.

Handing it to her, I said, "Here. Use this."

She dropped my hand to take the tie, leaving my fingers cold and empty. Turning the silk tie over in her fingers, she said, "I'll ruin it."

"I don't care about the fucking tie, Abigail," I snapped, and I instantly regretted my tone as her face closed down and went politely neutral.

Most of the time, Abigail's dignified act turned me on, especially now that I knew how hot she was in bed. When she used it to put distance between us, it just pissed me off.

I opened my mouth to tell her to knock it off when my brain kicked into gear and reminded me that I was the one who'd put that look on her face in the first place, and if I wanted it gone, I might want to try not being such an asshole when she was scared and hurt.

Forcing myself to calm down, I said, "I don't care about the tie, sweetheart. You're bleeding, and it looks like it stopped, but it'll be easier to tell if you clean it up a little. Okay?"

She dropped her eyes and nodded. I pretended I didn't see the sheen of tears as she gingerly used my tie to dab the blood from her temple. It didn't take long before it was apparent the cut wasn't bad. It was still bleeding, but only a trickle.

Head wounds always bled a lot, so if this one was clotting already, it wasn't a big deal. Good to know, since it felt like we'd been sitting in the van for an hour. The road outside was quiet.

"Abigail," I started, not sure what I planned to say, when the distant rumble of an engine cut through the early morning quiet.

My stomach tightened as I realized I was hearing the approach of motorcycles. Another squeal of tires, less than a second before the grinding crash of metal on metal, and we were flung in the opposite direction.

Lightning crashed behind my eyelids, an explosion of pain in the side of my head. My hand was again torn from Abigail's.

Fuck.

They had reinforcements, and if the motorcycles weren't a coincidence, then the Raptors had gotten tired of waiting for Big John to make his move.

My vision flickered in and out for a few seconds before I was able to focus my eyes.

Everything clicked into frame at once—the cracks in the front windshield of the van, the figures moving outside, fighting. The frightened pitch in Abigail's voice as she said, "Jacob! Jacob, say something, please, Jacob."

"I'm okay," I assured her. My head was killing me, and the side of my face was warm and sticky. Keeping my head turned away from Abigail so she couldn't see, I lifted my right hand to touch my cheek.

My fingers came away red, my blood gleaming in the slowly brightening morning light.

Shit.

I grabbed my tie from where it lay abandoned on the seat between us and used it to mop up the blood on the side of my face.

"What do we do?" Abigail asked. I wished with everything I had inside me that I had an answer. Stupidly, I wasn't even carrying a gun.

"Hold tight," I said. "Cooper was prepared for an ambush. This van is bulletproof. The smartest thing we can do right now is stay put and wait for the Sinclair team to get us out of here."

Abigail nodded and reached her hand out for mine. I took it, squeezing tightly, trying to convey absolute confidence that everything would be all right. I mostly believed it would.

I wanted to pull her over to my side of the van and cradle her in my arms. I didn't like her being so far away when we were in danger.

It was instinctive, an urge in my gut and in my heart to protect her from any threat. But I had to be smart. Unbuckling her seatbelt when we had been hit twice would be lunacy.

I wouldn't endanger her to make myself feel better, so I settled for stroking my thumb over the back of her hand as we waited and hoped.

More gunshots. A squeal of tires. Through the cracked windshield, I saw a hulking black SUV, the kind most of the Sinclair team drove. It was joined by a second black SUV. The doors opened, and men with guns poured out.

No more shots were fired, and shouts bounced back and forth, the words indistinguishable through the closed doors of the van.

We both jumped when the driver's side door opened and the figure in black slid inside.

Cooper didn't spare the time to look at us. He just started the van, threw it into gear, and hit the gas, swerving and veering around the vehicles blocking our way.

He sideswiped two bikes but managed to get us clear of the mess in the road, and we took off, flying down the back road and turning on to another two-lane road. Cooper didn't relax until we'd put several miles between us and the scene of the ambush.

Meeting my eyes in the rearview mirror, he said, "You two okay?"

"Okay," Abigail said in a quiet, strained voice.

"We're okay," I confirmed. "A little banged up. We both hit our heads pretty hard."

"Bleeding?"

"Yes," I said. "I think Abigail's has stopped, and mine slowed down."

"I'm taking us to the hospital then," Cooper said. "The police will meet us there. Are you up to talking?"

"Yes," Abigail said. "But we didn't see much. It happened so fast, and we never got out of the van."

"Good, that makes it all easier," Cooper said. "Just tell them what you know, answer their questions, and it'll be fine. We need to get this on record. They already know you're the linchpin in a dispute between Big John and the Raptors. Both of them had men there, and they didn't look like they were working together. Since we don't know how this is going to play out, it makes sense to give the police everything they need up front. You haven't done anything wrong."

"It's fine," I said. "Just take us to the hospital so we can get this over with and get home."

"Just hang in there," Cooper said. "It should all be over soon."

CHAPTER
TWENTY-FIVE
ABIGAIL

We didn't get home from the hospital until early afternoon. We were ushered into a curtained room as soon as we arrived—I sensed Jacob's influence there—and the police were both kind and patient.

Between a battery of tests to make sure we hadn't cracked our skulls or otherwise injured ourselves, and the procession of officers and detectives who wanted to talk to us, it was hours before we could leave.

Jacob stayed home long enough to share lunch before he disappeared with Cooper, reminding me not to leave the penthouse.

I understood that he wanted to get in on the action, and I knew him well enough to know all his instincts told him to lock me up tight where I was safe.

Honestly, I didn't want to be in on the action anyway, but being on my own gave me too much time to think.

After Jacob left, I took a shower. Unlike Jacob, I hadn't needed stitches. It was probably stupid to try to wash my hair.

The water and soap stung badly, bringing tears to my eyes, but I couldn't stand the dried blood caking my scalp any longer. I stood under the steamy spray, my mind blank, and let the hot water wash away the last twelve hours.

I was grateful Jacob had taken me to see my mother. She'd been so frail, as if she'd diminished in the weeks we'd been apart. She wasn't going to live much longer.

Maybe I should have felt some relief at that, both for her and for myself. I didn't. I couldn't. It was selfish, but I wanted her to stay with me longer, even if she didn't know me anymore. Even if she never opened her eyes again.

I pushed the thought away and got out of the shower, carefully squeezing water from my damp hair and wrapping myself in my fluffy cotton robe. My mother's fate was out of my hands, and what I wanted didn't matter. I had to think about my own fate.

Jacob had thrown our whole deal on its side, moving me into his bedroom, introducing me to his family, and taking care of me when I was sick. We hadn't agreed to any of that.

He'd told me he didn't want emotional complications, and maybe he was disciplined enough to do all those things with me and still feel nothing. I wasn't, not even close. If I took a minute to stop fooling myself, I'd admit I had feelings for Jacob.

A lot of feelings.

Too many feelings, not just love. I liked him. I enjoyed spending time with him, eating dinner with him, and seeing him when he came home from work every day.

Liking was bad enough. I wasn't supposed to like him. I was supposed to do my job—cook for him and be available for uncomplicated sex. That was it. Whether I liked him was irrelevant.

So how much worse was it that I was in love with him?

I hadn't wanted to fall in love. I'd known it was stupid, that it would only lead to heartbreak, and yet here I was, head over heels in love with Jacob Winters.

Normally, I don't like it when women play games—or men, for that matter. Game playing just made things more complicated. But in this case, our whole relationship had been a game, a business deal, really, but a business deal and a game weren't that different.

Emotional honesty had never been part of our agreement. In fact, the whole point of the agreement was to avoid emotions entirely, at least on Jacob's part.

I didn't know what he was playing at by moving me into his bedroom and introducing me to his family, but I did know it had to stop. I couldn't walk out on him. Not while I had my mother to worry about. But I could insist that he play by the rules he'd set up.

My stomach rolling with nausea at what I was about to do, I went to Jacob's closet and began to empty my side.

Clenching my teeth and ignoring the tears in my eyes, I walked back and forth, my arms filled with my clothes, until I'd erased all signs of my presence in the master suite.

Once that was done, and Jacob still wasn't home, I paced the penthouse, wondering what to do next. I knew there'd be a confrontation when he discovered I'd moved out of his room, and waiting for it was driving me crazy.

I ended up in his office, sitting behind his desk. It seemed it was my day for defying Jacob's wishes.

I wanted to see the picture again, and I couldn't very well ask him to show it to me. It hurt him too much to see it, and I wouldn't put him through that to appease my curiosity.

I tried his desk drawer and found it unlocked. He'd been distracted the last time he'd had the picture out and must've forgotten to secure it in his rush to leave his office and check on me.

I was pulling the envelope from the drawer when I saw it. An earring, a round, glowing pearl suspended from a diamond-encrusted ball.

My earring. I'd lost it at a charity ball over a year before. I'd looked everywhere for it, and its loss had led to a huge fight with John.

Why did Jacob have my earring?

If he'd found it, why hadn't he returned it? I set it on the desk and studied it. It was definitely my earring. It'd been custom-designed. There wasn't another like it.

I wanted to think it meant something, but I wasn't going there. I wasn't going to start spinning dreams based on an earring I'd found in his drawer.

I had too much at stake to risk any more of my heart than I already had. I couldn't help falling in love with Jacob, though I'd tried to stop myself. But that didn't mean I had to start having expectations. Hope.

I wasn't going to be that stupid. I placed the earring back in the drawer, nestling it between the pens where I'd found it. I was going to forget I'd ever seen it.

Resolved, I pulled the picture from the envelope and angled Jacob's desk lamp to throw light on the image, trying not to wince at the brutal scene it displayed. I'd originally thought it was a crime scene photograph, and it could've been. It's not like I'd seen a lot of those. Or any, ever.

But I would've expected a crime scene photograph to have some kind of date/time stamp. This picture had nothing like that. But it was definitely a photograph of the murder scene. So who had taken it? The press? Or the killer?

Gossip had called Jacob's aunt and uncle's death a

murder/suicide. The police had ruled it a double murder, but unable to find any clues after a year, the case had been put on the back burner.

As far as I knew, they'd never had any idea what had really happened. If it had been a murder/suicide, then this picture would have to have been taken by a private party at the murder scene, probably a member of the press.

If it had been the media who took the photograph, it would've been splashed all over the news, and though I'd been young, I was sure I'd never seen it before. Not then, and not when everything was stirred back up the year Jacob's parents had died.

If it wasn't the press, it had to have been the killer. Why would the killer send this photograph to Jacob? Was he in danger? And why Jacob? Why not one of James and Anna Winters' children—Tate, Vance, Annalise, or Gabe?

Too many questions, and I wasn't going to ask any of them. I wanted to know the answers, but I wasn't equipped to play amateur detective, and Cooper Sinclair and the police both had the picture. They'd taken fingerprints, they'd copied it, they'd studied it. They knew way more about the case than I did.

All I had was curiosity. Still, I examined every gruesome detail, looking for some hint as to why it had ended up in Jacob's apartment. It took me a while to spot what was off in the photograph. The tie on James Winters had been altered. It had been done so subtly, I'd almost missed it, but someone had colored it blue.

At the sound of the front door opening, I jumped in my seat, rolling it backward and almost tipping it over.

"Going to change, be right there," Jacob called out.

Panic crackling through me, I shoved the photograph back in the envelope, slid it into the drawer, and closed it.

The evidence safely hidden, I sat there frozen, waiting, knowing he was going to see the empty half of his closet when he went to change. He was going to be angry. Very angry.

It was one thing to exercise my defiance of his orders and move back into the guest room when he wasn't home. It was another to face the consequences of what I'd done.

I wasn't afraid he would hurt me. At least, not the way John would have. But this wasn't a playful error on my part, and I didn't think he would respond to this by spanking and making me come.

A few seconds later, Jacob appeared in the doorway of his office, still wearing his suit. Fixed on me, his silver eyes were hot and dangerous. In an even tone, heavy with expectation, he said, "Where are your clothes, Abigail?"

I drew in a breath and straightened my spine. I'd done the right thing when I'd moved out of his room, and I knew it, even if he didn't. "I moved back into the guest room," I said, fighting to keep my tone as steady as his.

"Why?" Jacob stepped into the room and leaned against the door frame, crossing his arms over his chest as if this were just a casual conversation. I wasn't fooled. I saw the bulge in his jaw muscle as he clenched his teeth.

"I don't belong in your bedroom, Jacob. You know it as well as I do. We have an arrangement."

"We do," he said, a hint of temper finally making its way into his voice. "And that arrangement is that you do what I say, and I told you to move into my bedroom."

"No, the arrangement was that I would be your pet, not your lover."

"What does it matter? Why do you have to make this so complicated?"

"I'm not the one making it complicated," I said, wiping

my sweaty palms on my cotton robe and wishing I'd taken the time to get dressed after my shower. With Jacob in a suit, and me in only a bathrobe, I felt defenseless and off-balance.

Jacob took a step into the room, his face softening as he said, "Is it so bad? Being here with me?"

"No, of course not," I said, shaking my head.

"Then why? Why do you have to stay in the guest room?"

"Because," I shot out, coming to my feet in exasperation.

Why did he not understand?

Again, I tried to explain. "I can't do this. We have an arrangement. I'm not your girlfriend. I'm your employee. I'm not here to play house. You're the one who set the limits. You don't do relationships, remember?"

"Is that what you want? You want a relationship? Why do we have to define everything? Why can't we just let it be?"

I shook my head, frustrated with him. Tears welled in my eyes, and I stared at the ceiling, blinking them back.

I was not going to cry.

Jacob always seemed to know what I was thinking. He probably knew I was in love with him. I wasn't going to cry and make myself even more pathetic.

"Do I really have to explain this to you?" I asked, wondering why he was making me spell it out. "I came to you because I needed help taking care of my mother. I still need your help. And as long as I do, as long as you're paying for her care, you're my boss. I can't pretend to have a real relationship with you. Don't you get it?"

Jacob threw his hands up in the air and let out a gust of breath.

"This is why I don't want a girlfriend. I will never

267

understand why women feel the need to overcomplicate every fucking thing. Your mother is taken care of, and we're enjoying each other's company. Why can't we just leave it at that?"

"I don't understand why you need to oversimplify everything," I shot back. "Sure, this is easy for you. You have all the power. You're the one keeping me safe, you're the one keeping my mother at Shaded Glenn. I'm completely dependent on your goodwill, and you can't see how that makes things complicated for me?"

Jacob re-crossed his arms over his chest and looked to the side, gritting his teeth, but saying nothing.

Unable to resist pushing harder, I said, "Why do you have my earring in your desk?"

Jacob shrugged, still not meeting my eyes. "I found it, a long time ago."

"A year ago," I clarified. "Did you know it was mine?"

Jacob nodded. "I did."

"Why didn't you give it back?" I pushed.

Jacob didn't answer at first. Finally, he said, "I don't know what you want from me."

"Neither do I," I said.

It was a lie.

I knew exactly what I wanted from Jacob. But he wasn't going to give it to me. I'd given him so many openings to tell me he had feelings for me, and he hadn't taken a single one.

I was vulnerable and dependent enough. I wasn't going to tell him how I felt. Anyway, he probably already knew. I was stuck for the moment, and the least I could do was protect myself.

Jacob met my eyes before he gave me a slow appraisal, taking in my loosely belted robe, his gaze lingering on the curve of my breast and my exposed legs before resting on my toes, then flicking away.

I saw heat there, and for a moment, I thought he was going to try to end our argument with sex.

Something inside me, some tiny bit of hope I hadn't realized I'd nurtured, shriveled at the thought.

If he did, if he wanted to fuck me, I wouldn't be able to say no. Saying 'no' wasn't part of our deal.

It had never been a problem before. I'd never wanted to say 'no' to Jacob.

Just then, raw and bruised from his rejection, I couldn't stand the idea of him touching me.

The thought that I'd have to let him do what he wanted, would have to fake it and pretend nothing had changed, turned my stomach and bruised my heart.

Maybe he saw something in my face, because his eyes cooled and he took a step back.

"I'm going back to work," he said. "I'll be late. Don't wait on me."

I flinched as the door slammed behind him.

CHAPTER TWENTY-SIX
JACOB

I nodded to the guards at the door and stalked back to the elevator. Rachel was still at her desk in my office. She looked up and hid her surprise at seeing me return so soon after I'd told her I was gone for the day.

I ignored her, and wisely, she did the same for me. I just barely stopped myself from slamming my office door. Instead, I closed and locked it behind me.

Helping myself to a glass of Macallan single malt from the bar in my office, a bottle reserved for guests, I shot back the first pour and refilled it, slamming the crystal decanter back on the bar.

I paced my office, glaring at everything in sight, especially the chair opposite my desk. The chair Abigail had sat in that first day she'd come to me for help.

What the fuck had I been thinking? It had seemed so simple at the start. I knew what I'd been thinking.

I'd wanted to fuck Abigail Jordan. She needed help, and I wanted to get her naked. It didn't get much more simple than that.

So how the fuck had it gotten so complicated? And

271

what was it about Abigail that turned me into such an asshole?

I'd been trying to ignore our situation from day one. Maybe if she hadn't so enthusiastically participated in everything I'd suggested, it would've been harder to pretend.

But it turned out that sweet, innocent, gracious Abigail Jordan had a kinky side. She loved everything, the spanking, the nipple clamps, eating dinner naked—everything I did with her, to her, she loved. So I fooled myself into thinking that made it all okay.

I didn't want to admit she was right. I'd been telling myself I could just order her to stay in my room and things would change between us naturally. But Abigail was right.

I had all the power, which meant that nothing between us could evolve naturally. I'd wanted to buy some time, time to figure out how to fix things. And, yeah, I won't deny it. I thought if I could talk her into bed, she'd forget she was so pissed at me.

At the flat, empty look in her eyes, I'd realized I was wrong.

Sex was not going to fix this.

Sex was the last thing we needed. Who would have thought I'd ever say that?

I'd stared at her, realizing she wore nothing more than a fluffy cotton bathrobe, and I'd watched her face go blank.

In that second, I knew. I understood exactly what she'd been trying to tell me.

As long as her mother was alive, as long as Big John and the Raptors were after her, she would never be mine.

She might give me her body, but I'd stolen her choice. I'd already figured out I wanted far more from Abigail than just her body.

I wanted her heart.

Her soul. I wanted everything that made Abigail, Abigail—her loyalty, her love, her affection. And I wouldn't get any of it unless I figured out a way to get both of us out of the mess I'd created.

I swallowed the rest of the whiskey, silently apologizing to the gods of alcohol for treating thirty-year-old single malt Macallan like cheap swill, before pouring myself a third and final glass and taking a seat behind my desk.

Picking up my phone, I said, "Rachel, put me through to Dave Price."

The receiver clicked twice before I heard ringing on the other end. If I knew Dave, he'd still be in the office. I didn't care what it cost. I'd give him whatever he wanted to draw up the papers I needed.

He couldn't help me solve all of my problems. A lawyer wouldn't help with Big John or the Raptors, but Dave was a start.

He picked up the phone, and I explained what I wanted. I hung up twenty minutes later, knowing at least one of the problems standing between Abigail and me was under control.

Sitting back in my chair, I surveyed my office and sipped the remainder of my scotch, trying to figure out what to do about Big John. I didn't think Abigail would leave Atlanta with her mother so weak.

That goddamned voice, the one I'd been running from since Abigail had walked into my office, the one that sounded suspiciously like my usually quiet conscience, piped up.

You could just tell her you're in love with her. That would fix everything, you fucking pussy.

I could. It wouldn't be a lie.

The more I ran from the idea, the more certain I was that this wasn't lust and it wasn't affection.

I was in love with Abigail.

Telling her should have been easy. But then, I was pretty sure she was in love with me, and she hadn't said a thing when we were fighting in my office.

Again, that fucking voice piped up—*That's because you have all the power. If someone's gonna say it, it has to be you.*

It occurred to me that if I manned up and told Abigail I was in love with her, maybe that fucking voice would shut up. I shook my head and took another sip of the scotch.

Easier said than done. I could count on one hand the women I'd said those words to, and I was related to every single one. I'd never said it to a girlfriend. I'd never had a reason to.

I looked at the stack of papers on my desk, evidence of the work I'd been ignoring over the past week.

I would deal with Abigail, and my unexpected feelings for her, later. I wasn't going home for dinner. I wasn't going home at all until I figured out what to say to her.

As it always did, work sucked me in. Rachel went home at least an hour after the rest of the office emptied. Dinner time passed, and I grabbed a sandwich from the fridge in my office, wishing Abigail had made it instead of the deli down the street.

No one cooked like Abigail. I ignored the impulse to go upstairs and beg her forgiveness, forcing myself to get back to work.

I'd caused enough trouble by being impulsive. I wasn't going to confront Abigail until I was sure I could win her over.

Seduction, I could handle. Baring my heart and soul to win the woman I loved?

I had no clue.

I might have stayed there all night, buried in work and avoiding home, if it hadn't been for the explosion.

At 9:13 pm, the building lurched with a violent surge of energy, and fire erupted in the street below.

It looked like I wouldn't have to figure out how to draw out Big John.

He was here, and he had a plan of his own.

CHAPTER TWENTY-SEVEN

ABIGAIL

J acob didn't come home for dinner. I didn't care. I didn't even bother to cook. I was heartsick and disgusted with both of us.

Jacob had behaved like an ass, but I should have expected that. He was used to getting his way. Why would he think I would be any different?

No, I was mostly disgusted with myself for debasing myself with this whole deal in the first place. I should have known it wouldn't end well. Never mind that I hadn't seen another way to take care of my mother.

Hadn't I also wanted Jacob?

I'd hoped, in the secret part of my heart, that I could keep my mother safe and have Jacob too. Stupid. I'd managed to keep my mother in Shaded Glenn, but I'd traded my body for security and lost my heart in the process.

All along, I'd told myself that falling for Jacob would make me the worst kind of fool, and here I was.

I ate a peanut butter sandwich for dinner, washing it down with a glass of milk. Nursery food, but it was comforting. I was still wearing my bathrobe. I hadn't been able to bring myself to do anything.

It was as if moving out of Jacob's bedroom had been my one big act of rebellion, and now that it was done and the confrontation was over, I didn't have the motivation to do anything else.

I'd never felt degraded by my deal with Jacob. I'd felt like I was getting away with something, sneaking a treat just for myself, and solving a problem at the same time.

Tonight, I hadn't been able to bear for Jacob to touch me. Knowing I loved him and he'd never return my feelings, but I'd still have to sleep with him, made me feel dirty for the first time. Sordid.

If I couldn't bring myself to touch Jacob, I'd have to leave. I couldn't live here if I wasn't capable of doing my job. And if I left, he might get angry enough to take it out on my mother.

My heart immediately rejected that thought. Jacob would never take his anger out on my mother. On me, definitely. But not on a sick woman. He could be an ass, but he wasn't a bad man.

I rinsed the crumbs from my plate and put it in the sink, along with my empty milk glass. I didn't want to go to sleep. It was barely evening.

Defeated, I curled up on the couch and turned on the television, settling for a random cooking show. Pulling my robe around my body, I stared blankly at the screen, blurred by the tears in my eyes.

I think I drifted off, but I'm not sure. All I know is that one minute, I was watching a baker artfully frost cupcakes to look like snow-capped mountains, and the next, the building shook so hard, the pictures on the shelves fell over.

I sat bolt upright, wildly looking around the empty

penthouse for a clue as to what was going on. I got nothing. Other than the shaking, everything seemed normal.

It wasn't an earthquake. We didn't have earthquakes in Atlanta.

Cautiously, worried the building might move again and knock me off my feet, I got off the couch and went to the window.

Smoke rose from the street level. My mobile rang in my robe pocket, startling me.

Jacob.

I answered, dreading the sound of his voice.

"Abigail. Are you okay?" He asked, sounding out of breath.

"I'm fine. What's going on? I see smoke."

"Get away from the windows," he snapped out. "There was an explosion in the street, and the retail level is on fire. It's contained for now. We're evacuating the lower levels, but I want you to stay where you are."

I got his meaning immediately. "The explosion was deliberate?" I asked.

"We think so. It's going to take me a few minutes to get to you. The stairwells are blocked off. You should be secure in the penthouse, but I want you to go to my office and hide in the closet. It's a safe room. Lock the door behind you and stay put until I get there to let you out."

"Are you okay?" I asked. Shouts and sirens sounded over the phone, the sirens echoing from the street outside.

"I'm fine. Get into the safe room now. Don't open the door for anyone but me. I'll be there soon."

The phone disconnected, and I stared at it for a second, trying to catch up. Lit by the moon and street lamps, the air outside the penthouse window was stained with clouds of dirty smoke.

I shoved the mobile in my pocket and turned for Jacob's office. Gunshots sounded on the other side of the penthouse door.

Pop. Pop. Pop.

Short and not as loud as I would have expected. A weight struck the door, the wood creaking as it hit.

I took off, running for Jacob's office, dodging around the coffee table and L-shaped couch, my eyes on the front door.

Another crash, and the door frame buckled, the wood around the deadbolt splintering. My foot caught on the leg of an armchair, and I went sprawling.

I should have been watching where I was going, but I couldn't take my eyes off the door. I scrambled to get to my feet, my legs tangling in my long robe, when the door slammed open, bouncing off the foyer wall.

A huge body filled the doorframe, blocking the light from the hallway.

My heart sank in dread.

They didn't call him Big John because he was the elder of the two John Jordans.

They called him Big John because he was huge.

At least six feet six inches tall and built like a line-backer. For a such a big man, he should have been slow. He wasn't.

I was just getting my feet back under me when he was there, his meaty fist swinging, catching me on the temple and knocking me back on my ass. My robe loosened, falling open around my legs as I sprawled on the carpet.

My stomach turned at the dark, hungry gleam in Big John's eyes.

"Look at the little whore, on her back with her legs spread. You re-thinking my offer, Abby?"

I desperately wished I'd bothered to get dressed earlier.

I didn't respond to his jibe.

Wrapping the robe around my middle, I wrenched the belt tight and tied it in a knot.

I didn't want him to hit me again—my head was pounding already, spots of light flickering at the edge of my vision—but I wasn't going to go quietly. Looking around from beneath my lashes, I eyed the door to Jacob's study.

So close, only fifteen feet, but it was on the other side of Big John.

"My son's dead, and you thought you could trade up? It doesn't work like that, you little slut. Once a Jordan, always a Jordan."

"You had John killed," I accused, slowly getting to my feet.

Getting Big John riled up was dangerous, but I needed to buy some time, and he wouldn't believe me if I pretended to cooperate. Not after all the trouble I'd gone through to escape him.

He shrugged and stepped closer.

"What if I did? The boy was dead weight. He was supposed to bring in business, but all he did was spend money."

"So you had your own son murdered?" I asked, edging to the side.

I was pinned between Big John and the armchair I'd tripped over. My shoulder nudged a narrow brass table lamp, almost knocking it over.

I spun to catch it, and Big John moved, closing the space between us in a second, grabbing my long hair in one big fist.

"I take care of business, Abby. You should know that by now. You thought you could sic the Sinclairs on me? Cause trouble with my shit? You don't know who you're fucking with, girl. John isn't here to protect you. Now it's your turn to pay up."

He used my hair as a leash, yanking me off my feet and dragging me across the room to the front door. It hung off its hinges, half-blocking the entrance. In the hall, I could see part of a black boot on the floor.

The guards were down.

Of course they were. Big John would never have gotten into the penthouse if the guards had been able to stop him. My heart sank. I hoped they weren't dead.

Alive or dead, it was clear they wouldn't be able to help me. I thrashed in Big John's hold, my scalp on fire, still gripping the lamp in one hand but unable to get the leverage to do anything with it. My heels thudded on the floor in an uneven drumbeat as Big John dragged me to the exit.

I screamed for help, gasping for air.

No one came.

I fought him with everything I had, but I was a butterfly batting its wings against a typhoon. I tried to flip over, only to be dragged on my knees.

I'd just about given up hope when the broken door split in half and fell to the floor, revealing a man larger than Big John, his eyes narrowed in rage.

The intruder was even bigger than Big John, looming in the doorway, his black clothes and hair turning him into a malevolent shadow against the elegant white foyer.

I caught a flash of apple green eyes through his shaggy, dark hair, an impression of bladed cheekbones and an unexpectedly lush mouth. I didn't have time to figure out what the new arrival meant for me.

Big John stopped moving so abruptly that the top of my head hit his foot. I managed to get to my knees, then my feet, yanking my hair from his loosened fist.

I stood, got my balance, and swung the lamp I still held at Big John's head.

The dense brass connected with his skull. Both of us staggered at the impact. The lamp fell from my fingers and I let it go, my only thought to get to Jacob's office. I ran, ignoring the shout of "Abigail!" behind me.

Jacob's office closet was in the far corner of the room, tucked behind his massive desk. I dove for the handle, not bothering to see if anyone was in pursuit. I couldn't afford to waste a second.

My fingers slid on the smooth metal handle before my grip tightened and I yanked it open. It swung toward me smoothly, but slowly.

If Jacob hadn't told me the closet was a safe room, the door would have tipped me off. It was too thick and heavy to be normal a closet door.

I threw myself inside and shoved the door shut behind me, my fingers feeling for the lock, the sound of my gasping breaths filling the small room.

My fingers closed on the bar of the lock, and I turned it as fists banged on the door, muffled and distant.

I sank to the floor in the pitch-black room, waiting for the pounding of my heart to slow. I didn't know where the light was or how long I'd be trapped in the safe room.

I didn't know what was going on in the penthouse, who the intruder was, or how he'd known my name. And I had no idea if the fire on the first floor was under control or if it was working its way up to threaten the penthouse.

I only knew that there was a thick door between me and Big John. And that Jacob would come for me.

No matter what was between us, I knew Jacob would come for me.

I just had to stay safe and wait.

CHAPTER TWENTY-EIGHT
JACOB

I should have expected Big John to make a move. I had expected it, just not this soon after the ambush at Shaded Glenn.

If the Sinclair team hadn't been covering the building, we might have had casualties from the car bomb in the street. As it was, there was plenty of property damage and a few minor injuries, but no deaths.

Not yet.

The second the building shook from the bomb, I wanted to go straight for Abigail. Our fight had been absurd, mostly because I was being an ass.

I loved her.

I knew she loved me.

All I had to do was tell her, and we could move past this bullshit. Instead, I'd played it safe and depended on our arrangement to keep her with me. The bomb shocked me back to my senses.

This was no game.

I loved Abigail, and Big John would stop at nothing to

take her from me. To destroy her. It was time for me to man up and stop being such a pussy.

I checked the window and saw the burning car and the people running in the street when my phone rang.

Cooper. I put him on speaker, my hands occupied with getting my gun from my desk drawer and shrugging into the shoulder holster. I had a license to carry concealed, but I almost never used it.

Pulling on my jacket, I said,

"Cooper. Report."

"You okay?" he asked.

"Fine. In my office. Abigail?"

"She's covered. I have men in the stairwell, men on the penthouse doors. No one is getting in. But we've got problems down here."

"Another bomb?" I asked, already moving for the door. I was the only one left in my office at that hour. At least Big John had picked a time when the building was mostly empty, except for the residents.

"Fire. We're not sure if it's from the explosion or a secondary source."

"I'm coming down," I said, taking the stairs three at a time. "Tate and Holden?"

"Both out at Manna with their women. We're evacuating the retail level and the residents. The sprinkler system is going off. Watch out for the water. Meet me out front."

I was almost to the first floor. As soon as I checked in with Cooper, I'd be up to watch over Abigail. If Big John had set off that bomb, he was here for her. Cooper's men were better protection than me, but I'd feel better if I were with her.

Until I could get to her, she should be in the safe room. I called her, relief spearing through my heart at the sound of her voice, concerned and confused but not frightened.

I filled her in on what I knew, told her to get into the safe room, and hung up. Talking to her just made the urge to go to her that much stronger.

But this was my building. I had to check on the evacuation and make sure the fire was under control before I went to Abigail.

Everyone here—the residents, the people stopping by for a coffee, anyone still working in the offices—were my responsibility.

Abigail had a whole security team watching over her. She was safe.

I knew she was safe, but my gut didn't believe it. I pushed open the door to the street to see Cooper pacing and barking into a phone, Griffen directing traffic, and police cars racing down the street. I was grateful for the officers' quick response, but I didn't want to talk to them. They'd try to keep me from going back in the building, and nothing was going to keep me from Abigail, not even the police.

Through the shattered front windows of the building, I could see the fire on the retail level. It wasn't raging out of control. That was something.

"Evacuation?" I asked. Cooper dropped the phone from his ear, but he didn't end the call. "We're double-checking the retail, but it looks like everyone got out in the first few minutes. We've been bringing them out the back exit, away from this."

He gestured around him at the shards of glass in the street and the burned-out shell of the car that had exploded. "I've got men clearing the office and residential levels. We've been tracking everyone who goes in and out, and we're clearing them as they evacuate."

"So we're good? I want to get upstairs."

Cooper gave a short nod. "The fire was more smoke than anything else. The flames aren't spreading. The evacuation is mostly a precaution, but—"

Cooper's hand shot to his ear, pressing an almost invisible earpiece as he said, "Say again?"

"What?" I demanded. "What's going on?"

"There's no response from the two guys I have in the stairwell on the east side of the building."

I took off at a run, not waiting for him to finish. Cooper's guys were closer to the east stairwell then I was, but I wasn't heading to the east stairwell. I was going straight for Abigail.

The elevator would have been fastest, but it would have been shut down when the sprinkler system went off, and I didn't have the time to bypass the system.

I pounded up the stairs, cursing myself for living on the top floor. Too many flights of stairs, too far away. I was in good shape, and I was fast, but not fast enough.

The top of the stairwell stretched above me, further away with every step, a funhouse tunnel of railings and endless stairs mocking me as I climbed faster and faster.

I should have passed people evacuating the building or Cooper's security. The floors went by in a blur, all of them ominously vacant. My lungs heaved for air by the time I got to the penthouse level.

I cracked the stairwell door and risked a quick look. In the narrow gap, I couldn't see everything, but the bodies on the floor and the streaks of red staining the carpet told me I shouldn't expect any help from the security team.

Fuck.

Movement at the door caught my attention. Someone was there, watching but not moving. For a second, I thought it was Big John until I realized this man had black hair and he was bigger than the elder John Jordan.

Bigger than Big John. That was a terrifying thought.

Over his black leather jacket, he wore a biker's kutte covered with patches, in its center, the image of a hawk poised for attack, its exaggerated claws dripping blood.

A Raptor's kutte. That meant his size was the least terrifying thing about him. Before I could figure out a plan, Abigail's scream for help sliced through the silence, spurring both of us into motion.

The Raptor, already at the door, beat me through. A thud, then someone shouting, "Abigail!"

I pushed through my ruined front door just in time to see Abigail disappear into the safe room. Big John lunged for the door, but she must have turned the lock because his meaty fists pounded uselessly on the thick barrier.

I drew my gun and pointed it at Big John, ready to swing it to the Raptor if he made a move for the safe room.

The Raptor drew his own gun and leveled it at Big John, ignoring me. Big John turned, bracing his back against the safe room door as if protecting his prize, and stared at the Raptor with a look he probably thought was defiant.

He didn't look defiant. He looked scared.

Shit.

The Raptor wasn't just bigger than Big John Jordan. He scared the hell out of him. Not good.

Whatever happened, they weren't getting Abigail.

"What are you doing here, Lucas?" Big John asked, his voice thready with nerves. "I've got this under control."

"Yeah, I can see that," the Raptor, Lucas, said, his voice holding a note of amusement. "Winters, for your own good, I hope that gun is trained on Jordan."

"It is," I said. "For now."

"Good. But don't shoot him. Big John is mine." He hadn't taken his eyes off his prey, but I could tell he was talking to Big John when he said, "I've been waiting for this for a long time."

"Don't!" Big John shouted. "Take out Winters, and we can get Abigail. We'll make our deal, and everything will go the way we planned."

Lucas laughed, a chilling sound that was distinctly unamused.

"I don't want Abigail. I only asked for her to get her away from you. She's better off with Winters. You fucking think you know everything, Jordan, but you're a fucking moron. You still don't know who I am, do you?"

"What?" John spluttered, his face paling. He leaned against the safe room door, more in need of support than as a mark of possession. "What are you talking about? You're Lucas Jackson."

"Remember your son? The job that took him out? You sent your assassin after two men that night. Who were they?" The Raptor's voice was low and deadly.

"I gave you everything," John protested. "If I hadn't had Gunner killed, you wouldn't be leading the club now."

His entire body a rock, Lucas didn't move except to squeeze his trigger finger. Big John screamed and fell to the floor, blood pouring from his leg.

"I never wanted the fucking club. I was only there for Gunner. Gunner Jackson. My brother. I took over the club to help them take you down. Killing you is just the beginning. We're going to dismantle your entire organization until what's left of your family has nothing."

"No, please, Lucas. I didn't know. He didn't go by Jackson. I didn't know he was your brother." Big John blubbered, but as far as I could tell, it had no effect on Lucas.

"Like it would make a difference. Gunner was in your way, so you killed him. You killed your own son the same night, you twisted fuck. The thing is, family means nothing to you, but it means something to me. My brother was a criminal, but he was family."

My head spun. All this time, I'd seen the Raptors as an equal threat to Abigail, but if Lucas was telling the truth, he wasn't my enemy. He claimed he'd been protecting Abigail.

I wasn't ready to believe it was going to be that easy.

Big John tried to get to his feet, slipping in his own blood, his injured leg unable to hold his weight. He aimed his weapon at Lucas and pulled the trigger, the shot going wild as he slid to the side, his knee buckling beneath him.

Lucas, apparently done with his revenge scene, shot three times in rapid succession. The first opened a neat hole in Big John's wide forehead. In case that wasn't enough, the next two drilled the left side of his chest.

Big John slumped to the side, his gun falling from his hand.

That quickly, it was over.

Lucas Jackson turned to me, shoving his own gun in a holster at the small of his back. I lowered mine, but didn't put it away.

I wasn't ready to trust the President of the Raptors.

Not yet.

"Keep that pointed at the floor, and we won't have any trouble," Lucas said, turning his back on Big John's body.

"You were playing Big John this whole time?" I asked.

Lucas lifted a shoulder in a half-shrug.

"Gunner wanted to get in bed with him. That part was real. After he died, we voted to use the deal to take him down."

"So why bring Abigail into it?" I asked. "You made her a target."

Lucas let out a bark of laughter, both bitter and amused. "I fucking kept her alive. As soon as Big John figured out she wouldn't whore for him, he was going to get rid of her."

"Why did you care?"

I had to know what his interest in Abigail was. Now that we had Big John out of the way, I needed to know if anyone else was coming after her.

Lucas shook his head. "Relax, Winters. Your woman isn't my type. She's gorgeous, but the last thing I need is a society girl."

"Then why put yourself out there to save her?" I asked, a little relieved that Lucas wasn't going to make a play for Abigail.

She loved *me*, not this oversized biker, but his ease with killing Big John, and his obvious size, meant I'd have a fight on my hands if he decided she was going with him.

He sighed, as if he'd hoped to avoid explaining. "She was nice to me, okay? Big John had us over a few weeks after it all went down, and he made her play hostess. It was obvious she didn't belong there. I knew her husband was dead, and she was terrified—of Big John, of a rowdy group of bikers in her home. But she treated us like honored guests. She was gracious. Like a flower in the midst of a cesspool."

Lucas looked away, embarrassed at his poetic turn of phrase.

"She deserved better than to be stuck at Big John's mercy. I looked into her and didn't like what I found out. We decided to make her part of the deal after Big John said he was done with her."

"So what happens now?" I asked, looking at Big John's

body on my office floor, his blood staining the handwoven rug.

"I'm heading out," Lucas said, turning for the door. "When the cops make their way up here, tell Detective Ryan Brennan what happened. He knows where to find me for any follow-up."

I watched Lucas leave and pulled my phone out of my pocket. Voices filtered in from the hall, but I wanted to check on Abigail before anyone else showed up.

The safe room was almost impenetrable, but I'd made sure a phone could get a signal. I didn't want to be stuck in there, safe but with no way to communicate.

"Jacob?" Abigail said, her voice low and hesitant.

"It's me. Are you okay? Did he hurt you?"

"No, I'm fine. I'm in the safe room."

"I know. I got here just as you locked yourself in. Big John is dead, but I want you to stay in there until we confirm the building is clear." A long silence. "Abigail? Say something."

"Big John is dead?"

"He is. I promise." Cooper entered through the smashed doorframe, several policemen and a man in a brown blazer trailing behind him. "I have to go for a few minutes, sweetheart. I'll call you back as soon as it's safe."

"Okay. But first, can you tell me where the light switch is? It's too dark in here."

Too dark would be an understatement. Had she been sitting in there in the pitch black this whole time? The switch was hard to find, a design flaw, but I'd created the tiny room just for me, and I knew where it was, so I'd never bothered to fix it.

"Reach into the shelves to the left of the door. Behind the boxes." Shuffling sounds, then a click. "Got it?"

"I got it."

"Good girl. I'll call you back as soon as it's safe to come out."

I hung up and turned to face Cooper, ready to get the details out of the way so I could set Abigail free.

CHAPTER
TWENTY-NINE
ABIGAIL

I'm sure Jacob didn't leave me in the closet for too long, but it felt like hours. I could hear sounds through the thick door, muffled voices and footsteps, but nothing I could decipher clearly.

Finally, he called me back and told me it was safe to come out. I unlocked the heavy door and swung it open to find Jacob standing right in front of me.

"Close your eyes," he said, scooping me into his arms and swinging me away from the safe room door. I obeyed, but not fast enough to avoid the sight of Big John's dead body, blood soaking his shirt, a neat bullet hole in the center of his forehead.

Not sure what else there was to see, I squeezed my eyes shut and let Jacob carry me away from the carnage.

He set me down on my feet in the guest bedroom and pulled me into his arms, holding me tightly, his cheek resting on top of my head.

"I thought I'd lost you," Jacob whispered. "I saw the guards and thought he had you."

I waited for him to step back and let go, but he kept me

there, tucked into his solid body, until a fist pounded on the door of the room.

"Winters, we need to get her statement."

Jacob raised his head and said, "In a minute."

He took my face in his hands, his mouth hard as he took in the swelling on my temple where Big John had hit me. I wasn't sure if it was lucky or not that he'd struck me opposite where I'd slammed my head into the van. Now both sides of my head ached, but at least I wasn't bleeding.

"We need to get ice on this," he said. "Did he hit you?"

I nodded. "I'm okay," I said. "Really."

Jacob made a sound in his throat that reminded me of a growl and tilted my face up to his, his silver eyes gleaming with an emotion I was afraid to read.

"Abigail," he whispered, and lowered his mouth to mine. He kissed me, nipping and sucking at my lower lip until I melted into him, opening my mouth and tasting him, pouring all my fear and hope into our kiss.

I was lost, and all I could do was sink my fingers into his shoulders and hold on.

Voices filtered in from the hall, and Jacob pulled back.

"The police need you to tell them what happened. After that, we're going to go stay with Aiden for a few days while they get this mess cleaned up. But first, you can change out of that robe and pack a bag."

I nodded, too overwhelmed to speak. I had questions—a long list of questions—but I couldn't seem to make my voice work.

Instead, I went to my closet and chose a pair of jeans and a loosely woven knit shirt. I wasn't normally a jeans kind of girl, but after the past few hours, I wanted something comfortable, fashion be damned.

I tugged on underwear, the jeans, and a camisole for

under the knit shirt before I found a bag in the bottom of the closet and hastily threw together a few days' worth of outfits.

Taking the bag to the bathroom, I pulled a brush through my tangled hair and packed my toiletries. The whole time, Jacob stood by the door, arms crossed over his chest as if to ensure no one interrupted us.

I was as ready for the police as I'd ever be. Holding an ice pack someone had brought me to the side of my head, I sat in the armchair in the corner of the room, Jacob beside me, and told the officer everything I remembered after Big John broke into the penthouse.

A man in a brown blazer, who introduced himself as Detective Ryan Brennan, asked me a few follow-up questions before they both left, warning us they'd be in touch.

"Are we in trouble?" I asked Jacob after they'd gone. He shook his head.

"No, sweetheart. I didn't kill Big John."

"Then who?" I remembered the dark-haired intruder. "Someone came in right before I made it to the closet."

"Lucas Jackson. President of the Raptors."

"Oh. He killed Big John? Why?"

Jacob took the overnight bag from the bed, where I'd left it, and wrapped his arm around my shoulders, steering me down the hall and angling me toward the front door so I couldn't see into the office. His gym bag, stuffed full, sat by the ruined front door.

He stopped short and turned to me.

"Close your eyes, Abigail." I opened my mouth to speak, and he shook his head. "Please. I'll tell you anything you want to know, but it's a mess out there, and I don't want you to see it. Humor me and just close your eyes. I'll lead you out."

I closed my eyes, letting him guide me across the hall to the elevator. There were a lot of things I wanted to argue about, but if Jacob didn't want me to see the hallway, I wouldn't fight him.

Common sense told me that nothing good had happened to the guards on my door. Not if Big John had managed to break into the penthouse.

"The fire?" I asked as we descended to the garage.

"Mostly smoke damage. Only minor injuries."

"And the Sinclair team?"

Jacob didn't answer, just let out a breath, his arm tightening around me. Finally, he said, "One down. Three guys are in the hospital, one in critical condition. No one you know."

I felt sick at the idea that men had died and been injured because of my mess. I knew Big John had done the damage, not me, but they wouldn't have been anywhere near him if I hadn't gone to Jacob.

I fell silent as we got in the car and drove north to the Winters estate in Buckhead. I'd never been there before, but I'd heard about it. This late at night, it was a quick ride from Jacob's building.

He stopped the car in front of black iron gates that remained shut until he reached above his head to the visor and pressed a button on what looked like a garage door opener.

The gates swung open smoothly, closing as soon as we cleared the entrance. I couldn't see much of the grounds in the dark, but the driveway wound up to the house, lined with live oaks arching over the road, every other tree lit with strategically placed spotlights.

We reached a second gate, this one also black iron, but more delicate, blocking the entrance to a porte cochere.

Jacob hit another button on the remote on his visor, and this gate opened as well. We drove through the porte cochere into a square courtyard with a lit fountain at the center.

Looking around, I realized that the Mediterranean style house surrounded the courtyard on all four sides.

The largest section, with a huge carved wooden double-door, was two full stories, while the other sides of the square were only one, wrapping around the courtyard with covered galleries, tall windows, and French doors.

I'd guessed that the Winters estate would be big, but this was beyond my expectations, and I'd been raised around the wealthy of Atlanta. I couldn't begin to guess at the square footage. I'd seen hotels that were smaller.

I was a little awed as Jacob parked the car and came around to let me out. "I'll get our bags and move the car later," he said.

I looked up to see his brother, Aiden, standing in the entrance to the house, his height dwarfed by the tall double doors.

"Don't worry about it," Aiden said. "Your rooms are ready for you, and there's a tray of sandwiches and tea. Just settle in and relax. We can talk in the morning." To me, he said, "I'm glad to see you're well, Abigail."

My manners kicked in, and I said, "Thank you for having me." Aiden smiled, stepping back to hold the heavy door open for us.

"This will always be Jacob's home, even if he doesn't live here."

"See you tomorrow," Jacob said to his brother, whisking me out of the main entry and down a high-ceilinged hallway.

We turned a corner, and he stopped before a set of

carved wooden doors that mimicked the front doors, but smaller in scale. Opening the doors, he ushered me into a sitting room that reminded me of his penthouse.

Elegant but comfortable, with creamy walls and dark woodwork, the sitting room had a small desk, a huge flat screen on the wall, a gas fireplace, and a deep leather couch that made me want to curl up with a book.

Off to one side, an open door revealed a bedroom, the crisp white sheets on the bed already turned down.

Spotting the tray of food on the desk, I said, "Do you want something to eat? I don't know if you got dinner—" I babbled, suddenly nervous to face Jacob after our argument earlier.

"Abigail," Jacob interrupted, taking my hand and leading me to the couch. "I have some things I need to say, and I want you to let me talk before you tell me what's on your mind."

I nodded, bracing myself for what might be coming. I tried to take a deep breath to settle my nerves, my lungs tight.

Accusations from our ugly fight pinged through my head. So much had been wrong between us. I waited for Jacob to say something.

He shifted on the couch and took a deep breath of his own. Was Jacob nervous? What did Jacob have to be nervous about?

"Abigail," he said, and stopped. When he opened his mouth again, words poured out, spilling over each other. "I created a trust for your mother. For her care. It's irrevocable, and it pays for medical and living expenses for the rest of her life."

I stared at him, too tired and anxious to keep up. "I don't understand. A trust?"

"No matter what happens between us, you never have to worry about your mother again. If you decide to walk out the door, whatever you want, she's taken care of."

"Why?" I asked, both terrified and thrilled at the gesture. "Why would you do that?"

He was talking about a lot of money. A lot. So much that trying to cover the expense had nearly destroyed my life.

"Abigail," he said again, looking uncomfortable, his eyes moving around the room before coming back to meet mine.

Leaning forward, he took my hands in his and said, "I love you. I did it because I love you. And I want you with me because you love me too, not because you need to take care of your mother."

My fingers tightened on his in reflex as I tried to understand what he was saying.

He loved me?

"You love me?" I whispered, afraid to give voice to the words.

"I love you," he said, his lips inches from mine.

"Oh," I said stupidly.

Love, I hadn't expected.

Not from Jacob.

"Abigail?"

"Hmm?" I said, still trying to take it all in.

"This is the part where you tell me you love me, too," Jacob said, his silver eyes glinting with amusement and a shade of nerves.

"I do," I said, the words a breathy rush.

I blushed a fiery red at my words. He was telling me he loved me. We weren't getting married. One thing at a time.

"I love you," I said. "I've loved you since the beginning. I think I started falling for you before—"

301

I stopped, unable to admit I'd had feelings for Jacob while I was still married to John.

"Will you stay with me?" Jacob asked. "Move into the penthouse with me? Forget about the deal we made and just be with me because you want to?"

"Yes. Yes, Jacob."

Jacob leaned forward and kissed me, his mouth claiming mine in a thorough, endless kiss. I wound my arms around his neck, dizzy with joy and the need to touch him.

Jacob Winters loved me.

I'd known for a while that I was in love with him, but I hadn't dared to imagine he'd ever love me back. Not after the way we'd begun, with me trading my body for his protection.

His hands slid under my camisole, pushing the material up and over my breasts slowly, baring me to his hot silver eyes.

"Abigail," he murmured, lowering his head to take one hard nipple in his mouth. I arched into him, wondering if he'd thought to pack any of our toys. I'd find out later.

Too impatient to wait, I unsnapped my jeans and shimmied them off, leaving me naked. If Jacob didn't get the hint and strip his own clothes off, I'd do it for him.

Now that I didn't have to be afraid, I wanted nothing between us.

He rubbed his cheek into the side of my breast. "I love you, Abigail. I'm sorry I couldn't say it sooner. But I love you. I loved you when I made this stupid deal with you. I just didn't know it yet."

He stood, lifting me off the couch and carrying me to the king-sized bed in the other room. I lay on top of the covers, naked, waiting for him to join me and getting more aroused by the second. I loved watching Jacob get undressed.

He shed his civility one layer at a time until all that remained was a hungry man who wanted to fuck me. His fingers unraveled his tie and his eyes burned. He was going slow just to tease me.

If he didn't get a move on, I'd show him some teasing.

A knock sounded on the door.

"Fuck," Jacob said, pulling his tie free and tossing it on a nearby chair. "Don't move. I'll be right back."

He drew the covers over my naked body before leaving the room. Tucked so sweetly into the bed, I rolled on my side, hoping Jacob wouldn't be long. I heard him open the door, the murmur of voices, then nothing at all.

I woke sometime in the middle of the night to feel Jacob's body wrapped around mine, keeping me safe and protected, even in sleep. He loved me. Tears flooded my eyes as I replayed his confession the night before.

He *loved* me.

The best I'd hoped for was affection. Maybe to continue our affair once Big John was out of the picture. I hadn't dared to expect love. There would be people who would think I was reaching too high.

I'd heard what William Davis had called me. *Tainted.*

Jacob had been pissed, but in a way, William was right. According to the rules of the society we knew, I *was* tainted. If Jacob didn't care, neither would I.

I would ignore the people who gossiped and make my own place in our world. Not as my parents' daughter, John's widow, or Jacob's love.

I'd make a place for myself as Abigail, and anyone who didn't like it could go to hell. With Jacob at my side, making something of the fragments of my life wasn't a scary thought.

We loved each other. We could do anything.

With that in mind, I rolled over, pushing Jacob to his back. I'd fallen asleep before we could get to the good part. My head was still tender, but it no longer ached.

I rose onto my elbows and studied Jacob's naked body— the cut lines of his chest, his ridged abdomen, his narrow hips. Even in sleep, his cock was half-hard. Maybe it sensed what I was up to.

Sliding down on the mattress, I rested my cheek on Jacob's hip, my lips an inch from the head of his swelling cock.

I flicked out my tongue and tasted him, loving the musky, salty flavor that was all Jacob. I never imagined I'd love a man's cock, but Jacob's was all mine.

Wiggling closer, I dropped my mouth over his length, his cock fully hard after my experimental lick. I nudged his legs apart, moving between them and taking him into my throat, my hands roaming, stroking every inch of skin I could reach while I sucked his cock with everything I had.

"Abigail. Sweetheart," Jacob moaned, his fingers threading through my hair. "Fuck, baby."

His hips bumped up, not hard enough to interrupt my rhythm, just enough to tell me he wasn't entirely in control. I sucked harder, drawing my lips up his length from base to tip, twisting as I went, until he let out a low moan.

I'd had a lot of time to learn what drove Jacob crazy, and I was using it all, loving the sounds he made as he moved beneath me.

It was all over a second later. Jacob jackknifed up and flipped us both, laying me out on the sheets and coming over me, his silver eyes gleaming with heat in the dark room.

Gripping my leg behind my knee, he pushed back, opening me wide, and fucked his cock into me, filling me in one long thrust. I came in an explosion of light on his second thrust, my body trembling, my fingers locked on his shoulders.

He slowed as my orgasm waned, then started thrusting again, slowly, building me up again until I teetered in the edge.

"I love you, Abigail. More than anything. Always and forever. I love you."

I parted my lips to tell him I loved him too, and he kissed me, his tongue tangling with mine, his mouth branding me as his.

I fell into bliss, my body and heart holding Jacob close, far too in love to ever let him go.

Epilogue

Abigail

One Month Later

Life went back to normal a few days after Big John's attack at the penthouse. Well, it didn't go *back* to normal. Rather, Jacob and I made a *new* normal.

With Big John out of the picture, I was free to visit my mother again. I was spending most of my days at Shaded Glenn, sitting by her bedside. She rarely woke, and when she did, she didn't know who I was.

The end was coming. I knew it, but at least I'd be with her.

I usually got home in time to make dinner, or like today, I cooked ahead of time. It had been a long day, but dinner was warming in the oven and I was curled up on the couch with a mug of tea, waiting for Jacob to pry himself free of the office.

He worked late more often than not. I imagined once I finished school and got a job of my own, I'd have a few late nights myself. While I waited, I flipped through the course atlas for the upcoming semester.

Without asking me, Jacob had put in an application to Emory and begun the process of having my credits transferred.

High-handed, but I was used to that. Since I'd love to go to Emory and wasn't sure I had the grades to get accepted on my own, I wasn't going to argue. I had a position waiting for me as an intern in the Winters Foundation, so I could get the job experience I needed while I finished school.

My start date was still undetermined. The way things were going with my mother, I didn't want to get invested in school and work. I wasn't sure how much time we had left, but I knew it wasn't much.

The door to the penthouse opened and I got to my feet, carrying my tea with me to the foyer. Jacob dropped his gym bag on the floor—he'd played racquetball with Vance that morning—and came toward me, his lips curled in a smile.

"Good day?" he asked, pulling me in for a kiss. I held my tea away from him so I didn't dump it on his suit and leaned into his kiss, breathing deeply of his familiar scent.

The after work kiss was one of my favorite parts of being with Jacob. No matter how late he worked, I always got a kiss as soon as he walked in the door.

"Long day, but good," I answered. "You?"

Jacob took my tea and set it on the table in the foyer before backing me down the hall to the bedroom. "Good enough. Vance cancelled on racquetball, so I didn't get a workout in."

"That's too bad," I said, laughing into his lips as he dropped another kiss on my mouth. He crowded me though the bedroom door, stripping off his suit as he walked.

"You know, I don't like to miss a workout," he said, pushing his suit pants to the floor, his hard cock bouncing free, jutting aggressively in my direction.

"I know," I said, my hands going to the zipper on my dress. All innocence, I asked, "Did you want me to work out with you?"

"That's the idea," he growled, tossing me on the bed the second my dress pooled around my ankles. He was on me a heartbeat later, raising my arms to the discrete leather loops in the bed frame.

"Hold on," he ordered. I did, gripping the leather hard as he pressed my thighs apart and swiped his tongue over my pussy. Sometimes, Jacob took the time to buckle me into the restraints, but other nights, like tonight, he was too impatient to bother.

He knew he didn't have to strap me down. I had no problem following orders in bed. Not when they came from Jacob.

I was already coming when he lined up his cock and sank inside me. Pulling on the leather restraints, I lifted my hips and wound my legs around Jacob, fucking him back as he filled me over and over. It didn't take long before orgasm took us both.

Jacob rolled to the side, idly stroking his fingers over my breasts while I lay sated, loosely holding the leather loops.

"Are you hungry?" I asked, my own stomach threatening to growl.

"Not anymore," Jacob said, pressing a kiss to the side of my breast.

"For food."

"Oh, food. I could eat. What are we having?"

Reluctantly, I let go of the restraints and rolled from the bed. After a quick stop in the bathroom to clean up, I headed for the kitchen, Jacob following behind.

"I made a polenta casserole with sausage and mushrooms. Rachel gave me the recipe."

"Sounds good." Jacob got the plates, and I dished out the meal, carrying it to the table while he poured us wine.

Tonight, I was eating in my robe, as I often did. This wasn't the first time Jacob's after-work kiss had ended up in the bedroom. Some nights, I still ate naked, decked out in the entire set of erotic jewelry he'd bought me.

More than a few times, I'd cooked wearing nothing but my apron. Those nights, I made sure I picked a recipe that didn't need much attention.

We didn't talk about anything of importance over dinner. Life was wonderfully quiet for the moment. Nothing more had come from the mysterious picture of his aunt and uncle's murders.

I'd eventually told Jacob about the tie, but as I'd suspected, the Sinclairs had already found it, and no one knew what it meant.

They'd all agreed to ignore it and hope it was a one-time thing. I didn't think they had much choice, with no more clues to go on.

The Jordans were no longer a problem. Lucas Jackson had steered clear of us, but Cooper kept us updated on his activities.

He'd led the Raptors into a full-scale attack on Big John's criminal empire, stripping the remaining Jordans of product and associates until there was nothing left, just as Lucas had promised.

To everyone's shock, once the Jordans were destroyed, he'd handed the Raptors over to his Vice President and dropped out of sight.

I didn't want to get mixed up with a biker club, especially not the Raptors, but I wished I'd had a chance to thank him. If Lucas Jackson hadn't been looking out for me, I might never have made it to Jacob in the first place.

Maybe someday, he'd turn up again. For now, I wasn't looking for trouble. I was happy with the quiet life as long as I could spend it with Jacob.

After dinner, we went into the living room to watch a game on the TV. I wasn't interested in the game. Sports weren't really my thing, but I didn't feel like reading, so I lay draped across Jacob, my head on his chest, drawing random designs on his t-shirt with my fingertip.

His phone, lying on the cushion beside us, beeped with a text. Holden.

You talked to Vance today? He's not answering his phone.

Jacob read the text and typed something back, then held the phone to his ear, stroking a hand over my hair as he waited for an answer.

He must have been denied, because he looked at the phone, tapped it again, and put it back to his ear. The third time, I heard a click followed by Vance's voice, sounding out of breath and irritated.

"This had better be an emergency."

"Holden's trying to get you. Why aren't you answering your phone?" Jacob demanded, "Where are you?"

"I'm at home," Vance said. "And I can't talk right now, okay?" The loud, squalling cry of an infant cut through his words, so loudly I could hear it clearly, despite my distance from the phone.

"Is that a baby?" Jacob asked, sounding incredulous and amused. "Why is there a baby in your house?"

"It's a long story," Vance said, sounding tired. "I have to go. I'll call you tomorrow."

"Vance—" Jacob didn't get a chance to finish whatever he was going to say.

A woman's voice interrupted, yelling, "Vance Winters,

you put down that phone and get that bottle over here right now, or so help me, I will *end* you. Do you hear me?" She sounded frazzled and furious.

"Is that Magnolia?" Jacob asked, not bothering to hide his laughter.

"Yes, and she really will kill me if I don't get off the phone. I can't afford to piss her off right now. I need her help. I'll call you tomorrow."

We could hear him yelling something back at his assistant before the phone cut off.

"Now I really want to go over there and see what's going on," Jacob said, still laughing, and tapped out a text on his phone.

"What's Vance doing with a baby?" I asked. "Is it Magnolia's? A relative?"

"I have no idea, sweetheart, but I'm going to find out."

"Tomorrow," I said, taking Jacob's phone and tossing it on the coffee table. "I don't think he can handle an invasion of family right now."

"Tomorrow," Jacob agreed. "I have better things to do tonight than bug my cousin."

"Better things?" I asked, raising an eyebrow. "Like what?"

"Like you, sweetheart. Always you."

He clicked off the game and rolled over on the couch, pinning me down with his long body. Then he proceeded to show me exactly where I ranked on his list of priorities.

At the very top.

Just as he'd promised, he showed me how much he loved me. More than anything, always and forever.

Keep reading for a sneak peek of Vance & Magnolia's story, The Billionaire's Promise.

SNEAK PEEK
THE BILLIONAIRE'S PROMISE

CHAPTER ONE: MAGNOLIA

T-MINUS 2 YEARS

I couldn't breathe.

He opened the door and my breath was sucked from my lungs in one big whoosh.

If you'd been there, you'd understand. One second I was standing in the hallway, waiting impatiently to be interviewed for a job I wasn't sure I wanted.

The next second, the door was swinging open, and he was there, filling the door frame, six and a half feet of panty-melting hotness.

A towel slung loosely around his waist, barely clinging to his lean hips, drops of water sliding down his broad, defined chest, he leaned against the door and looked down at me, his eyes scanning me from head to toe.

Was it too late to run?

There was no way I could work for this man.

Vance Winters. Heir to billions, renown artist at the young age of twenty-eight, and secret angel investor in up and coming tech companies. All of that was intimidating enough.

I hadn't taken into account the impact he would have in person. I'd seen pictures, in the society section of the paper, in glossy magazines. They didn't scratch the surface.

First, he was tall. I'm right in the middle, neither tall nor short, and he towered over me, all of him sculpted muscle and smooth golden skin decorated with elaborate inky black tattoos.

From the way the towel dipped across his abs, showing every inch of the cut V of muscle between his hips, as well as a stark tan line, I knew the golden skin came from the sun. He must spend a lot of time outdoors.

I tried not to imagine him jogging without his shirt. Or swimming, that too-long, dark blond hair pulled back, powerful legs propelling him through the water. I definitely didn't imagine tugging on the towel to get a better look at the white skin below the tan.

Absolutely not.

I blinked hard. What was wrong with me? I had a boyfriend. He was a good guy, a med student, and we'd been together for years. He wasn't in Vance's league, but he was very attractive. Brayden. I had to think of Brayden.

I was quiet, but not easily intimidated. Not usually. There was something about the way Vance lounged in the door, his blue eyes lazily hooded as they studied me. He threw me off balance. Then he grinned and said, "Are you coming in?"

My knees went weak.

That grin. Holy crap.

With his blond hair, vivid blue eyes, and all those

314

golden muscles, he reminded me of a Viking. A debauched Viking with a killer grin.

I don't know where it came from, but in a crisp, cool voice I said, "I don't know. Are you going to get out of the way?"

Another grin, and a wink. Vance Winters was trouble.

Fighting the weakness in my knees, I straightened my spine and followed him into his loft, ready to get this over with.

"Can you make coffee?" he asked, gesturing to his ultra-modern kitchen. "Consider it part of your interview."

Again not sure where the attitude was coming from, I said, "Are you planning on getting dressed?"

He looked down at his lack of attire and shrugged. "Do you want me to?"

His tone suggested I'd be crazy to cover up all that gorgeous. He was right. Telling Vance Winters to put on clothes was a crime against nature. A man with a body like that should be naked all the time.

But I was there for a job interview. I wasn't looking to get laid. Brayden. I had Brayden. I wasn't into casual hookups anyway, even if I were single.

Vance Winters was known for many things and sleeping his way through Atlanta was one of them.

"Please," I said, as cool and professionally detached as I could manage.

Not waiting for his response, I turned to the kitchen to start a pot of coffee. I heard him leave and let out a breath I hadn't known I'd been holding.

What was I doing here? I didn't need the job. Well, I did, and I didn't. I had money. My grandmother had left me well provided for. I wasn't wealthy, not like the Winters family, but I had a beautiful home - my grandmother's - and enough money to live on if I was careful.

Six months ago I graduated from Emory with a degree in Business, after staying an extra semester to complete dual concentrations in Finance and Accounting. I'd planned on working for a year or two, then going for my MBA.

A month after I'd finished school, my grandmother had died.

I should have seen it coming. She'd been almost eighty, and for the last few months of her life she'd been unusually tired. She'd refused to go to the doctor, saying she was fine.

She'd been wrong. Losing her had leeched every drop of vitality from my life. For as long as I could remember, my grandmother was the only adult I could depend on.

She remembered my birthday. She gave me a home for summer vacations.

That first year in boarding school, eight years old and terrified of being alone in England, she'd called me every night, the time difference be damned.

Iris Henry had loved me like no one else, and then she'd died on me. I'd imagined I'd be able to return the favor one day, envisioned caring for her as she aged.

Instead I was rattling around in her house, alone, losing my bearings more and more with each day that passed.

I'd been drifting for months when I'd run into Rupert Stevens, an old bridge crony of my grandmother's. I'd known him since I'd been a child, and if Rupert wasn't family, he was the closest thing to it.

It hadn't taken him long to size up my situation. Two days after we spoke, his wife Sloane, Vance's manager, had called me with a job offer. I knew if I didn't at least drag myself out of the house and go see Vance, Rupert would call in the calvary.

I was having a hard enough time dealing with my grandmother's death. I didn't think I could take an intervention from her bridge club, no matter how well meaning.

So I was here, willing to let Vance Winters interview me to see if I'd fit the role of his assistant. I hadn't been sure I wanted the job when I'd knocked on his door. Now, after seeing him in the towel, I thought my best option might be to tell him 'no thanks' and go home.

I remembered the ridges of his six pack and my mouth watered. I hadn't had sex for over a month. Brayden was never home lately and when he was, he said he was exhausted.

I caught the scuff of a bare foot on hardwood and turned to see Vance prowling toward me, his magnificent body covered by a pair of jeans so old they were worn white at the knee and an equally threadbare t-shirt with the faded logo of a classic rock band.

All that luscious tanned skin was covered, only the trailing vines of a tattoo visible on his left arm. His streaky dark blond hair was wet and loose around his face, his vivid blue eyes dancing as they took in the full mug of coffee in my hands.

"That mine?" he asked, sliding onto a stool at the counter built into his kitchen island. I nodded and placed it in front of him. He took a sip and let out a low hum of approval. "Good coffee. You're hired."

"That fast?" I asked, raising an eyebrow as I took a sip of my own coffee.

He was right, I did make good coffee. I'd worked as a barista in college and I knew everything about coffee. It was my only addiction.

"I haven't agreed to take the job."

"True. Do you want it?"

"I don't know what it is," I said. "Sloane said you needed help with your schedule and errands. I'm at loose ends right now, but I'm over-qualified if that's all you need."

Vance shook his head. "Sloane has no idea what I need. But Rupert speaks highly of you, said you had a business degree and a sharp mind."

"I do," I said.

His eyes narrowed on my face and he said, "I was sorry to hear about your grandmother. I didn't know her, but my brother Aiden did."

I nodded and choked out, "Thank you."

I still wasn't used to the sharp stab of pain every time someone told me how sorry they were. I knew they meant it, but the kind platitudes were miles away from my own raw emotions and they always left me frustrated.

I was bereft. Furious she'd abandoned me, guilty for being angry - a jumbled mess of pain and hurt I couldn't quite hide from the world - hence my drifting through life.

Vance must have sensed my mood, because he broke eye contact and went on, "Sloane told you I need an assistant. That's accurate, but doesn't really cover the scope of what I have in mind. Do you know what I do?"

"Some of it," I said, glad to be back on familiar ground. "I know you're a sculptor, working primarily in metal. Large pieces mainly, a combination of your own inspiration and commissions. You also act as an investor on occasion, mostly for small tech companies, though last year you branched out and went in with your brother and cousin on a nightclub."

"You do your research," he said. I sipped my coffee without responding.

He went on, "I want help managing my life. I have a lot going on between my work and the investing and other things. I need someone who can keep track of mundane shit like my dry cleaning and dentist appointments, but can also stay on top of my investments - vet proposals, keep an eye on the books, that kind of thing. You'd have to be flexible - every day is different around here."

It sounded intriguing. I wanted to use my degree, but I couldn't see myself in an office, even though that had been my plan while I'd been in college. I opened my mouth to ask more about the details when a toilet flushed on the other side of the loft.

I sat up straighter. I'd thought we were alone. Vance slouched over his coffee and muttered, "Sorry about this."

A door shut, and a woman appeared, her micro mini and strappy top straight from a club. So was her big hair and smoky eye make-up. I'm sure she'd been stunning the night before. With smeared mascara under her bloodshot eyes and badly in need of a comb, she wasn't that appealing.

I knew her type. When she stumbled on her spike heel on the way to Vance, I looked away. She ignored me, didn't even bother to ask who I was or why I was there, her focus all on Vance.

She slipped her arms around his torso from behind, leaning forward to nip his earlobe, saying, "Vance, baby, come back to bed." She eyed me with vacant disdain. "Get rid of her. Or bring her with you. Whatever, it's cool with me."

Out of the corner of my eye I saw her hand slide into Vance's lap. I swallowed and stood. I wasn't a prude, but this was just weird and uncomfortable.

I had no interest in being the third wheel in another woman's awkward morning after.

As if he had a lot of practice - and I imagined he did - Vance twisted from her embrace and stood, turning the woman to face me.

"Not now. I have a full day. Ms. Henry will show you out."

I raised an eyebrow at him, caught between annoyance and reluctant amusement.

Vance had balls, I'd give him that.

Taking in his expectant look, I understood. My job description would include managing his morning afters.

Ugh. If rumor was half accurate, this happened a lot.

I thought about walking out. I didn't need this. I didn't much like his one-night stand, but I didn't want to humiliate her either.

My irritation let me see through the mask of Vance's beauty to the red lines dulling his eyes, the faint circles beneath. He was as hungover as she was.

Vance had the looks and talent of a god, but he was really just like every other party boy I knew. Thinking over my options, I got to my feet and took the confused woman's arm in a gentle grip, steering her to the door.

She glanced back over her shoulder at Vance, almost losing her balance in her high heels, and I got the feeling she was going to plead her case. I shook my head, nudging her through the door.

"Do you need me to call you a ride?" I asked gently. She snatched her arm from my hand and stalked to the stairs.

Guess not. Locking the door behind her, I turned back to finish my interview.

"Thanks," Vance said from across the kitchen. He refilled his coffee and held out the pot. I shook my head. We had more to talk about before I decided if I was staying for a second cup.

"Does that happen often?" I asked, again in a crisp tone. I realized I sounded exactly like my boarding school headmistress, minus the posh English accent.

Vance shrugged. "Often enough," he said with unashamed honesty. "Why, interested in taking her place?" His electric blue gaze caressed my body with indolent interest. "I don't usually mix business and the bedroom, but I could make an exception for you."

He raised one eyebrow as if daring me. For a second, I thought about slapping him.

"Are you kidding?"

He shrugged. "Not really, but I'm getting the idea sex isn't in your job description."

"Sex is absolutely not part of my job description." I was both offended and flattered.

Yes, flattered.

I know, I know.

I should have given him a good smack and walked out. My only excuse is that no man who looked like Vance had ever hit on me.

Granted, Vance's standards weren't that high, but still, the sex deprived woman in me appreciated the offer. There was no way I'd ever sleep with him, but it was nice to be asked.

"I figured you'd say that." Vance shrugged again, amusement glinting in his red-rimmed eyes. "It was worth a try. Now that we've gotten my obligatory pass out of the way, here's how I see this working. You'll show up by ten every day, evict any guests, make me breakfast and get my lazy ass out of bed.

Once I get rolling, we'll go over business, then I'll head down to my studio and you'll do whatever you've got on for the day."

"So you need a combination babysitter, errand girl, and business manager," I said, disarmed by his upfront explanation.

"Something like that," he admitted. "Interested?"

He named a salary that wasn't outrageous, but was more than generous. I was tempted. It wasn't a long-term plan, but it would get me out of the house and force me to move forward with my life. I couldn't keep going as I was.

"Can I bring my dog?" I asked. I'd gotten Scout a month after my grandmother had died and I didn't want to leave him at home alone all day.

"What kind of dog?

"A mutt. A boxer/corgi mix."

At the look on his face, I pulled my phone out of my pocket. It was impossible to describe Scout unless you could see his absurd cuteness for yourself.

He had the face, ears, and long, low body of a corgi, with the stance and fur of a boxer. He wasn't the brightest dog, but he was all love. We were a perfect fit.

He'd needed a home, and I'd needed someone to hold on to.

Vance took my phone and flipped through the pictures of Scout, smiling down at my adorable dog. He stopped on a picture and held my phone up.

On it was a shot I'd taken of Brayden, backing up as Scout went for his bagel. Brayden didn't like dogs, and Scout returned his lack of affection.

"Who's this?" Vance asked. "He looks familiar."

"My boyfriend. Brayden," I took my phone back, turning off the screen and sliding it in my pocket.

"Brayden Michaels?" Vance asked, an incredulous look on his face.

"You know him? How?"

"School. I was in the same class as his older brother. Brayden's a twat."

Before I knew what I was doing, I stood.

Brayden wasn't perfect, but he was mine and I wasn't going to listen to this dissipated playboy put him down.

Picking up my keys and my purse, I said, "This isn't going to work, Mr. Winters. I'll see myself out."

"Wait," he said, shoving back his stool and coming to his feet. "Magnolia, don't leave."

Against, my better judgement, I stopped and whirled to face him.

"I don't know that I want to work for you," I said bluntly. "You're rude and immature."

Vance shoved his hands in the back pockets, dragging his jeans down an inch to reveal a strip of taut golden skin. I shouldn't be tempted. I didn't even like him. I dragged my eyes away, forcing myself to look at his face.

His blue eyes were shadowed when he said, "Yeah, I am. Rude, immature, sometimes a complete asshole. I'd be a pain in the ass to work for half the time."

"And the other half?" I asked.

"You'll get more hands on experience with me than an entry level job at a bigger company. My personal shit aside, I get first look at some very interesting investment opportunities and you'd be involved at every level. You'd get personal exposure to some of the biggest players, not just in Atlanta but across the country. When you're ready to move on, you'll have connections you'd never be able to make sitting in a cubicle. All you have to do is put up with me."

When he laid it out like that, how could I say no?

Wondering if I was making a huge mistake, I held out my hand. Vance took it in his, his strong fingers closing around mine with possession. I tried to ignore the spark of heat as we touched.

"So you'll take the job?" Vance asked, holding onto my

hand when I tried to tug it free. I gave a hard yank and took a step back.

"On a trial basis," I said in what I was starting to think of as my headmistress voice. "If you're too much of an asshole, I'm quitting, and I want a guarantee of six months severance."

"Agreed," Vance said, grinning down at me. "But the severance is only payable if you leave because I'm an asshole."

"Does sexual harassment count as you being an asshole?" I challenged. I'd admitted to myself that I was flattered by his offer, but if he kept it up I'd walk out.

"It would, if I was planning on harassing you. I won't pull that shit. I'm an asshole, but I'm not a complete dick." He ruined it by leering at me and saying, "Anyway, when we finally sleep together it'll be because you can't keep your hands off me."

"And that's strike one. Jury's out on whether you're a complete dick."

To my surprise, Vance laughed. "Cross my heart." With two fingers he swiped a cross over his chest. "I have a twin sister who'd kick my ass if she thought I was harassing a woman who works for me. Give me a chance, I promise the job will be worth it."

"Fine. I'll start tomorrow." I turned on my heel and walked out. I'd had as much of Vance Winters as I could take for the day. His voice followed me into the hall.

"Ten A.M. Don't be late, Magnolia."

Like he would notice if I was. I'd bet my inheritance Vance would be passed out in bed when I showed up, another nubile, hungover, girl beside him.

On the drive home I tried to convince myself I'd done the right thing.

It wasn't easy.

The truth was, my first instinct was spot on. Vance Winters was trouble; Six and a half feet of dangerously beautiful mayhem.

I should have taken one look and run in the other direction.

I should have told him to take his job offer and shove it up his tight, perfect ass.

But hindsight is 20/20. By the time I knew what was coming, it was already too late.

For Vance, and for me.

Also by Ivy Layne

Don't Miss Out on New Releases, Exclusive Giveaways, and More!!

Join Ivy's Readers Group @ ivylayne.com/readers

THE HEARTS OF SAWYERS BEND

Stolen Heart

Sweet Heart

Scheming Heart

Rebel Heart

Wicked Heart

THE UNTANGLED SERIES

Unraveled

Undone

Uncovered

The Winters Saga

The Billionaire's Secret Heart (Novella)

The Billionaire's Secret Love (Novella)

The Billionaire's Pet

The Billionaire's Promise

ABOUT IVY LAYNE

Ivy Layne has had her nose stuck in a book since she first learned to decipher the English language. Sometime in her early teens, she stumbled across her first Romance, and the die was cast. Though she pretended to pay attention to her creative writing professors, she dreamed of writing steamy romance instead of literary fiction. These days, she's neck deep in alpha heroes and the smart, sexy women who love them.

Married to her very own alpha hero (who rubs her back after a long day of typing, but also leaves his socks on the floor). Ivy lives in the mountains of North Carolina where she and her other half are having a blast raising two energetic little boys. Aside from her family, Ivy's greatest loves are coffee and chocolate, preferably together.

VISIT IVY
Facebook.com/AuthorIvyLayne
Instagram.com/authorivylayne/
www.ivylayne.com
books@ivylayne.com